Eugene's .ale

EUGENE'S TALE

A LOOK INTO THE CULTURE AND SUBCULTURE OF THE POLICE

T.L. ALLEN

ISBNs
978-1-80541-348-6 (paperback)
978-1-80541-349-3 (eBook)
978-1-80541-350-9 (hardback)

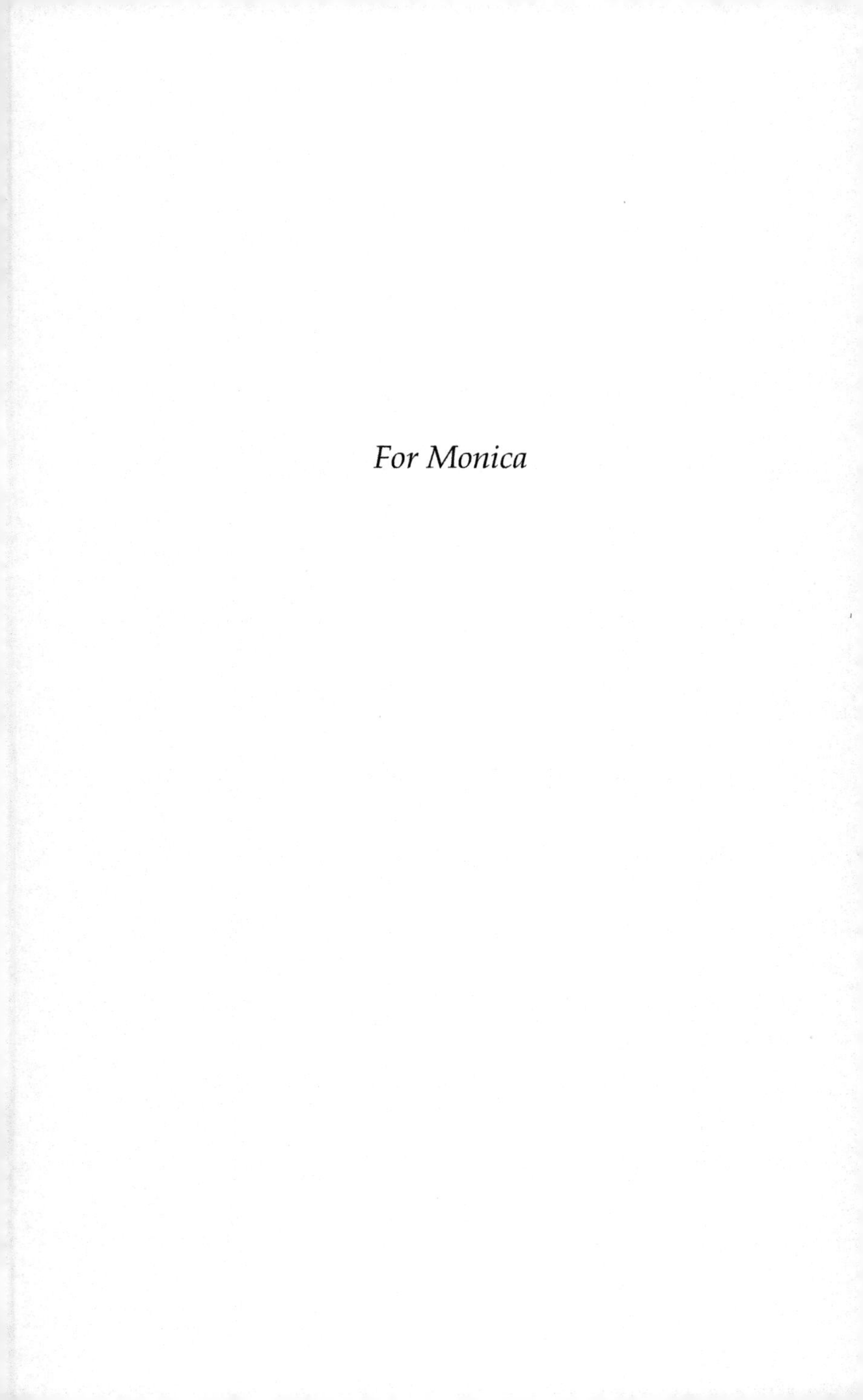

For Monica

About the Author

T.L. Allen served as a police officer with Thames Valley Police for 30 years. He is also a qualified psychiatric nurse. This is his first novel. He resides in Berkshire.

CHAPTER 1

The morning shower for Eugene Elphick was something of a ritual, without it things just weren't right. That was Detective Inspector Elphick's special time, his private time, a time when he could plan his day, sort his mind, and relax under the reassuring warm water. The shower was a time for Eugene of meditation, thinking his most inner thoughts, as near to prayer as he ever got these days, but nevertheless a kind of prayer in its own way.

But, that private time was interrupted today by Sandra, Eugene's wife, calling through the slightly open bathroom door, raising her voice above the noise of the shower.

"Gene, there are some lads from the station downstairs who want to see you."

"What at this hour?"

It had just tuned 7:00am. It must be something urgent, he thought, something pretty serious had occurred during the night, but why had they not telephoned?

Eugene exited the shower, the room now silent from the noise of the shower motor.

"I must get that motor seen to, it's getting very noisy," he thought.

Just the noise of the gurgling water as it exited the cubical making its escape down the plughole. He could hear muffled voices in the room below; no doubt Sandra would be offering his colleagues some tea. He dried himself and dressed ready for his day. Nothing too taxing, well so far as he knew. A strategy meeting, some appraisal work and a mountain of mundane paperwork that had been growing on his desk.

Wiping the condensation off with a sweeping hand, he looked in the mirror. Yes, he was looking a little older that his 42 years, more grey hair by the day it would seem. No time to waste, the lads were waiting.

Eugene moved quickly downstairs and entered the sitting room. Two men who he did not recognise stood up. One was in his 50s, the other a little younger than Eugene, both dressed in sombre inexpensive business suits, the younger man clutching a black briefcase, old fashioned style. The older man spoke first.

"Mr Eugene Elphick?" Eugene noticed how the man emphasised the mister.

"Yes."

"I am Superintendent Matthews from the Professional Standards Department at Headquarters; this is my colleague Inspector Preston."

Eugene noticed that Preston was not making eye contact with him at all. He remained staring down at the battered briefcase which he held in both hands to his front.

Eugene enquired, "Is one of my team in trouble then?"

Matthews answered softly, "Not exactly."

The awkward atmosphere was punctured as Sandra appeared with a tray of tea.

"I thought you could do with this," she said cheerfully and with that special smile that was reserved for people who she didn't know well.

She placed the tray on the coffee table. Gene noticed that she had used the best china – white porcelain cups with an ivy leaf pattern, a wedding present and seldom used. He couldn't help but think the cups were too small for a decent cup of tea.

"Katie and I will be going in about 15 minutes, Gene; she's got a hockey game this afternoon and I have shopping so we'll be home around six."

She didn't wait for a reply and exited the room.

"Please sit down," Eugene said to the two men. Matthews sat down, and Preston only did so a few seconds, and after Matthews had taken his seat.

Eugene said nervously, "What's all this about?"

Superintendent Matthews looked at Eugene without saying anything for a few seconds – a few seconds that seemed an eternity.

"Mr Elphick...."

"Please call me Gene, Guv."

Matthews had never been a CID officer and smarted at the use of 'Guv', preferring to be addressed as 'sir' – strictly uniform all his service, apart from now. 'Guv' seemed too familiar and disrespectful for him, but he didn't say anything.

"OK, Gene...tell me a little bit about you. What service have you?"

Eugene realised immediately that Matthews was stalling, playing with him holding back – a basic tactic to unnerve and keep the suspect in suspense, but why?

"I started in the job young; I was just gone 20. I served my probation at Slough. You know, usual stuff: walked the High Street and Farnham Road, drove a Panda, and did some unit beat/neighbourhood work at Manor Park."

Matthews said, "I see you've spent some time on CID, so how did your career move along that route?"

Eugene could see that Matthews was still stalling, unwilling for some reasons to get to the point but he thought that he shouldn't appear too nervous or concerned although, in fact, Matthews' tactics were making him very nervous. He could feel his heart beating, his mouth was dry and how he wanted to drink the tea from the white porcelain cup with the ivy leaf pattern, but as neither of the other men had made a move towards theirs he decided not to.

"Whilst at Slough, the opportunity came up for some acting DC work at Langley. I applied, got it and that was the start. It was mainly bike thefts and credit card stuff, but I suppose I got the 'bug' from that; most of my service has been spent in CID."

"Nick here," Matthews indicated Preston, "has spent a lot of time in CID...at Oxford, so he knows a lot about bike theft."

Matthews allowed himself to laugh at his own small joke. Preston remained stony faced.

From out in the hall Sandra called, "We're off now."

Katie, called, "'Bye, Dad."

Eugene tried to reply with a 'bye', but the word stuck in his throat and a croaky, barely audible sound emitted. Eugene felt as if he was going to cry; he was welling up inside and didn't know why.

"They're going early," Matthews said.

"Katie attends a breakfast club at school three mornings a week, it's a sort of social thing. Sandra drops her off and then goes on to work." He continued, "With respect, I need to get to work myself soon"

"You don't have to concern yourself with that. Your supervisors know we're here and what's happening," said Matthews.

But what the hell is happening, thought Eugene? Nothing has been said.

"Now your family have left the house, Mr Elphick, we can get down to why we're here. I was anxious not to cause any unnecessary embarrassment." He paused, and then said, "You see I have been appointed by the Deputy Chief Constable to carry out an investigation following certain allegations that have been made against you."

"What allegations?"

Eugene could hear the defensiveness in his own voice.

Matthews paused again then said, "We've received information from another police force that a number of people have been downloading pornographic material onto their computers – you're named as one of those people."

Eugene, again hearing the defensiveness in his voice, said, "That's absolute rubbish".

There were a few seconds silence. He could now see that Preston, who up to this point had not made eye contact at all, was staring at him intently.

"Pornography? What pornography?"

Matthews said, "I regret to say Mr Elphick, the allegation is that you have downloaded child pornography."

The words hit Eugene hard just as if he had been hit in the solar plexus by a professional boxer; he felt sick, he was finding it difficult to breathe, his heart was beating fast and loud and all he could hear in the background was Matthews' voice sounding more and more droning, featureless and flat.

"I think for your safety and mine I should caution you."

Matthews then recited the caution perfectly. "You do not have to say anything, but it may harm your defence if you do not mention when questioned something you later rely on in court, anything you do say may be given in evidence, do you understand?"

Eugene thought, 'What a stupid question,' of course he understood. He had given the caution probably thousands of times, but now it was being given to him in such circumstances the whole thing took on a totally different context. It seemed so surreal. Eugene wondered if he were in fact dreaming and would wake up soon, but the stark realisation that this was fact and actually happening here and now was all too real.

Preston, who had not spoken at all up to that point, then said, "Where are your computers?"

Eugene noticed that his tone was harsher, brusquer, not necessarily rude but different to that of Matthews.

Eugene said, "We have a laptop which is on the dining room table."

Whose computer is that?"

Again, Preston spoke in a brusque tone which Eugene thought most unnecessary. He also noticed how broad Preston's Oxfordshire accent was.

"It's the family computer – we all use it".

"Any others?"

"Katie has her laptop. It's there."

Eugene pointed to a small writing desk in the corner of the sitting room upon which sat a white laptop.

"Any others?"

"Oh, there's an old desk top in the garage, but it hasn't been used in a long time."

Preston then said, "I don't know which part of 'where are your computers' you don't understand but please tell me where all your computers are."

Preston was now sounding brusque to the point of rudeness and had emphasised the word 'all'.

Eugene said, "There's no need to be so rude." He continued, "That's it. Exactly what I have already told you."

Preston then left the room and went outside.

Matthews then said, "I know this must be difficult for you, Mr Elphick, but please just try to cooperate at this stage. It'll make things much easier for you and us."

Before Eugene had a chance to reply, Preston had returned clutching large plastic property bags and red plastic numbered property labels.

He said to Eugene, "We'll need to seize all of your computers, and these will need to be examined by a specialist department."

Matthews then said, "To make it clear, we'll be taking your computers to Oxford, so outside the area where you are known, for further examination. They'll be returned to you when they have been examined by the technical side of the Paedophile and Cyber Investigations Unit."

Eugene exclaimed, "You can't do this; I haven't done anything." His words seemed so futile even to him. He sounded as if he was pleading and hated himself for that. Don't the guilty always plead in this pathetic manner he thought.

He continued, "You can't take Katie's laptop; she needs it for her schoolwork."

Matthews said, "I'm sorry, Mr Elphick, it has to be done. However, I'll ensure that Katie's laptop is examined first, but as you know these things can take some time."

Preston then went to Katie's computer, but Eugene said, "Hang on, shouldn't you have a search warrant?"

Preston exhaled through his nose in a display of his own frustration. He left the writing desk and returned to the battered black brief case that was beside the settee where he had been sitting. He withdrew a sheaf of papers. As he did so Matthews stretched out his arm and Preston placed the sheaf of papers in his hand.

"You're quite right Mr Elphick," said Matthews, "Here's a search warrant obtained locally from a magistrate last evening."

He showed the warrant to Eugene and then continued, "The warrant authorises us to search these premises and any annexes or outbuildings for computers, accessories and component parts .Oh yes, We'll also need to search your car."

Eugene was silent, everything was beyond his control. There was nothing he could say; he felt totally helpless.

"Inspector Preston will bag up the two computers down here. I'll now call in a search team that I have standing by, and they'll carry out a more thorough search."

"Search team?" enquired Eugene. "I've told you where everything is, I don't want people going through all our personal things."

"It's the way it's going to happen," said Matthews,

"As you know you'll be given a receipt for any property seized and provided with a full inventory."

Eugene sat down. He felt physically weak. 'Why is this happening?' he thought. Who is behind this? So many questions passing through his mind all jumbled up, all trying to make sense of a senseless situation. Matthews handed the papers back to Preston who returned to the writing desk and started to pack the two laptops. Matthews made a short phone call and within a few minutes Eugene saw through the front window three quite young people, two men and a woman, walking toward the house. As he watched them he saw the curtain of the house opposite twitch. Matthews let the trio in; they were all dressed in blue jeans and sweatshirts. Eugene noticed that they all wore Magnum boots. He thought that Sandra would be upset to think of those boots trapesing through the house.

Preston asked if there was access to the loft and Eugene said that there was a loft ladder and a light to the loft, and that the loft had a lined floor. Preston and the three young officers moved upstairs.

Matthews said, "You can be present if you wish Mr Elphick."

Eugene did not reply. He didn't feel he could move. In fact, he felt as if he had been beaten up. He merely said, "There's nothing in the loft except some boxes of books, a couple of suitcases and the Christmas decorations."

He could hear Preston speaking to the young officers upstairs in as brusque a manner as he had spoken to him,

"You two up there, you start on the kid's room."

How had that man had survived in CID with such an attitude was beyond Eugene.

Matthews then said, "If you're staying here perhaps you could answer a couple of questions." He continued, "I would remind you that you remain under caution. Have you a mobile phone?"

"Yes, a work phone and my own phone."

Matthews said, "Are they smart phones, or not?"

"No, one is Nokia – the work one – and mine is a Samsung."

"Can you place them on the table please?"

Eugene took a phone from his shirt pocket and went to the kitchen to retrieve the other. He placed them both on the coffee table.

Matthews looked at them and said, "You can put your own phone away, leave the work phone there." He continued, "Does your wife or daughter have smart phones?"

Eugene replied, "My wife does, my daughter has a Samsung similar to my own phone."

Matthews said, "Could you place your locker keys, any keys to your desk and filing cabinet and any electronic pass keys to the station on the table please?"

As Eugene was dressed for work he only had to take the keys from his pocket and the electronic keys from his wallet. He felt as if he was gradually being stripped of all his authority and power and sat with a feeling of being naked and beaten.

Eugene did not really know how long after, time seemed irrelevant for the moment, but Preston and the officers came downstairs. The young officers did not look in Eugene's direction, but he saw one of them staring at a photograph depicting him in a group graduating from the Detective Training School at Wakefield which hung on the sitting room wall.

Preston said, "It's clear up there, Guv."

"Thank you, press on then," Matthews replied.

Preston then detailed one officer to the kitchen, the dining room and hall and one to the sitting room. Eugene watched as the young officer systematically worked his way around the room. Wearing blue disposable gloves he looked in a cupboard and drawers, taking things out and carefully replacing them again. He came to the centre of the room and even searched down the back of the chairs and asked Eugene and Matthews to move whilst he searched the back of the settee they were sitting on. He removed a two-pound coin which he placed on the tea tray. Eugene thought the officer was efficient and professional.

Preston and the young officers gathered in the hall momentarily and then exited the house, Preston saying as he did so, "Are the garage and shed open?"

"No, I'll get the keys."

"And your car keys please," called Preston.

Eugene got up from the settee, his legs hardly bearing his weight. He got the keys from the kitchen and gave them to Preston who took them but said nothing. Eugene took his seat.

Matthews said, "Have you any debit or credit cards?"

Eugene said, "Yes, two: an HSBC debit card and a Santander credit card."

He took them from his wallet and Matthews quickly glanced at them and said, "Any others?"

"No."

Matthews said, "Are the cards in your name?"

Eugene replied, "The HSBC is a joint account, the Santander is in my name."

Again, after a period of time, the length of which was beyond Eugene's comprehension, the four returned from outside. The female officer and a male officer each carried the base unit of a desk top PC each wrapped in a plastic property bag.

Preston seemed as if he could hardly wait to say, "I thought you said there was only one computer in the garage."

Eugene looked and then recalled the old Tiny brand computer that had been replaced long ago and had been stored out there ever since.

He said, "Oh, yes," pointing to the computer held by one of the male officers. "That one's very old. That was the first computer we ever owned. I had forgotten about that. The make is obsolete now."

"Really," Preston said, not seeking to hide the sarcasm in his voice.

"OK, have we finished now?" asked Matthews,

"Yes sir," replied the female officer.

"Inspector Preston, please complete the paperwork and give the necessary copies to Mr Elphick."

"All done Guv," said Preston, who handed a sheaf of papers to Matthews and a sheaf to the female officer.

Matthews gave his papers a cursory look and then handed them to Eugene.

"Please check these Mr Elphick and if you are satisfied that they are correct please sign."

Eugene didn't check them, he couldn't, he just signed. Matthews took the papers back, retrieved the bundle from the female officer and gave her his. Preston seemed to slightly blush as his basic error. Matthews then gave the other bundle to Eugene.

"These are yours."

Instructions were then given to the search team as to where to take the seized property and, without further ado, they left. Eugene watched them walk down the pathway each carrying a plastic bag containing his property. As they left he was sure he saw the curtain at the house opposite twitch again.

Matthews and Preston stood in front of him and then sat; Matthews sat next to him and Preston in the chair opposite. Matthews looked at Eugene and Preston was again staring at him intently.

Matthews gave what seemed like a little sigh and said, "Mr Elphick, the Deputy Chief Constable has authorised that you will take paid leave until further notice. You're not being suspended at this time, but you're advised not to go to, or contact your own, or another police station, or make contact with any police staff. I'll be taking your keys and your phone, and your office will be searched. Your team will be told that you're taking leave and they'll be instructed not to make contact with you. You'll retain your warrant card for the time being. I would advise you to make contact with your Police Federation Representative and arrange to see him or her here or at the Federation office at Thame. Once our initial enquiries have been completed we'll be in touch with you again. Have you any questions?"

Eugene had a thousand questions mulling around in his head, but he merely said, "No…no thank you."

Matthews continued, "Just before we go, Mr Elphick, have you given us everything? Can you assure me that there is nothing else, no hidden computers, portable hard drives, USBs and such like."

Eugene said, "No, you have everything".

Both Matthews and Preston stood up and made towards the front door.

Eugene followed. Preston was the first to leave and as Matthew's left he quietly said to Eugene, "Try to keep busy, that's the best advice I can give you." The two then walked away and did not even glance back toward Eugene.

Eugene stood at the doorway watching the two men drive away in the steel grey Vauxhall motor car. Even after they were out of sight he remained at the front door trying to fathom out what had happened. He looked at his watch, it was nearly 11:15; the whole process had taken some four hours. Four hours that occasionally seemed to have passed in a flash otherwise had taken an eternity. He turned, shut the door, and leaned his back against it. He placed his head in his hands, thought of his wife, child, and mother, and burst into tears. He stumbled into the sitting room and sobbed for what seemed a long time.

CHAPTER 2

Preston had driven away from outside Eugene's address. After a reasonable distance Matthews instructed Preston to pull over. He did so in a small layby off the main road on their way back toward the M40. Preston stopped the engine, and they both sat in silence for a minute or so.

Matthews said, "Tell me Nick, what do you think?"

"He's definitely guilty Guv, a real shifty character. I didn't like him from the start. I wouldn't be surprised if he's been at it for ages."

"Um," mused Matthews, "I'm not so sure. Of course we won't know anything until the hard drives on the computers are examined." He continued, "We don't even know what to expect."

"Child porn, that's what we expect, Guv. Have you seen any of what he's alleged to have downloaded?"

"No, and neither has anyone as yet. The Deputy just said that it's supposed to be pretty serious stuff, pretty hardcore. The Deputy implied that they're still waiting for some information from America, that's where, apparently, it all originated."

Preston said nothing but was clearly thinking hard about the various implications.

"There's nothing else to do now - let's make our way toward somewhere where we can at least get a cup of coffee and then should get back to headquarters."

Eugene had composed himself, washed his face and changed out of his work clothes. He picked up the tray containing the stone-cold cups of tea in the white porcelain cups with the ivy pattern and the two-pound coin. He poured away the tea and milk and placed the cups, saucers, and jug in the dish washer, and the coin in his pocket. That was as much as he could manage. He just didn't know what to do. How was he going to explain this to Sandra and Katie? He poured himself a glass of water and drank it down in large gulps; he hadn't realised just how thirsty he was. He looked at the clock - 2pm; anther four hours at least before his family would be home.

During that long afternoon, Eugene tried to read but couldn't, went into the garden and came back in again, tried to go for a walk but got to the end of his road and came back, lay down on his bed but couldn't rest. Each time he closed his eyes the scenario of Matthews and Preston marching in and searching his home played back. His mind was so active with so many thoughts rattling around inside his head - many connected, but as many totally unconnected. Why he would be thinking about holidays spent as a child he had no idea, and why was he thinking of his long deceased father, and of his mother who had been so proud of his entry into, and progress within, the Police Service? He started to feel emotional again with tears welling up in his eyes. He switched on the TV; and flicked through the channels which seemed to portray cooking programmes, antiques programmes, and an American police drama which he certainly did not want to watch. He switched off and the afternoon dragged on.

Eugene saw the clock was creeping toward 6pm and he knew that his family would be coming through the door at any time now. Paradoxically, he wished for that moment but dreaded it, too; this was going to be the next difficult part of this exceedingly difficult day.

Eugene stood near to the front window until at last he saw his wife drive onto the driveway. He saw her and Katie alight from the vehicle and Sandra staring at his car for a moment. Both took a bag of shopping from the boot of Sandra's car.

Katie came through the front door first calling out, "Hi Dad. Had a great game…you're home early." She was still talking as she came into the sitting room, "I scored for once!"

Eugene, not really taking in what Katie was saying and on auto pilot, replied, "That's great Katie, well done!"

Katie moved with her bag of shopping to the kitchen.

Sandra came into the sitting room with her bag and said, "Gene, I didn't expect you to be here yet."

Eugene didn't reply.

Katie came out of the kitchen and said, "I'll get the other bag, Mum."

She went outside, and Eugene said to Sandra, "There are a few issues, I'll explain later."

Katie came in with the final bag of shopping which she took to the kitchen and then returned to the car to retrieve her school and sports bag.

Sandra was saying, "What issues, Gene? Who were those men this morning?"

Eugene didn't think he could answer anything just at that moment despite having rehearsed over and over in his head how he would broach the dreadful subject, and could only utter again, "I will explain a little later, Sandra."

Katie returned to the sitting room.

"I'm just going to have to tell everyone about that great game today…" She paused and then said in a much quieter voice, "Where's my laptop?"

Eugene noticed that Katie was wearing half school uniform and half hockey kit, her knees muddied, her hair untidy, one sock up and one down; she looked so vulnerable, childlike, and innocent. For a moment she looked much younger than her 14 years.

Eugene cleared his throat and said, "Those men that were here this morning were police officers. They're making enquiries into a serious matter; someone has told lies about your dad and your laptop, along with ours, has been taken to be examined. They'll be returned once they've been examined and your dad's name cleared."

Katie was silent for a moment and then exploded.

"What are you talking about? Why my laptop? I have school work on there. How am I supposed to access Facebook and Skype?" She was becoming hysterical. "I'll be an outcast, a pariah! Why me? I hate you and I hate the fucking police."

Sandra exclaimed, "Katie!"

Katie screamed, "It's so unfair. I hate you both!"

Normally an adolescent daughter saying she hated her father would be like water off a duck's back to Eugene, but today those words hurt...hurt a lot. Katie made for the stairs and Eugene thought quickly.

He called after Katie, "And don't tell anyone that the police have your computer...please!"

Katie shouted back from the top of the stairs, "Bollocks!"

Eugene turned to Sandra and said, "It's very important, Sandra, that Katie doesn't tell anyone that her laptop has been taken by the police; it could interfere with an investigation." Eugene was aware that if Katie told all and sundry that the police had her laptop somebody, somewhere, would put two and two together. He ended the sentence to Sandra with a pleading, "Please...please, go and speak to her now."

Sandra said, "I'll go and speak to her, but I want a full explanation about this when I come down, Gene, do your hear me?"

Eugene went to the kitchen and put away the shopping that had been left out. He could hear Katie shouting and crying upstairs and Sandra talking to her in soft comforting tones. Within a short time, he couldn't hear any further crying or shouting, and an eerie silence once again took over the house.

Sandra came back downstairs.

"She's going to have dinner in her room; she's really upset. I'll make us all a salad now, take hers to her and then we can talk."

"Can I help?" enquired Eugene.

"No, just keep out of my way for the moment, watch TV or something, leave me to prepare dinner," she looked at him angrily.

Eugene didn't switch on the television, he just sat. He'd probably spent more time in this sitting room today than on any day, ever. He sat staring at the blank TV screen, his own nightmarish programme playing away in his head.

Sandra took Katie's dinner to her room and then called Eugene to the dining room. She had prepared tinned red salmon with salad and microchips. A jug of water was also on the table. Gene sat down and helped himself to a glass of water.

Sandra spoke first.

"What's this all about Gene?" she said, in a seemingly very controlled way.

Gene told her about the bland Superintendent Matthews who had tried hard to be as pleasant as possible but who wanted everyone to know that he was very much in charge, and the brusque and sometimes outrageously rude Detective Inspector Preston. He told her that they had both been from Professional Standards at Headquarters, and that an allegation had been made that involved officers using computers, and that he had been one of those named officers. Sandra mostly listened without comment and only asked if Eugene knew who the other officers were who had had similar allegations made against them, and he had said that he didn't.

Sandra ate her meal as Eugene gave his explanation. He steered clear of any mention of child pornography and did so for two reasons - one, that Sandra would, understandably, overreact and two, once the computers had been examined the allegation would be nullified and life would resume as normal - at least he hoped so. Eugene skirted around exactly what the allegation was despite Sandra's questions, saying that it involved quite complicated issues related to 'trolling'. But he knew that Sandra wasn't one hundred percent convinced with his explanation.

Katie then appeared in the doorway; she was in her night attire holding her empty dinner plate.

She put the plate on the table and said, "Someone's been in my room and gone through my things." She said it quietly, in a nervous kind of way.

Eugene said, "Yes Katie. I'm afraid the police searched your room; they had to do that, but nothing has been taken apart from your laptop."

Sandra interjected, "Has our room been searched as well?"

Eugene replied, "Yes, they had a search warrant. Everywhere has been searched; it's just routine."

Katie said, "But my private things have been looked at," and she started to cry.

"Routine!" exclaimed Sandra as she threw her knife and fork on to her plate with such force that it was a miracle the plate didn't break. "Routine? Routine is when some toe-rag says you were too robust making an arrest. The searching of a Detective Inspector's family home where the private things of his wife and daughter are mauled over by some oaf is not routine – it's an outrage, a violation."

She paused took a breath and continued, "I can't bear to think of those two men going through my things."

In an effort to ease the situation Eugene lied, "They didn't do it. It was a search team; a female officer did the search of ours and Katie's room."

"And that's supposed to help, is it?" shouted Sandra.

Katie had stopped crying and was staring a little open mouthed at her mother who she had seldom heard raise her voice, let alone shout in this manner.

She softened her voice and said to Katie, "Go to your room love, I'll be up in a minute."

Sandra, was silent for a moment, composing herself, then said in a quietly controlled voice, "When you go into work tomorrow, you'll get my daughter's laptop back and you'll get this sorted."

Eugene replied, "I'll not be going to work…they've put me on 'gardening' leave."

"You've been suspended?"

There was silence and after a moment Eugene said very precisely, "I have not been suspended, I'm on authorised paid leave, hopefully for not too long. It's different these days… the search, the leave, it's all to do with moral conduct and the service being seen as transparent, that sort of thing. Anyway, you can pick up a cheap laptop from Argos for Katie."

Sandra half closed her eyes, something she did when angry or being ultra-sarcastic and said, "You pick it up – you've got precious little else to do now, have you?

Eugene didn't reply; he thought it best not to.

After a pause, Sandra said in that meticulously controlled manner of hers, "I'm now going to try and pacify my daughter. I'm then going to have a bath and go to bed. You can clear up here and what you do after that I couldn't care less."

She left the room and Eugene listened as she went upstairs to their daughter.

Eugene sat looking at his plate of food. He had hardly touched it and realised that he hadn't eaten at all that day. He picked at the chips and the salmon but left the salad. He got up, cleared the table and went back to the sitting room and sat. He could not get the images of the day from his mind, the voices of Matthews and Preston, images of the search team, the contents of the plastic property bags, the taking of his keys and phone – he felt violated, Sandra's word, just as violated as her in his own way.

He did not know how long he sat there but made his way to the bedroom at some point. He got into bed and lay on his back. He watched the reflections of the lights of passing cars in the road outside moving across the ceiling like moon-beams. He was thinking – thinking all the time. Thinking about all the searches that he had authorised and been present at, hundreds probably. Thinking how he must have left people feeling just as he, Sandra and Katie were feeling now, and never giving it a second thought. How many family lives had he violated?

Sandra lay on her side with her back toward him. He knew that she wasn't sleeping but he said nothing. He closed his eyes but again the events of the day replayed in his mind, quite different and distorted in relation to the real thing.

"Are you awake, Gene?" Sandra said in a very quiet voice.

"Yes."

Sandra turned and lay on her back looking up at the ceiling. She took Eugene's hand in hers.

"I'm sorry for being so rude earlier. It was just the shock of that whole unfortunate episode."

He could only whisper, "I'm sorry, too".

She continued, "It must be so hard for you; I hadn't thought of that."

She let go of his hand and turned to face Eugene. "There's one good thing to come out of this, though."

"What could possibly be good about it?" asked Eugene.

Sandra continued, "Do you know, I'm glad that you aren't working for a while; you've been under such strain, you don't look well, and you certainly haven't been sleeping well."

"Haven't I?" he said, surprised. "I thought I was sleeping OK; I haven't felt unwell."

"I think you're stressed, Gene – talking in your sleep, not concentrating, often not hearing what Katie or I have said, agitated, getting up in the night preoccupied with something."

Eugene didn't reply straightaway He hadn't realised. "You've not said before."

Sandra said, "No, and perhaps I should have. Look, I love you, Gene, and whatever this is we'll get through it, we'll get through it together."

For the first time in many hours Gene had a warm feeling inside, a feeling for once that he was not alone after all.

He whispered back, "I love you too."

She leaned forward and kissed him, and they made love – the first time in quite a while.

Eugene awoke and initially all seemed normal but within seconds the events of the previous day flashed through his mind, reminding him that all was far from normal. Looking at the luminous dial of the clock on the bedside table he could see it was 3:10am. He felt wide awake. He could hear Sandra slowly breathing and knew that she was asleep, so he gently slipped out of bed, went downstairs and made tea. He sat at the breakfast bar in the kitchen and once again turned the thoughts, feelings, actions, words, frustration and hurt of the previous day over in his mind. It was going to be another long session of self-inflicted mental torture, looking for clues in what had been said to him, looking for answers where there were none. The whole process was so exhausting.

Later the family gathered around the breakfast table, which was a rare treat. A slower start today as Katie didn't have a breakfast club. Conversation was congenial and the events of the previous day weren't mentioned but were upon everyone's mind. Eugene said he would drop Katie off at school and he told her that he would be purchasing a temporary laptop for her. Breakfast over Eugene and Katie left, and Sandra had time for another cup of coffee before she left for her own work. Mondays, yesterday, were always the busiest day of the week. It was the only day that Sandra worked a full day; the other days she only worked until 1:30pm. The full day coupled with Katie's breakfast club made it an early start. Today, with Eugene doing the school run, it was much more leisurely. She had time to dwell on what was happening.

She was 41 years of age. She had previously worked as an admin assistant at Slough police station which was where she had met, fallen in love with and married Eugene. Sandra had left her job at Slough when she had become pregnant with Katie and had remained as a full-time mum until Katie had attained the age of 10 and had started at her present school in Ascot.

Looking back, Sandra felt her time at Slough was a huge waste of time. How she now hated the culture that existed there which she believed held her personal development back. Although she wasn't a police officer she was young, impressionable, and working with frontline officers. She was aware of how that which is termed 'police culture' had robbed her and Eugene, and countless other young police staff of the day, of their innocence. The hidden unpleasant characteristics of machismo, sexism, racial prejudice, distrust, elitism, the primitive symbolic language, homophobia, and above all the siege mentality all took their toll.

She hadn't realised how bad things were until she had left. Whilst pregnant, and soon after the birth of Katie she studied part time for a diploma in child development and the people that she met whilst studying outside of the 'job' were so different. She so wished that she had never been part of that way of life at Slough. Eugene had become a fully participating member of that culture, especially so when he had moved to CID some 2 years or so after they had married. She realised that he probably had no choice. She was aware of how suspicious and distrusting he had become through time, of how life beyond the police did not really exist for him.

Oh yes, she was aware of how he embraced the culture of elitism within CID and how he quickly derided his uniformed colleagues early in his CID career, referring to them as 'Woollies' and 'Wooden tops'. The affairs, too, which were so common – she knew that he had had two affairs over the years. She was sure that Eugene didn't know that she was aware, but by God she very much was. It was as if the need for a clandestine affair was as important to the progression of a CID officer as much as the 'feeling collars', drinking, and staying out all hours. Affairs seemed to be notched up as a rite of passage. Eugene had said that things had changed now and that the 'culture' no longer existed; she was not so sure. The whispered telephone conversations, the secrecy, the arrogance all suggested that nothing had changed. She was only glad to be out of it but realised, of course, that she could never be really 'out of it'. She suddenly felt cold, shuddered, looked at her watch and hurried off to work.

Sandra had what she would describe as an 'odd feeling' during the rest of the morning. She couldn't put her finger on why she felt as she did – she just did.

Sandra left work at the usual time of 1.30. She hadn't really decided what to do but knew that she didn't want to go home right at that moment. She drove out of the surgery car park, turned right instead of left and drove toward Runnymede.

She drove to the large car park at the Staines end of Runneymede Park and parked the car. She could get quite close to the river. It was a sunny afternoon and there were a few other cars there. The occupants were mostly elderly people drinking tea from flasks, others sitting on folding chairs staring at the passing river.

The place got quite crowded at weekends but during the working week it was much quieter, and one could appreciate the surroundings. Sandra sat for a moment then got her walking shoes out of the boot, put them on and made her way along the tow path in the direction back toward Old Windsor. She noticed how the sun played on the river making complicated shapes in shadows as the sunlight moved through the trees, the dark blueish colour of the water, the lush green of the grass and foliage. It was pleasant.

'Why don't I do this more often?' she thought. But she was avoiding the very reason she had come. She mentally pulled herself in line and resumed the thoughts of the morning. Sandra started to think about Eugene's two affairs, the ones that she knew about, anyway, and the ones that he had no idea that she knew about. The first one, that lasted about six or so months was with a girl called Ann-Marie Curtis, a female police officer, a girl about the same age as Eugene, unmarried and pretty. The affair ended when she apparently moved to the Traffic Department. It was a long time ago and Sandra had, in her mind, forgiven that transgression. She paid that matter little heed. It was the other one that caused her the most anguish.

CHAPTER 3

Eugene had enjoyed taking Katie to school that morning. It was a pleasure that he had not afforded himself of that much, but now it was something he intended to do on a much more regular basis. The embarrassing situation of the previous night wasn't touched upon, and the conversation centred on hockey and the new laptop that Eugene had promised to get her.

As usual Katie had asked Eugene to drop her a good hundred yards from the school entrance; the unfounded embarrassment of adolescent girls in respect of their parents never ceased to amaze Eugene. A quick peck on the cheek and Katie sprinted off to join her friends.

Eugene drove off in the general direction of Bracknell but stopped at a layby. The thoughts of the previous day had caught up with him again, the respite from those thoughts whilst he chatted to Katie and took her to school was short lived. The anxiety in relation to what had occurred the previous day again became very acute. He could feel his heart beating fast, he was finding it difficult to breath with his breathing coming in short shallow breaths, he felt as if he were choking , and felt that he might be having a heart attack.

There came a feeling of impending doom, he was sweating and his hands were trembling - he didn't know what was happening. He opened the car windows and felt the cool air enter but it didn't do anything to help immediately. Eugene griped the steering wheel and held on to it tightly. Gradually the symptoms subsided, and he was left with a feeling of light-headedness. What was happening? What's wrong with me? he thought. He sat for a while and gradually started to breath more slowly again.

He realised that what had occurred was a reaction to the events he was embroiled in. He realised that he had, for the first time in his life as far as he knew, endured a panic attack. But why? He asked himself, what is so serious to cause me to react in this way? He examined his thoughts and concluded that it was not the process of the Professional Standards people - it was the subject material, child pornography. The words echoed around and around in his head - it was those words that made the whole thing unbearable. How had his name come up in whatever enquiry was being considered? Who had caused this to fall at his door? Who was making such mischief for him?

He didn't know how long he sat there but after a while he felt better and well enough to drive on to Bracknell. He did so, and manged to get a laptop at a good price, which he felt was as good as, if not better than Katie's original. He wandered around a few shops and made his way back to his car and home. Eugene reflected on the morning, not least about what he believed to be a panic attack and wondered what to do. He began to set up Katie's computer. She would probably do it better than him, anyway, but he made a start. He wondered if he should he speak to his GP. Should he contact the Police Federation office? Whilst contemplating his options the land-line telephone rang.

Sandra was still making her way along the tow path at Runnymede, now thinking intently about the other woman, the one who had caused her the most anguish – Shelia Marshall. Shelia Marshall was a PCSO at Reading, previously by all accounts, a supervisory Traffic Warden. Sandra had never seen her but was told she was about 45, tall, brassy, promiscuous and loud. Whatever Eugene had seen in her she didn't know. From what she had been told Eugene and Marshall had had a torrid affair for a number of months, at least seven, and probably more. At the time, about 2 years ago, there had been a lot of 'overtime' that Eugene said he had to carry out, a lot of late nights. Looking back, there had been lies, deceit, and much suspicion on her part. She had been told about both affairs by her friend Joan Clarke, who worked at Slough admin office, and who had a good knowledge of what had been going on with Ann-Marie Curtis, but a much more limited knowledge of what had been going on with Sheila Marshall. In consequence Sandra conjured up thoughts of what was going on in her mind and everything had seemed to grow out of proportion. There were times that she had contemplated confronting Eugene but had resisted, doing so, mainly she thought, because of Katie and that she believed the situation would burn itself out. It did so eventually, but not without leaving it's mark indelibly printed on Sandra's mind and heart. The marks of betrayal, of suspicion, mistrust, and malice.

Sandra had by now reached a café at the Old Windsor end of the Runnymede Park. She crossed the road to it and went inside. Sandra had driven past the place on numerous occasions but had never before gone inside. The building was a typical, fairly large, Victorian tea house. Inside it had a high ceiling and was decorated in a boring dark green paint which must have been applied many years ago. There were some large photographs on the wall depicting day trippers boarding and alighting from steamer craft that must have given trips to the masses up and down the river. There were only a few people inside, probably much busier at weekends and in the high summer, thought Sandra. She looked at what was on offer and ordered tea and an Eccles cake which she took to a table toward the back of the room.

She resumed her thoughts on the issues surrounding Shelia Marshall and again felt the feelings of betrayal. It was the betrayal that she believed had the most profound effect upon her. Betrayed by the person who professed to love her, betrayed by the father of their child – a child who by definition must have been betrayed. Betrayed by the lies. She imagined Eugene and that woman engaged in intimate acts, visions that had circulated in her head from time to time and had now resurfaced, because she knew that since yesterday Eugene would, for a time at least, revert to that 'lost little boy' state of helplessness, relying on her. At this moment in time she resented him for that, and resented him for his acts of betrayal. She hated Shelia Marshall, a woman she didn't know and had never seen. For all she knew Shelia could be that woman at the opposite end of the café cooing at a small child who was standing on a chair tackling a Knickerbocker Glory with an enormously large spoon.

She crushed the Eccles cake in her hand and let the crumbs fall onto the plate in front of her. She saw the lady at the counter who had served her raise an eyebrow and look quickly away. Sandra allowed herself a brief inner smile as she thought the woman must have thought there was something wrong with the Eccles cake.

Sandra couldn't help herself from returning to the thoughts of Shelia Marshall. Why had she not confronted Eugene at the time – she wished she had. She had spoken to, confided in, her mother, but her mother had told her to wait and that things would 'blow over,' it was a mistake, least said soonest mended, all in her subservient style. But it was not one 'mistake', it was two, and twice could not be a 'mistake'. Two that she knew of, but she didn't tell her mother that! Sandra thought that she should confront Eugene now but then thought that this wasn't the best time – he was at his weakest, it was too late, and the affair had long ended. She knew exactly when it had ended when Eugene started coming home on time, bringing silly little gifts and tokens, talking of foreign holidays, and taking her and Katie on outings. She knew but had said nothing. She knew, but the pain did not ease and had not eased. She hadn't touched her tea and got up and left it, and the crumpled Eccles cake, and started her walk back along the tow path to her waiting car.

Eugene answered the telephone; it was Benjie, Benjie (Benjamin) Jacobs who was a Detective Sergeant on Eugene's team. They had known each other since a time when they were

Detective Constables together, he at Langley and Benjie at Slough. Benjie was the only Jewish police officer that Eugene had known. Benjie was old school, fiercely loyal and a good, as they say, 'thief taker'. He did not 'suffer fools gladly' and that was a phrase that he proudly related had appeared on quite a few of his annual appraisals. Benjie was quite prepared to stretch the rules a little but in no way, could be said to be 'bent'.

"What's going on, Gene?"

"What have you been told, Benjie?" enquired Eugene.

"Well, we were told that you were off for a while, that we're not to contact you at all and that you may or may not be coming back. We were given the impression that you weren't well, stressed out or something like that."

"Professional Standards are investigating me; they were here yesterday."

"I knew it, C and D."

Benjie used the old fashioned initials which stood for Complaints and Discipline and were often used for Professional Standards by more long standing officers, especially those who had encountered that department along the way.

"I knew this had their stamp all over it."

Benjie had had more than his fair share of dealings with Professional Standards but officers like Benjie saw that as part of the job, a mere occupational hazard. Benjie saw complaints by those he would term 'villains' as inevitable. Such complaints usually comprised of allegations of assault, evidence 'fit ups', being a little rough in making an arrest, but Benjie had never been disciplined and had never attended a discipline hearing. Benjie went on to say that Eugene's office was now locked up and stated that he personally had not seen anyone in it.

"So, what's the score Gene, what are they saying the allegation is?"

This was the question Gene was going to find hard to answer, he disliked lying to his friend but felt that he had to. He used the same story as he had to Sandra previously, he said that his computer and that of Katie had been taken and it was some allegation about trolling. After he had related his half true and half not true story there was silence at the end of the phone for what seemed an eternity. Had Benjie, using his well-honed detective skills worked out exactly what was what.

But he exclaimed, "Ah, I know what this is, Gene." He paused and said, "Remember, a few months ago at Reading Crown Court, when we had those Dodson brothers sent down for distraction burglaries, do you remember?"

Eugene said that he did remember, and Benjie continued "And do you remember Kenny Dodson turned to us and said, 'You'll live to regret this,' the idiot, do you remember?"

Gene indicated that he did vaguely remember. Benjie said,

"Well they've made some sort of complaint, without any evidence of course. They would have made it to the governor of the prison, and he would have sent it straight to the Chief's office, the Chief would've winged it down to C and D and because it came direct from the Chief they would've overreacted in the way that those sanctimonious bastards do. I bet they were HQ C and D weren't they?"

Eugene said, "Yes, they were, actually: a superintendent Matthews and his bag carrier, a bloke called Preston."

Benjie said, "I don't know either of them, but I can see what's happened here - there'll be no evidence - you haven't been suspended, have you?"

"No, I'm on gardening leave."

Benjie said, "Well, I don't know why they've gone to these lengths in such a futile matter initiated by a couple of villains, I suppose it's that 'transparency' and 'ethical and moral conduct' bollocks we keep hearing about now. Don't worry Gene, there's nothing to this you'll be back in no time."

Benjie and Gene then talked about football for a short while after which Benjie drew the conversation to a close by saying, "Look Gene, I know how this sort of thing can affect you. It's no use me saying don't worry because anyone would worry, but just remember, I'm only a phone call away and if you want to meet for a chat, Gene, we can do that."

Feeling a surge of gratitude Eugene replied, "Thanks Benjie, I really appreciate that."

After the call ended Eugene saw that it was time to go and collect Katie from school and he was already late. For the time being his focus was on collecting Katie.

Sandra remained angry as she left the café and the walk back along the tow path seemed shorter than the walk out. Perhaps she was walking more quickly but whatever it was by the time she had got back to her car her anger had subsided. She got to the car and as she climbed in she decided that she wouldn't be saying anything; she would not be confronting Eugene. The damage had been done and there was nothing that could be achieved now that would undo that damage.

The journey back home was short and the traffic light. Sandra arrived home and found that Eugene had left to collect Katie. The new laptop was on the small writing desk in the living room, Katie would be pleased.

Sandra started to tidy around and within a short time her family arrived home. Katie was naturally excited about her new laptop and she and Eugene settled down to complete the set up. In the meantime, Sandra's thoughts were very much focussed on the revelations of the afternoon. She had a shower and imagined the negativity of the afternoon washing away and her now focussing on her maternal duties. She desperately wanted to keep Katie separate from all that was going on. She returned to the kitchen and attended to the dinner preparation and called her family to the table.

Talk over dinner comprised of Katie's school day and the laptop, and as soon as dinner was over Katie returned to her laptop. Sandra and Eugene remained in the dining room.

"How was your day?" asked Eugene.

"Yeah, OK. I had a walk at Runnymede this afternoon; it was good, allowed me to clear my head a little. And yours?"

Eugene paused, then said, "Not too bad."

Sandra thought that he looked a little more relaxed and less preoccupied this evening.

"Benjie called. I think the conversation with him helped – it put things into perspective in a way. His theory is that a couple of villains that we both know are trying to cause trouble for me."

Sandra was silent for a moment and then said, "But why have the job reacted in the way that they have, not allowing you to go to work, searching our house. And I can tell you Gene, I'm having difficulty coming to terms with that."

"Benjie, and I to a certain extent, think that it's this obsession with the police today being seen to be transparent and morally correct in all things."

"Well, I think it's over the top."

Eugene went on to explain the panic attack of the morning and Sandra listened with a concerned look on her face.

"Gene, I'm not surprised. I don't think you've been well for a long time, As I said yesterday, your sleeping has been poor; you talk in your sleep and seem agitated. Look at the state you were in last night. Why don't you make an appointment to see Dr. Bennett?"

Eugene hadn't realised until yesterday when all this kicked off that Sandra had known of how disturbed his sleep had been. In fact, he hadn't even been aware of it himself.

"Well, we'll see. I'm feeling a little better this evening. This'll blow over Sandra, don't worry".

The evening passed, as most evenings did, with little activity save watching TV, and almost no conversation to be had. Katie was engrossed in her new laptop and Sandra and Eugene lost in their own thoughts.

The family retired as they did, no real conversation having taken place between Eugene and Sandra. Eugene started to drift off and soon found himself in that strange place between being asleep and being awake. There, conversations and scenes played out which seemed to have no connection with each other and no real sense of reality.

Suddenly he awoke, wide awake devoid of thought for a moment, then the thoughts of Benjie's conversation came into his head coupled with what Matthews had said.

He could hear Matthews saying, "We've received information from another police force that a number of people have been downloading pornographic material...you are one of those people ."

Eugene tried to analyse the words – "another police force". But which one?" He thought that it must be the force in the area in which the prison was where at least one of the Dodson's were locked up, "Yes, that's it," thought Eugene. He continued to analyse Matthews words,

"A number of people have been downloading pornographic material...you are one of those people."

'Yes,' he thought. 'The Dodson's have made that particular allegation because they assumed, correctly, that the Force would overreact and choose the subject that they considered, again correctly, that would have the most impact.' His analysis and Benjie's words satisfied him for a time.

Eugene's mind was racing very much in overload. He glanced at the clock: 3:23am. 'But would the Dodson's be able to think in that way, plan in that way?' he asked himself. He assumed that they would, and in any case, there was no evidence to back up their story. He returned to Matthews words "...that a number of people have been downloading...". What did that mean, a number of people? Had the Dodson's made allegations about others; other police officers maybe? But the Dodson's worked locally and if they had made any allegations of this nature they would have done so against local officers, and if that were the case then Benjie would have said something. In fact, Benjie would have been one of them. He returned to the words, "... A number of people..." What did that mean? He turned the words over and over in his mind until they became jumbled, meaningless and torturous. He was becoming restless and decided to get out of bed so as not to disturb Sandra.

Eugene sat in semi darkness in the lounge, turning the words of Matthews and Benjie over and over in his head until the words of each were seemingly in competition with each other. Why could he not work this out? He was a professional detective after all. He noticed that his breathing was becoming fast and shallow and his heart pounding in his chest again, and he thought he might be having a heart attack. He couldn't breathe properly, and now he was sweating and shaking. He tried to call out but couldn't; was this what dying was like?

He was grasping his throat and all the time trying to breathe, but it was as if he couldn't.

The light suddenly went on and Sandra stood in the doorway, "Gene, Gene are you OK? Whatever's the matter?"

Eugene couldn't reply - he was still finding it difficult to breathe. Then Sandra was sat beside him, holding his hand.

"Just try to calm yourself, just breathe slowly; breathe in through you nose and out through your mouth…slowly… slowly, Gene."

She took him into her arms, and he placed his head on her chest.

"Slowly, deeply Gene, It's OK."

She was saying the words in a very soft voice, he felt like a distressed child but her soothing voice and her own rhythmic breathing which he could feel as he lay against her, calmed him.

Gradually, he started to breathe more slowly and deeply, the shaking stopped, and a great sense of peace enveloped him. It reminded him of being held by his mother in a similar manner. But this wasn't his mother - it was his wife, and he raised his head.

"Just don't say anything, Gene. Just breathe slowly and deeply," urged Sandra.

Eugene felt as if he was in a childlike state and Sandra at the same time thought how childlike he looked. Eugene leaned back against the settee that he was sitting on and gave a long sigh,

"What's happening to me Sandra?"

"This needs to be looked into, Gene. I want you to make an appointment with Dr. Bennett. If you won't, I'll make one for you."

Eugene thought that he should see the doctor but what could he tell him? He couldn't tell him the whole truth, could he?

Sandra made some tea and they drank it together in more or less silence. Finally, they returned to bed and Eugene mercifully drifted off to sleep.

CHAPTER 4

The morning came soon enough, and Eugene awoke as Sandra pulled back the curtains.

"You stay there, Gene; I'll take Katie to school."

"No, I'll do it."

Eugene immediately got out of bed, grateful for the few extra hours of undisturbed sleep he had enjoyed. He felt that he needed to talk to his daughter, just to make sure of a few things. He went to the bathroom had a quick shave with the electric razor and washed his face. He didn't really feel like showering, he just didn't feel motivated to have one. 'What was the point, he thought? I'm not going anywhere.'

It was a Breakfast Club morning, so Eugene and Katie left early.

As they left the house Sandra called out, "Don't forget to make an appointment with Dr Bennett."

"I won't."

Eugene and Katie commenced the drive to school.

"Katie, I want to ask you one or two things."

"Dad?"

"They're a bit personal, but I want to ask you if you've ever downloaded anything on the computer that you shouldn't have done – you know what I mean?"

"Like what?" asked Katie,

"You know, things that you would know it's wrong to download, or even see."

Katie replied indignantly, "No Dad, I'd never do that. I know some girls do things like sexting, but I've never done that."

"Have you downloaded any, you know, rude pictures?"

"If you are asking if I've downloaded any pornography then again, the answer is no, I 've not, and I wouldn't."

Eugene was shocked; he had never even contemplated that Katie would even know the word pornography. 'They grow up so quickly,' he thought.

Katie continued, "Anyway, my old computer had parental control on it. You haven't put it on this one, by the way."

"Oh, haven't I? Katie have you ever sent messages to people that were unkind?"

"No Dad, of course not. Why are you asking me these things?" she asked, crossly.

Eugene thought how sophisticated Katie sounded, how well controlled, not losing her temper at being asked questions which must be embarrassing for her.

"I had to ask love, because you know the police took your computer and I just wanted to make sure that there wasn't anything on it that could cause you any embarrassment."

"Well there isn't. I just wish you would trust me more, just drop me here."

Eugene stopped a good 250 yards from the school and Katie jumped out. She didn't offer the usual goodbye kiss, didn't say goodbye, and didn't glance back as she made her way toward her friends a good distance away. Eugene felt guilty that he had angered his daughter, but he felt that he needed to ask the questions. But he took on board what she had said, and he believed her without doubt.

Eugene couldn't remember the drive home. He contemplated how strange it was that one could drive for long distances on a sort of auto pilot and not remember the journey. He wondered how acute, or not, concentration was at such times. By the time he got back Sandra had already left for work.

Eugene made himself a cup of coffee and picked up one of the books that Sandra was currently reading. He gave it a cursory glance but couldn't read. He didn't seem able or motivated to do very much beyond more automatic operations such as taking Katie to school, although this morning he was aware that he had annoyed her with his questions but convinced himself that they needed to be asked.

Later he made his appointment to see Dr. Bennett, which Sandra had cajoled him into. The appointment was for Thursday. Eugene couldn't eat anything; he just didn't feel hungry at all. He tidied the kitchen and the sitting room. 'Try to keep busy…'. He thought about what Matthews had said. He just felt so lost and didn't know what to do. He telephoned his mother. She was a widow living in Shaftesbury where Eugene grew up. She lived in a small house and enjoyed a good social life within the local OAP scene. Eugene thought as he dialled the number that he had not visited her for some months, which he felt was selfish and decided there and then he would take Katie to see her gran very soon.

Eugene's mother answered. They exchanged greetings and she said,

"My darling, what a surprise! You don't usually call in the mornings. There's nothing wrong is there?"

"No Mum," Eugene said, putting on his 'all is well' cheerful tone. He said that he'd a day off and that Sandra and Katie were well.

They chatted about nothing in particular, but Eugene felt a sense of calm for the few minutes that he spoke to his mother. They said their goodbyes and afterwards he thought about his mother; he kept her shielded from most things and would, of course, do so in respect of current events. He felt close to her at this moment and wished that he were with her, I will go and see her soon he thought.

He thought about his mother safely cocooned in her pleasant little lifestyle, oblivious to the cruel nature of the real world, seeing only the best in all people and all things, offering a smile and a kind word to all who she met. As he thought of these things and his neglect of her, he was overwhelmed by his feelings of loneliness and desolation, and of how he just wanted to sit in her kitchen and drink tea with her. He wept.

The day passed with Eugene achieving very little. Sandra called during the morning to ask if he had made the appointment and to inform him that she would collect Katie from school in the afternoon. Eugene sat around; such a lack of activity allowed those nagging, almost persecutory thoughts to re-enter his mind. 'Why hasn't anyone apart from Benjie called?' he thought and then realised that it had only been three days. How he wanted just to talk to someone who might understand, but who would? They would just assume, like Benjie, that it was an unfortunate allegation made by a known villain and that the Force had overreacted, - end of, no big deal. Eugene just hoped that was so.

Some 47 miles, roughly north of where Eugene lived, was the headquarters of Thames Valley Police at Kidlington. Situated at the very back of the Headquarters complex was a single-story building, tucked away from view, very much like a 'Special' clinic at a city hospital, were the offices of Professional Standards.

That unit which would state that Thames Valley Police can only maintain the trust and confidence of the public if their service responds expeditiously and professionally to any person seeking to complain or express dissatisfaction about the conduct of police officers and/or police staff. They seek to promote the highest of standards of professional behaviour and personal professional integrity.

That is what they would say, and Superintendent David Matthews would certainly embrace that sentiment. In reality, the unit was disliked and distrusted by rank and file police officers and largely unknown to the public. Many police officers, and such would include Eugene, struggled to know why people would want to serve in a unit that investigated and hounded its own kind, but many do. Officers such as Eugene satisfy themselves that officers that serve within that unit do so for one of two reasons: a misplaced sense of career progression at the expense of their fellows, or because they are past their best and have been 'put out to grass'.

David Matthews would very much occupy the latter group. That afternoon Matthews was in his office not doing very much. He tended to spend a lot of time looking at an expanse of grass outside his window, looking at birds coming to feed on the food that he scattered there after his lunch each day, and feeding from the feeders that he had placed in the branches of a tree at the far end of the patch of grass. He had been looking at two investigation files; the investigations had been completed and he was checking the files and would make his recommendations before they were returned via the unit's chief officer. From there they would go back to the Deputy Chief Constable who would make the final decision on the matters. One related to a young PC who had entered into an inappropriate relationship with a known prostitute in Aylesbury. It was suspected that he may have passed sensitive information on to her but that couldn't be proved. Matthews wondered, as he often did, how police officers could get themselves into such situations. The officer was young in service and his conduct fell far below the moral conduct that was expected of a police officer. Single, with no previous disciplinary record, and a mediocre service record, Matthews felt an example had to be made and marked the file in the recommendation box with "Disciplinary Proceedings".

It was likely that the young man would be dismissed if proceedings followed, and it was highly likely they would. The second case was one of driving with excess alcohol. A sergeant in Oxford had been found to be driving under the influence when off duty. He had appeared in court, pleaded guilty and had been fined and disqualified from driving for 1 year. He had been moved to duties which did not entail driving. Such a case was a difficult one to judge. It would have to go to a disciplinary hearing, but the sergeant's fate very much lay with the Gods. Matthews had, through time, known some officers get away with a reprimand and were allowed to carry on with their careers – some senior officers at that! Some junior officers, too. Others, of varying ranks, excluding senior ranks, were dismissed without further ado. The reasons for such a variance were unknown to Matthews and most others.

Was it simply if you were seen by the organisation as a 'good egg'? Or had a sponsor, maybe, then you would keep your job, but if you were seen as 'a bit of a shit' with no one in a position of authority rooting for you, then you walked. Matthews had no idea which 'camp' the sergeant would fall into as he wrote in the recommendation box 'Disciplinary Proceedings' and cared little. He consciously did not allow the fate of officers such as the young PC or the sergeant to affect him. He didn't dwell on the matters and believed that they were, at the end of the day, masters of their own fate. He pushed the files to the edge of the desk ready to be routed to the Chief Superintendent and on to the Deputy Chief Constable.

There was a knock and a young woman who Matthews recognised as working in the Deputy's office entered.

She carried a large buff coloured package which she handed to him saying, "Sir, the Deputy wanted you to see this today".

Matthews, thanking the young woman, took the package. He placed it on his desk in front of him. He saw the postage stamps of the United States of America, the customs declaration stating that the package contained "Urgent documentation".

The package, addressed to the Deputy Chief Constable, had been opened and a routing slip paper clipped to the front destined the package to him. Matthews withdrew the bundle of papers which formed a thick file. He noticed at the top of the covering letter in bold print the words "Operation Nabokov". 'It will take some time to wade through this,' he thought. He left his office to get a cup of tea which he thought would help sustain him through the long read ahead of him for the rest of the afternoon.

Eugene's afternoon was dragging; he tried to rest but couldn't, tried to cut back some rose bushes but quickly tired and became bored with the task. He just felt unable to do anything. He was feeling cut off from the rest of society. It wasn't easy for him to call any of his colleagues although he wanted to. Nothing was easy anymore. Each day started with such good intentions, but those intentions quickly faded and by the end of the day little was achieved. Eugene was aware that he had not eaten anything again; he didn't feel hungry, just an overwhelming feeling of emptiness. He thought he should have something and prepared some cheese and crackers. He was also aware that he had not, so far, washed or shaved that day. Nothing seemed to be going well for Eugene. He realised that he had lost interest in almost everything, could not settle, could not concentrate. He thought, 'Perhaps Sandra's right, I'm more stressed out than I thought'. Eugene consoled himself with the thought that he would be seeing the doctor the following day. He ate his crackers but didn't bother to wash or shave.

Sandra came home at the usual time after picking up Katie. She slammed the front door, which was so unusual.

Throwing her bag onto the breakfast bar she abruptly said, "Katie will be having her tea with Suzi this evening; I'll pick her up around 7 – I'm going up to change".

Eugene thought that Sandra sounded agitated, but he had no idea what could be wrong. She returned after a while and settled in the dining room Where she called Eugene to join her. She didn't say anything for a moment.

She then looked directly at Eugene with those half-closed eyes and said, "What the hell were you asking Katie when you took her to school this morning?"

"Asking her what?"

But Eugene knew full well what Sandra meant.

"Asking her if she'd downloaded pornography, if she'd been sexting or sending inappropriate messages to others – what was that all about?"

Eugene could feel his heart in his mouth; he wanted to explain his reasons without causing more upset.

"I had to ask her those things. I didn't mention sexting, she did, but I needed to know if there was anything on her laptop that could cause embarrassment or problems."

"She's fourteen!" exclaimed Sandra. She continued, "She's angry and upset that you should be asking her such things and so am I."

"I was doing it for the best," said Eugene.

He really didn't know what to say. He knew that he had angered Katie and now it was clear that Sandra, although controlled, was very angry, too.

"I don't know why you were asking her about pornography. You told me that this investigation was about trolling, so why?"

"I just wanted to make sure there was nothing on there."

"Anyway, there's a parental lock on her laptop, we've always insisted that she uses the laptop down here and not in her bedroom to ensure there's nothing untoward going on, so what's your problem?"

Eugene said, "Yes, she reminded me of the parental lock, I'd overlooked it."

He suddenly remembered that he needed to apply the parental lock to Katie's new laptop. Sandra again looked at him with those half-closed eyes that significantly betrayed her mood.

She said slowly and precisely, "I don't know what the hell is going on here, Gene, but I tell you now, you keep our daughter out of it. You make sure that that vile job does not affect her or interfere in her life the way that it has ours."

Eugene was becoming defensive and said, "That 'vile' job as you call it has given us a good living."

"Yes, but at what expense?" demanded Sandra, angrily. She continued, "That vile job has changed us, changed our lives; at best you're suspicious all the time, at worst almost psychotically paranoid. You can see the good in no one and feel that everyone is operating with some ulterior motive."

"You're exaggerating, Sandra."

"No, I'm not. You don't see the way that cancer of a job grows to a point where it takes over lives; the lives of those that who are in it and the lives of their families. How many friends, and I mean real friends, do you have? I have about five, not through my own fault but because I'm married to you, a policeman."

Eugene realised that he didn't have many friends and hardly any outside of the 'job'.

Sandra continued, "That bloody job, that cancer, has taken over my life as well as yours. Do you know why we send our daughter to a private school?" Not waiting for an answer Sandra went on, "Not because I thought she would get a better education, but because I thought she would be bullied less than had she remained in a state school – bullied because of the fact that her dad was a policeman, that's why."

Eugene could see that Sandra was so angry that tears were welling up in her eyes and he decided not to reply at all. He was almost transfixed by her outburst.

"Just keep Katie away from whatever is going on, whatever you're mixed up in, and keep her away from anything to do with what you laughingly call a profession."

Eugene was glaring at her, his fists unconsciously clenching and unclenching.

He rose to the bait, if that was what it was, and said, "Well you were part of that 'profession' for long enough."

Sandra paused then said, "Yes, and how I regret that, and how much I regret that, you'll never know."

She pushed back her chair angrily and stood up and said to Eugene, "Just remember what I've said, you wallow in the filth of that job if you want to, but keep Katie away from it". She continued, "I'll go and collect her soon. If you want something to eat, get it yourself and say nothing to Katie when she comes home."

Eugene again, and it was happening so often these days, felt as if he had been beaten up. He felt as if he had no energy either physical or emotional; he felt so desperate and so alone and now he could feel that even his own family was turning against him. How he wished for this nightmare to end, for the telephone to ring to tell him all was OK, that he could return to work, to be told that their computers were clear and that no further action would be taken by Professional Standards. How he wished for that more than anything and how he wished to return to his lifestyle, which he considered far from being 'vile' 'polluted' or any other negative adjective that Sandra cared to use.

David Matthews remained in his office; he came to the end of the dossier of papers which had been brought to him. He glanced at the clock and saw that it had just gone 6pm. He rarely worked late beyond 4:30pm these days but today had been different. The file of papers had been compelling yet disturbing, and as he turned the last page he saw a blank piece of paper with one word in the middle written in bold letters -'End'. Matthews closed the file and pushed it aside. Not a man that was easily phased, offended or shocked, he placed his head in his hands and said quietly, 'My God'. He remained there for a moment, rubbed his eyes, and pushed the file toward the edge of the desk.

Matthews stared at the file. He thought that he should inform Preston straight away but realised that he would have finished for the day. He prepared a text for Preston which he hoped he would pick up first thing in the morning. This needed a joint consultation at the very least. Matthews pressed the 'send'. He waited for a few moments in case Preston called him, but he didn't. Matthews opened his filing cabinet and placed the dossier received from the US inside. He made sure the cabinet was locked shut, not once but several times. He left the office locking the door and made his way to his car in an unusually sombre and contemplative mood.

CHAPTER 5

Matthews arrived at his office before 9:00 the following morning. He hadn't slept particularly well and what he had read the afternoon before weighed heavily on his mind. Before even removing his coat, he picked up the telephone. There was an answer at the other end.

"Good morning, sir. Superintendent Dave Matthews here, Professional Standards. Are you able to see me at all this morning?"

He listened to the answer and replied, "Yes sir, I can come across straight away."

Matthews unlocked the filing cabinet, and took out the dossier that had been received from the US. He finally removed his coat, placed the dossier under his arm, locked the cabinet again and after securing his office, set off to meet the Deputy Chief Constable.

At about 9:30 Matthews returned to the offices of the Professional Standards Department. In the main office, he saw Preston talking to one of the admin staff.

"Ah, Nick, thanks for coming at such short notice, I know how busy you are." He placed his arm around Preston's shoulder and guided him towards his office.

"Take a seat Nick," said Matthews as he shut the door.

He placed the dossier on the desk between them,

"That dossier arrived yesterday, and I read it during the late afternoon and evening." And looking across at the closed door, he added confidentially, "It's pretty disturbing stuff."

Preston said nothing but stared at the dossier in front of him.

"Nick, I want you to take time out today and read those papers. As I said it's pretty disturbing stuff and I certainly don't want the file removed from the department. When you read it make sure no one else can see it."

He tapped the file with his fingers. "Don't leave the file unattended, lock it away; lock it away even if you leave your office to take a piss is that clear?"

"Yes Guv." Preston leaned across the desk and looked at his boss saying, "You can rely on me, soul of discretion and all that."

Matthews continued, "I'll give you a quick summary of what is contained within the dossier, but I want you to carefully read it fully, notwithstanding its disturbing contents."

Matthews opened the file and giving a slight cough began to read.

"About six weeks ago the police in Phoenix, Arizona received information from Microsoft that there was a person or persons unknown dealing in all manner of pornographic material, including child pornography, via the internet. They were able to identify the source of the computer activity to a suburb of Phoenix called South Scottsdale. Following some authorisation for more detailed electronic enquiries they were able to identify an actual address where they believed the activity was emanating from. The premises, which was a normal suburban house, was raided and a man and woman arrested."

Matthews gave another little cough, looked at Preston to ensure he was listening and continued.

"There was a considerable amount of electronic equipment in the premises: computers, video recorders and so on. It would appear that a lot of the straightforward pornography, for want of a better word, was sourced from within the US and uploaded on to the various sites that were run by the couple."

He cleared his throat with a cough and continued, "Neither the US police, nor we, had any particular interest in the straightforward adult porn...that's the word I'm looking for...It was the child porn that was so concerning and so disturbing."

Matthews stopped again and looked at Preston who was staring back at him intently.

"It would appear that some of the material was imported on VHS video tapes from Cambodia and Vietnam. There was some surprise at the fact that these imports had not been picked up by US customs, who are usually very good at that sort of thing apparently, but they were not, and those imports had been coming in for some time.

"Material was also distributed via the internet from the same two countries. The US perpetrators must have had a contact, or contacts, in those countries. It seems that the material, when received, was uploaded onto the various web sites. The one that we're interested in was called Phoenix Gate. Surprisingly, or maybe not so to those who know about these things, the website wasn't within the dark web but available on the regular internet. That said, once accessed, there were a number of 'gateways' to go through so whoever accessed the site would be fully aware that they were entering a child pornography site.

"It seems that once into the site there were descriptors and what are termed 'teasers' that would show so much but not all. To avail oneself of the material one would have to place an order, sort of picking things off a shopping list, and then pay by credit card. The material would then be sent to the computer of the customer. Both pictures and videos could be purchased in this manner."

Matthews stopped for a moment and Preston said, "And Elphick purchased material, did he?"

Matthews continued, "Yes, I'm coming to that. In the original briefing report, we were told that Elphick had purchased material as described by way of credit card, but we had not been told the details of the credit card. I did look at his credit cards when we saw him at his home address – he had an HSBC and a Santander card, but the purchase was made on a Lloyds card. We have the details now."

"So, he kept details of that card well hidden? It'll be gone by now," said Preston.

"Yes, I suppose so," said Matthews.

"Have we details of what Elphick purchased?" asked Preston,

"Yes, it's described in the dossier. There were a number of pictures, graphically described I warn you, and one video, again graphically described, which was streamed across."

"Are there any sample pictures?" asked Preston and Matthews noticed that he was touching, almost caressing the dossier moving his fingers across the cover as he spoke.

"No," said Matthews, "we only have descriptions of what Elphick is alleged to have downloaded." He waited for a comment from Preston but there was none, and he continued, "We now have to wait for actual evidence." He took a deep breath,

"And that evidence can only be gained from what is on the hard drives of Elphick's computers."

"So, how long do we have to wait for that?" The question hung in the air for a moment.

"That's why I went to see the Deputy this morning. I asked him if we could hurry these technical people along and he's agreed to that; I'll call them in a moment."

Preston sat back in his seat. "Shall I start reading the file now?" he reached across for the file.

"Not for a moment, Nick. I'll give you details of Elphick's Lloyds credit card, and you can obtain a statement of activity on that account via a statement obtained under the Bankers' Act."

Preston knew what to do and silently resented Matthews telling him how to do things.

"I'll contact the technical bods and speak to the officer in charge of the Paedophile and Cyber Investigation Unit. I think it'll be helpful to have one of them on board with us to advise."

"But we'll do the interviewing of Elphick, won't we?" asked Preston in a somewhat inappropriate anticipatory manner.

"Yes, of course," replied Matthews. "Now Nick, take this dossier and read through it, let me know when you've done so, and secure that statement from Lloyds."

"The statement will take a few days at least, Guv."

"Yes, I know, but let's just press on now." Matthews nodded toward the door giving Preston his cue to leave.

Eugene was walking toward the GP surgery at the same time that Matthews and Preston had parted company in Kidlington. His appointment with the GP, Dr Bennett, was for 10:30 and it was only a short walk from home. Eugene reflected on the evening before. It had been a difficult period, strained with something of a foreboding atmosphere where Eugene was fearful to say anything and decided to say nothing. Katie had returned home but there was little conversation between her and Eugene. He had in fact absented himself and spent time in the garden and then retired early. To his surprise he dropped off to sleep quickly but awoke early in the morning around 3:30am. Unable to get back to sleep, his mind racing, he got up and made tea. He sat alone in the semi darkened sitting room going over and over recent events which he knew at the time, and now was not at all helpful.

He entered the surgery, 'clocked' in at the automatic reception point and took his seat. There were only a couple of elderly people in the surgery waiting: one old gentleman with a hacking cough and an elderly woman who was telling the man with the hacking cough all about the pain in her knees. The elderly man looked totally disinterested and was clearly more focussed on his own concerns. Two receptionists chatted in the background, but Eugene couldn't see Sandra who was probably busy somewhere else in the building.

The neon sign in the waiting room flashed up "EUGENE ELPHICK ROOM 2 PLEASE". Eugene moved toward room 2 conscious of the stares of the elderly couple who were looking at him in silence, no doubt wondering why they had not yet been called. Eugene gave a light knock on the door and entered. There, waiting for him was Dr David Bennett, a jovial looking sort of man of about 60 years of age with a very florid face, which probably indicated that he had his own blood pressure problems.

Dr Bennett was sat at his desk, and he motioned Eugene toward an empty chair placed adjacent. Dr Bennett had known Eugene for some time; they had met socially when Eugene had attended work parties such as at Christmas, and they and David Bennett's wife, Marlene, had exchanged pleasantries.

"Hi Eugene, how can I help today?"

"I don't quite know where to start," said Eugene.

"At the beginning would be a good place," said David Bennett with a little laugh.

"Well, I've not been sleeping too well..."

"Tell me about that." The doctor gave an encouraging smile.

"Well," started Eugene, "I can usually get off to sleep OK, but it takes time, and then I do get off, but I wake up again early in the morning."

"What time?" enquired the doctor.

"Usually around 3:00. I can't get back to sleep and I usually get up and make tea and sit downstairs so as not to disturb Sandra."

The doctor didn't say anything, and Eugene continued, "Sandra has said that my sleep has been disturbed for some time. She says I was agitated and talking in my sleep and getting up." Eugene rubbed his eyes and sighed, "I wasn't aware of that."

"What about your appetite?" enquired the doctor adjusting himself in his chair.

"Not good, I just pick."

"Do you feel sad?"

"Yes," Eugene turned and looked out of the window.

"Do you cry?"

Eugene hesitated, "I never used to, but I have been doing so lately."

The doctor continued to ask similar questions about Eugene's libido, his concentration, his interests, all of which had been affected since the events of Monday, but according to Sandra well before that. The doctor asked about Eugene's energy levels, his decision making, and if any of his family had ever endured depression.

Then came the dreaded question, "What's happening at work?"

Eugene paused and said slowly, "I'm not at work right now?"

"Are you off sick or on holiday?"

"Neither. I'm on 'gardening leave."

"What does that mean?" asked Dr Bennett.

"It means that I'm not suspended from work, but I can't go into work. I'm under investigation by the Professional Standards Department."

"Is that sort of Internal Affairs?" queried the doctor.

"Well yes," said Eugene, "that would be the American equivalent." Dr Bennett gave a little cough which betrayed his embarrassment.

"May I ask what for?"

"That's the difficulty doctor, because my wife works here I'm a bit reluctant to be fully open about that. I'm not saying you would betray any confidence or anything, but Sandra and her work colleagues have access to notes, and you know a screen left open…something like that could cause problems."

Dr Bennett was silent. Eugene thought he might take offence and the silence seemed to go on for a while. The doctor finally said, "I can see your point; we won't pursue that for the moment. Suffice to say you're not working and under investigation, all of which is having a detrimental effect upon your health...would you agree?"

"Yes, very much so," said Eugene, again glancing out of the window.

The doctor said, "I want you to complete a questionnaire for me. Would you mind doing that?"

"No," replied Eugene glancing around the room and feeling a little trapped. The doctor went to his filing cabinet and withdrew a form on slightly yellowing paper. The questionnaire was entitled in bold letters at the top "BECK DEPRESSION INVENTORY (BDI). There then followed a series of statements and questions that Eugene had to score by circling a number.

Eugene worked through the questionnaire whilst Dr Bennett looked at his Daily Telegraph newspaper. Eugene quickly completed the questionnaire which he handed back to the doctor, who then went through it scoring Eugene's answers from a score sheet.

After a few moments Dr Bennett looked up and said, "This questionnaire is rather an old tool to assess one's level of mood at a particular time – a measure of depressive symptoms. It's not that scientific, but it gives me a baseline to work from." Adopting his most professional voice Bennett continued, "From what you've said in your questionnaire, it would appear that you're at the severe end of being moderately depressed."

"Severe?" asked Eugene with more than a hint of anxiety in his voice,

" As I said, it's not a scientific test, and I would like to make some enquiries with some of my colleagues who work in mental health."

The words mental health came as a shock to Eugene. 'Mental health,' Eugene thought 'Is he saying I'm mad, insane even. What would the job say about that?' He was aware that even in these more 'enlightened' times mental health issues did not evoke that much empathy within the machismo of the 'job'.

Dr Bennett leaned forward and enquired, "Eugene, could you pop back and see me for a short time, say at four this afternoon?"

Eugene hesitated, not knowing what for but mumbled, "Yes, yes I'll be able to."

Dr Bennett then asked, "One last thing Eugene, have you ever thought of harming yourself in any way?"

Eugene said almost immediately, "No, I'm a family man. Nothing of that sort has ever crossed my mind, Dr Bennett."

"OK, that's good."

Dr Bennett rose from his chair, put his hand on Eugene's shoulder, and guided him to the door. They said goodbye and

Eugene walked back through the waiting room. The room was much fuller now and Eugene felt a slight pang of guilt as he was aware that he had taken much longer than his allotted 8 minutes and that the full waiting room must be partly his fault. He stopped at the reception desk and asked to see Sandra who duly appeared from behind some shelves crammed full of old style GP records. She motioned Eugene outside and joined him in the car park.

"What did he say?" enquired Sandra.

"He said that I had a bit of depression," said Eugene, trying to minimise what had actually been said.

Sandra replied, "There, I told you, Gene. I told you that you've not been well for a while."

Eugene made no reply to Sandra's comment but asked, "Can you collect Katie from school, because he wants me to come back here at four this afternoon?"

"Yes, yes I was going to anyway."

Sandra started walking back to the building and almost as an afterthought said, "We'll chat later."

Before Eugene could reply, Sandra had disappeared back into the surgery. Eugene started his walk home. Meanwhile back in the surgery David Bennett did not immediately call the next patient. He sat still for a moment and thought about Eugene and that he had looked particularly rough. He clearly hadn't shaved and had probably not washed. The doctor felt that there was a lot more going on with Eugene than he had been told.

Within his office at Kidlington Dave Matthews lifted the phone and asked for the Paedophile & Cyber Investigation Unit at Oxford. The call was answered, and he asked for the officer in charge.

After a moment, a voice answered, "Detective Inspector Callaghan, how may I help?"

"I wonder if you can, Inspector. This is Superintendent Matthews, Professional Standards, could I speak to the technical support unit that deals with examining the hard drives of computers seized for enquiries?"

Inspector Helen Callaghan gave a short laugh at the other end of the phone and said, "The unit sir, comprises one technician. You can speak to him if you wish?"

"Well, perhaps you can help me," said Matthews. "I want to speak about the Elphick case. The case reference is DM/PSD/3221 of this year. I've spoken to the Deputy Chief Constable this morning and both he and I would like this matter treated as a priority."

Helen Callaghan said, "Just a moment please." Matthews could hear the tapping of computer keys and after a few minutes she came back and said, "Yes, there were two laptops and two PC base units that were brought in on Monday; they've not been examined yet."

Matthews said, "Well can they be examined straight away and treated as a priority please?"

Helen Callaghan replied, "I'm afraid not, sir. Monday is only a few days ago and we have a backlog of work, most of which has been prioritised in relation to pending Crown Court cases. I think it will be at least two weeks before the equipment you are interested in can be examined."

Matthews noted how soft and refined Helen Callaghan's voice was. He guessed that she couldn't be very old, but she spoke with confidence and didn't seem at all phased by the fact that she was being addressed by a senior officer from Professional Standards.

"Well, that's not good enough, Inspector," said Matthews. His tone of voice hardening.

Callaghan replied, "Well, in reality that's the best estimate I can give at this moment."

Matthews was getting annoyed with this seemingly young upstart of an inspector.

"Well, the reality is, Inspector, both the Deputy and I want the computer equipment examined," he raised his voice slightly, "as a priority! Which part of the word priority do you not understand?"

Matthews realised immediately that what he said was something that Preston would have said and not normally his style at all. He had in fact surprised himself at his own crassness.

There was silence at the other end of the telephone and then, in a calm, slow and clear voice, Helen Callaghan said, "Please do not take that tone with me, Superintendent. I'm just trying to put you in the picture as to the reality of the situation down here..."

Matthews interrupted her and said, "Young lady, I want the evidence that may be gleaned from those computers as soon as possible. If you want to be clever about this I'll go back to the Deputy and request that he calls you directly. The suspect in this case is a senior police officer from the south of the force and this matter needs to be bottomed out, pronto."

Even as he said it Matthews knew that he should not have told Callaghan that the suspect was a police officer, although with him being involved she had probably worked that out already. Nevertheless he was aware that he should not have said it and felt embarrassed by his own lack of professionalism. Again, there was a pause at the other end of the telephone. In the same calm and controlled voice Helen Callaghan said slowly, "There will be no need for that, sir, I'll ensure that the examination is prioritised."

Matthews felt a sense of satisfaction; he had won the argument with the young, female, intelligent upstart of an inspector, and he wanted to put her under additional pressure.

He said, "I want that evidence on my desk by noon on Tuesday next. I don't care if overtime must be worked; if it's needed you can put me down as authorising it."

Callaghan tried to interject saying, "It's not a matter of over…" but Matthews overtalked her and said, "If the evidence is not on my desk by noon on Tuesday a report from you detailing why it's not there will be, do you understand?"

There was a slight pause and Callaghan said, her voice still calm and controlled, "I will endeavour to have a report detailing the content of the hard drives on the computers with you by noon on Tuesday." She paused, and then added, "But is there a need for you to be so rude to me?"

Matthews ignored Callaghan's question, but just said, "Thank you."

Slamming down the telephone receiver. He sat back in his chair and considered the previous five minutes and in a hushed tone almost hissing through his teeth said, "Little shit, who the hell does she think she is?" He vowed to himself that he would be finding out more about Detective Inspector Callaghan.

After returning home from the GP surgery Eugene made himself a cup of coffee and realised that again he hadn't eaten anything that morning. He placed one slice of bread in the toaster and sat at the breakfast bar. He started to reflect on what Dr Bennett had said, and was only disturbed by the 'pop' of the toaster as it delivered his piece of toast. He didn't reach out for it and carried on with his reflections, wondering if he were 'depressed' as Dr Bennett had indicated, or was his mood just low because of events, which he rationalised would be quite understandable. Had he been in a low mood for a while as Sandra had indicated? Was he stressed as she had said? He just did not know.

All he did know was that each day merged into another with no sense of structure or purpose, he knew that he wasn't sleeping and that he felt unwell and weak. He felt that he was quickly losing his grip on things and that he was even losing his grip on family life. His daughter remained angry with him, and his wife distant. He hated the thought of being 'depressed' having a 'mental illness', being stressed. He had little knowledge of such things and didn't really want to know about them. So far as he was concerned, and the majority of his colleagues come to that, these things were a sign of weakness, a sign that one couldn't 'hack it'.

Eugene wandered into the garden, ignoring the fact that the grass needed mowing. He looked into the garage, still untidy from the search on that fateful day. Going back indoors he managed to watch the lunchtime news on TV but wasn't sure how much of it he took in. He didn't have lunch and later realized that he hadn't touched the piece of toast that he'd prepared a few hours earlier. He took some fruit and decided to have a bath prior to returning to the GP surgery for 4:00pm. He ran his bath and thought that his life was, at present, like descending a helter-skelter – totally out of control.

CHAPTER 6

During the late afternoon Detective Inspector Nick Preston went to the office of Superintendent Dave Matthews. He was carrying the large buff enveloped which contained the dossier that he had been reading in his office for much of the day. He knocked on the door of the office and waited for the 'come in!' from Matthews. He entered the room and Matthews immediately saw that Preston had an ashen look about him.

"Hi Nick, you OK? Take a seat."

Preston didn't speak immediately but seemed to be carefully formulating what he wanted to say. He was staring directly in front of him. He placed the dossier on the desk still in its envelope.

There was silence in the room for a while and then Preston said slowly, "I've read the dossier, the dossier of filth, the dossier of unnatural acts the like of which I have never come across in my entire life before, the like of which I had never even thought about or imagined. The dossier of mistreated, abused, violated, and tortured victims, victims who are children. There are no pictures as you know, but that makes it worse in a way because reading the detailed descriptions you picture the acts. Acts which are totally alien to you, in your own mind. I must say, Guv, I found it a horrible experience. When you read of men gang raping a child, putting them with animals..."

Matthews interjected, "Alright Nick, I've read the file, I know exactly what you mean. It's horrible."

Preston continued, "I want to go and arrest that creep Elphick right now and do you know why? Because what we read about is going on somewhere right now and it's going on in the main because bastards like Elphick are prepared to pay money to view and satisfy their demonic perversions. Not only would I desire to arrest him, Guv, but I would very much like to..."

Preston put his left hand up to his forehead and Matthews, for a moment, thought he was going to cry, but Preston was far too angry for that.

Just then a knock came on the door and Matthews bellowed out in a loud voice, "Not now!"

Whoever it was went away. Preston was saying nothing. Matthews was somewhat surprised to see this human, emotional side of Nick Preston which he had never witnessed before. He had worked with the man for nearly 6 months but didn't 'know' him at all.

To break the silence he asked Preston, "You a family man, Nick?"

"I was married but I'm divorced now; no children. But that doesn't mean I didn't feel for those kids that I had to read about. Those images, when we see them, the pictures will be level four and five without a doubt!"

Another silence and Preston then said, "What about you? Are you a family man, Guv?"

"Yes, I'm married with a grown-up daughter. That dossier does leave its mark. I would suggest you try and do something tonight to take you mind off it. Matthews continued, "What are your commitments tomorrow?"

"I have to see a couple of PCs over in Witney. A complaint was made that they drove past this old girl who was driving her car and they were both wearing those rubber masks of old men, they waved to the old girl and frightened her apparently. She made a complaint. In comparison to what we are dealing with here, it's crap. I don't think it will go anywhere. They'll probably deny it anyway. There's no evidence."

Preston, relating that story, lightened the mood a little and Matthews said, "Get yourself home now. What time will you finish with that Witney job do you think?"

"About lunchtime I'd think," said Preston.

"Well," said Matthews ,"when you finish, take the rest of tomorrow off and we'll touch base on Monday. Try to have a relaxing weekend."

"Thanks Guv," said Preston, "I appreciate that."

Preston left the room leaving the envelope containing the dossier on Matthews desk which Matthews picked up and carefully placed in the lockable filing cabinet. As he did so the telephone rang. Matthews picked the phone up.

"Yes sir, yes sir. I'll be there, that's 2:00pm on Monday? Yes sir."

Matthews replaced the receiver and just hoped that the Deputy would not be giving him another case similar to the Elphick one when they met on Monday.

Eugene Elphick made his way back to the GP surgery, arriving there just before 4:00pm. There was no one in the waiting room and the receptionist, a lady called Carol, who Eugene knew vaguely, said he could go straight into Dr Bennett. Eugene walked to the room gave a light tap on the door and entered. Dr Bennett almost rose to his feet and greeted Eugene in his normal agreeable manner.

"Eugene! Come and sit down". He continued "I've spoken to my colleague, Dr Shen Bekhit - he's a consultant psychiatrist. If I referred you to him, you would see him anyway, but it would take around six weeks for an appointment. I've asked him if he would, as a favour to me, see you more quickly and as he's had a cancellation he can see you at his office at Maidenhead tomorrow afternoon at 3:30pm - could you make that?"

Eugene hesitated - him having to see a psychiatrist! He never thought it would come to this, but he replied, "Yes, yes I could go there."

Dr Bennett wrote Dr Bekhit's office address down, and he gave it to Eugene.

The doctor continued, "I'm prescribing you something that may help with your chronic insomnia," and he gave Eugene a ready prepared prescription.

Eugene glanced at it, and it read "Amitriptyline 10 mg nocte - 28 days".

Dr Bennett said, "Take one of these at night; they'll help you sleep through the night. However, one of the side effects is a very dry mouth so have a glass of water at your bedside for when you wake up. Also read this leaflet for the other side effects."

Eugene took the leaflet, folded it, and tucked it into the inside pocket of his jacket without looking at it.

"Is there anything you want to ask Eugene?"

Eugene said, "No, I don't think so," as he placed the prescription and address details in his pocket.

"Ok then, I think you will find Shen very helpful and remember you can always come back and see me." He again rose and shook Eugene by the hand, and said, "Take care, Eugene." They parted company and Eugene walked slowly home, stopping to get his prescription filled on the way.

When he got home Sandra and Katie were both there. They all greeted each other in a superficial way. Katie and Sandra were in the kitchen seemingly having a 'girlie' chat. Eugene sat in the living room mulling over the day's events. He took the small bottle of tablets from his pocket and looked at them wondering again how things had got this far. He still wasn't sure if he would take any of them or not.

The evenings were beginning to take on something of a routine that never existed when Eugene was working. They had dinner, Katie usually attended to homework, chatted to friends on her laptop, texted, watched TV or listened to music. She usually went to bed around 9:00. Sandra cleared away after dinner, sometimes read, listened to music with her headphones or attended to domestic chores; she seldom watched TV these days. Eugene seemed to place himself in front of the TV but whether he 'watched' it or not was a different matter. He tended to exhaust himself going over and over current events, trying to seek clues, to fathom out what was going on, and on who it was that had orchestrated this 'trouble'. This evening was no different.

Once Katie had gone up to bed Sandra came and sat beside Eugene, switched off the TV via the remote and said, "So, what happened with David Bennett this afternoon?"

Eugene paused as he was not totally clear as to what really occurred. He said after a moment, "Well, as I told you this morning, he thinks I've a bit of depression; he wants me to see a psychiatrist."

Eugene paused waiting for some sort of reaction from Sandra but not knowing what reaction to expect. There was in fact no reaction.

He continued, "He's arranged for me to see a Dr Bekhit at Maidenhead tomorrow afternoon, so if you can pick up Katie again...?"

Sandra automatically said, "Yes, of course." She was quiet for a moment and then said, "Well, let's bring this to a head now. You've been unwell for a while in my view, agitated, not sleeping well and more recently getting up at night and not concentrating."

Eugene replied, "Well, part of that is to do with what's going on, I suppose."

"Did he say anything else?"

"He gave me some tablets to help me sleep," and he took the bottle of tablets from his pocket and showed Sandra who took the bottle, looked at the label and gave the bottle back to him.

She said, "I'll make a warm drink. Why don't you take one of the tablets and have an early night? And maybe you should try sleeping in the spare room tonight?"

"Do you think it will help?" asked Eugene.

"It'll help me, Gene. Your sleep is pretty disturbed at the moment which affects my sleep."

"Ok, I will then," said Eugene not quite knowing what he thought of the idea.

Eugene awoke with a start. He couldn't quite work out where he was for a second. He could hear either Sandra or Katie in the bathroom. He looked at his watch which he was still wearing and saw it was 7:45. He realised that he had slept for some 11 hours and without waking up during the night. He was very thirsty, and he didn't feel refreshed and thought it must be the aftereffects of the medication. But at least, he had slept!

Eugene was lying there not thinking of anything in particular when there was a slight tap on the bedroom door and Sandra appeared with a cup of tea.

"How do you feel?" enquired Sandra.

"Well, I appear to have slept well but I feel a bit groggy."

"You were up again in the night though," said Sandra. "I heard something and saw the downstairs light on so I went down and found you sitting at the dining room table. You were just staring into space as if you were in a trance. I spoke to you, but you didn't reply, and I guided you back to bed. Are you OK now?"

"I didn't realise," said Eugene somewhat pensively.

Sandra continued, "It was a bit scary. Perhaps it was the medication, I don't know but you should tell the doctor when you see him this afternoon."

Eugene said he would. He started to get up and Sandra left the room.

By the time Eugene had readied himself and got downstairs Sandra and Katie were in the process of leaving the house.

Katie came and hugged Eugene saying, "Have a good day Dad, see you later, love you." She hadn't done this for a day or two and Eugene felt very pleased that she had made this gesture.

"I'll be home before you go this afternoon, Gene, so we'll be able to have a chat then," Sandra said.

They all said their goodbyes and Eugene was alone again. Being alone and feeling alone was par for the course these days. He made himself a cup of coffee and sat in the kitchen, the start of the process of allowing the day to drift along with the only focus being his appointment that afternoon.

The day did drift along, with Eugene doing very little. He tried to watch some daytime TV, but the content was so banal and his concentration so poor that he switched the set off very quickly. He toyed with his mobile phone. He thought about when it rang incessantly to the point of annoyance, and of how now it hardly ever rang. He thought about his colleagues and how none of them except Benji had contacted him. He wondered how much they knew by now; they were, after all, police officers and would naturally want to know and find out. He thought about Benji and considered calling him but decided against it as Benji would naturally ask questions that Eugene did not want to answer right now. He made numerous cups of coffee which he didn't drink, spent a long time staring into space and tried to listen to the lunchtime news on the radio without success. He made a sandwich which he didn't finish and drank half a mug of tea. Time seemed so very irrelevant and passed by at seemingly different paces.

By around 1pm Eugene was beginning to feel very restless and somewhat agitated. He didn't want to wait for Sandra to return because there would be more questions; questions, questions, someone always seemed to be asking him questions, that is if there was any someone at all.

Eugene felt the strain of spending so many hours alone, something he was certainly not used to. He got ready, quickly made sure that he had everything he needed and that he had the piece of paper with the address of Dr Bekhit's office which he placed in the inside jacket of his pocket. He felt another piece of paper there, pulled it out and saw it was the leaflet on side effects that David Bennett had given him the previous day. He put it back in its place in the inside pocket, again without looking at it.

Eugene made his way to his car and drove to Maidenhead via the outskirts of Windsor, through Water Oakley and then on into Maidenhead. He was ridiculously early but parked his car in the multi-story car park. He made his way to the High Street and walked slowly along. He looked at the address on the piece of paper that he was given it read Simply "Dr Bekhit - CMHT - Reform road" and a sort of shorthand giving directions - "High Street > Bridge Rd turn right into Waldeck Road T junc. turn left CMHT at bottom on left". Eugene knew roughly where it was, on a small trading estate. He thought how depressing the High Street here was.

Eugene arrived at the bottom of Reform Road and saw a double doorway, a sign saying, "Berkshire Healthcare Foundation Trust, Maidenhead/Windsor CMHT" to the left of the door, and to the right a sign saying, "Screw Fix - Training Department". He stood looking at both signs. A strange thought entered his mind - 'Screw loose to the left, screw fix to the right'. He didn't smile but just thought that even in these bizarre and somewhat tragic circumstances he found himself in, the black humour of the police force still managed to get through.

Black humour, he thought, and had always thought, was just another means of relieving stress notwithstanding how cruel it may seem. Eugene went through the outer door and saw a glass fronted door to the left displaying the sign "CMHT". He entered and saw that he was in a well-lit room with blue plastic chairs around three of the walls, surrounding a small table with a few well-thumbed and tattered magazines displayed.

In one corner was a large-framed woman bent over almost double looking into a Tesco carrier bag that was on the floor in front of her. She seemed intent on looking for something inside the bag. At the far end of the room was a glass fronted office, obviously reception. He went over and noticed how thick the glass was with an aperture at the base for documents to be placed through and a circular area in the middle with the words 'speak here' above.

Inside the office sitting behind a desk was a female of about 50 years. She was looking at a computer screen and although she must have known that Eugene was there, didn't look in his direction. Eugene just stood there looking around the office picking out little details with his trained eye: dirty coffee cups, a child's photo in a cheap plastic frame, lots of coloured pens in a mug marked 'Keep calm, it's nearly the weekend'. Eventually the woman looked up and made her way toward him.

"Yes?" she enquired without really looking at him.

"I am here to see Dr Bekhit...umm...I have an appointment at 3:30."

"You're early," the receptionist informed him, "Just take a seat".

Eugene moved back into the body of the waiting room, where the Tesco bag-woman wearing a somewhat dirty off pink coloured coat which was totally unsuitable for the outside temperature, continued to search through her carrier bag, muttering to herself. She took things out and then put them back again, over and over again. Eugene was quite fascinated with it all, but had no idea why this woman was behaving in the manner that she was.

The woman from reception then came into the waiting room and addressed the woman in the off pink coat in a patronising manner, "Annie, Clare said that she can't see you today."

Annie replied, "But she's here, why can't she see me?" While Annie was talking she was still looking through her Tesco bag.

The woman from reception gave a loud exasperated sounding sigh and said, "Clare said she would see you next week at home as arranged."

Annie replied, "Why can't she see me now?"

The woman from reception appeared to get more agitated and said, "Well, she can't. She's very busy. You're not her only patient you know. Go home now."

Annie seemed defeated. She stopped looking inside her bag, stood up and Eugene noticed what a tall woman she was, and how the lenses of her spectacles were so dirty he wondered how she could see out of them.

Annie just said meekly, "Alright," and made her way out of the building.

The woman from reception sighed again and returned to her office. Eugene looked at the tattered magazines, titles such as Woodworker, Peoples Friend, a Saga travel brochure were there but Eugene didn't pick anything up. The room was quiet, a door along the corridor to his left opened and a young woman appeared. She was holding a tissue to her face and appeared to be crying as she quickly egressed from the building.

Eugene waited and glanced at his watch - 3:29 - and as he did so the door along the corridor opened again and a slightly built, in fact quite thin man, who looked Asian, and was wearing a light brown suit which seemed tight and too small for him walked towards Eugene.

"Mr Elphick?"

"Yes," Eugene stood up.

"Hi, I'm Dr Bekhit." He stretched out his hand and smiled. The two men shook hands and Dr Bekhit said, "Please come this way."

They both entered the room that the woman had come from earlier; it was a fairly small room with no window. There was a desk against the wall, a chair in front of the desk and one to the side of the desk. At the far end of the room were two more comfortable looking chairs and a small coffee table between them, on the table was a box of tissues. On the wall above the desk was a picture of 3 seagulls walking along the wet sand of a beach with a cold looking sea in the background.

"Please sit down," said Dr Bekhit and Eugene took the chair that was beside the desk. Dr Bekhit sat at the desk; there was a laptop in front of him which bore the logo in blue and white, 'Berkshire Healthcare Foundation Trust'. Dr Bekhit closed the laptop and said "My friend, Doctor David Bennett, contacted me and has emailed me a letter which I've read. I see he carried out a Beck's Depression Inventory, a copy of which I have. Now, I want to ask you some questions, many of which he's already asked you but please bear with me as I need to do this."

Eugene just replied, "OK."

He noticed that Dr Bekhit spoke in perfect English with no trace of an accent, and Eugene assumed that he must have been born in the UK, but he could still not work out what the doctor's national or cultural origins were.

Dr Bekhit said, "May I call you Eugene?"

Eugene replied, "Yes, but I prefer Gene.".

"OK, Gene." Dr Bekhit then proceeded to ask Eugene many questions, as he had said often repeating what David Bennett had asked him the previous day; his personal details, where he was born, where he went to school, qualifications, marital status and so on. Dr Bekhit then asked how Eugene's appetite was.

"Well, I suppose its reduced to what is was. Thinking about it, I don't feel like eating much these days."

"And, what about your sleep?"

"Well, not as good as I thought it was. I hope that the medicine that David Bennett gave me will help, but my wife informed me I was getting up in the night again, she said I'd been doing this for a while, but I was unaware of it. I can usually get off to sleep but either wake up in the small hours or seemingly sleepwalk."

There was a pause and Dr Bekhit said "How long has this been going on?"

"I'm not sure," replied Eugene. "Not long, I think."

There was another pause and Dr Bekhit asked, "Have there ever been other episodes of sleepwalking in the past?"

Eugene said, "No, at least not that I know of." As Eugene answered each question Dr Bekhit made a note in a spiral bound notepad. He sat at his desk but facing Eugene and Eugene couldn't help noticing how one ultra-thin leg crossed the other, exposing woollen socks of a slightly different blue hue and how Bekhit's brown shoes had been scuffed into a light brown, shoes that obviously had never seen any polish. Questions, questions, and more questions some fairly innocuous such as: 'What leisure pursuits do you have?' 'Are you able to pursue them now?' to the more bizarre such as 'Were you, as a child, cruel to animals?' 'Were you afraid of the dark?' 'Did you bite your nails?'

So many questions and then, "I understand you are a police detective inspector; tell me about you career to date."

Eugene started to give a potted history of his career, of the milestones, how he met Sandra, married, promotion.

"Do you enjoy your work?" asked Dr Bekhit.

"I did, yes, very much up until recently."

"I'll come back to recent events shortly, but tell me, is there anything in your career that stands out for you, and I'm thinking more of traumatic events, things that have occurred that have stayed in your memory."

Eugene thought, and the room fell silent for a minute or so.

"I don't know..."

Dr Bekhit interjected, "Anything in your service that unnerved you, upset you, caused you to dream about it, anything you can think of."

Eugene thought again briefly and said, "There was something. It was a good while ago, I was a uniformed PC at the time, a tutor constable, I had a young WPC with me...yes, there was something."

Dr Bekhit said in a quiet reassuring soft tone, "Go on Gene."

"It was at night; we were sent to a point just west of Iver Railway Station to a report of someone on the railway track. We got there and I could see someone laying on the slow goods track. It looked as if the head may have been missing...I told the WPC to stay where she was and I approached the...the... body. The head was in fact attached, it was her coat that had come up over her head."

Eugene paused again, a little longer this time and Dr Bekhit did not interrupt the silence.

Eugene continued, "Her left leg was missing and so was her right foot...I was surprised at the lack of blood, there just wasn't that much. The body was cold. I radioed in what I'd found and asked for the slow goods track, where we were, to be closed. I was told to leave things as they were, and that assistance would be sent. I called the WPC over. She was a bit shocked by the whole thing and I said she could go and sit in the car, but she didn't."

Eugene paused with no response from Dr Bekhit who was listening intently.

"I walked back to the road bridge. Underneath the bridge I saw that beside the track were a number of spent matches and cigarette butt ends. There were also some pieces of paper which turned out to be letters. They were addressed to various people, I remember, to her mum, and other named people. The letters were written in pencil, beautifully scripted; they spoke about the ancient Stoics of Greece, of how it was natural to love someone of the same sex and so on, how it was natural to love a younger person. There was also an account of the woman's feelings as she sat under the bridge. Looking at the number of matches and butt ends she must've been there a good while."

Eugene stopped again and there was no interruption of the silence so he continued.

"She said in one of the letters that she was waiting for a goods train and wanted to jump between the trucks as she didn't want to alarm the driver. And that's what I think she did. After a while other officers, an inspector with a PC, and the duty CID sergeant and DC arrived. The CID officers were concerned that the woman may've been pushed off the bridge but when they were satisfied that this wasn't so, they left. The

Inspector gave me and another PC a black plastic bag each and told us to walk along the track to see if we could spot any human remains and to place them in the bag."

Eugene stopped again seemingly lost in thought, and again Dr Bekhit allowed the silence to prevail. After a little while Eugene continued.

"He was quite a vile man, that inspector, lacking in any compassion, lacking in common decency. I remember he treated the whole thing as a bit of a joke, making crude and unnecessary comments. He never asked us how we felt, or if we were OK. He did say to the WPC as he handed out the plastic bags, 'Not you love, this is a bit too gruesome for you' which only served in humiliating her. We, the other PC and I, did what the Inspector had asked, and the other PC had the unfortunate task of retrieving the missing leg and foot – I wonder how he must have felt...The police doctor arrived to examine the body and formally pronounced the body dead. After that, the British Transport Police arrived, and they took over the scene. I was asked to make a statement which I did later.

Do you know doctor, I could write that statement today, right now! I can remember her name even her date of birth...I later found out that the woman had appeared in Court in London earlier that day, had been charged and bailed to the Crown Court for indecency with under aged girls. She just couldn't hack it, I suppose. She was a classics teacher at some posh London boarding school; the scandal would've been colossal and that's why I suppose, she killed herself."

There was a long pause and Dr Bekhit said, "Have you ever spoken about this before?"

"Not so much…no, not really".

Dr Bekhit continued, "What stands out most in the matter for you, the most prominent thing?"

"The letters I think, what must've been going on in the woman's mind."

"How did you feel about the woman?"

"I don't know. I suppose I felt sorry for her."

"Tell me, Gene, how did this matter affect you at the time?"

Eugene thought for a moment and said, "I'd seen a dead body before but not one that'd been as traumatised as this one had. I used to dream about it."

"Do you dream about it now?"

"Not so much."

"What about flashbacks to that scene?"

"Yes, I've had them, but not generally that much over recent years although when talking to you a few minutes ago, I was there - right back there again."

"And what about the area, do you go there?"

"Not much now, but you can approach from different sides and do you know, I've never driven over that bridge. I've avoided it. I don't know how I would react if I had to go down to the track there again."

"I understand," said Dr Bekhit". He then continued, "What form of debriefing of that incident took place?"

"None. Debriefing of incidents like that didn't take place then. I think it's a bit different now, but no, nothing; no one asked us anything about it, about how we were feeling, if it affected us, nothing."

Dr Bekhit gave a little sigh, did not reply but seemed lost in thought for a moment. He then said, "Eugene would you like a little break?"

"No, I think I'm OK, thank you."

Dr Bekhit then said, "I want now to turn to more recent matters. You've already told me you are currently on enforced leave so something has happened at your work, has it?"

"Yes," replied Eugene.

"And is this what you were reluctant to disclose to Dr David Bennett?"

"Well, yes, because my wife works there, at that surgery and so on."

"Yes, I understand. Would you like to share this with me?"

There was again silence which was not interrupted by Dr Bekhit.

"It's just a few days ago, it seems much longer. Officers from Professional Standards came to my home, searched it, and took away the family's and my daughter's computers and said that allegations had been received that I'd been downloading material on to a computer."

"What material?"

"Well…child pornography."

Eugene consciously looked for a reaction in Dr Bekhit but there was none. He merely asked, "And did you? Did you download that material?"

"No, of course not," said Eugene.

"How did it get there then?" enquired Dr Bekhit.

"We don't know that it is," said Eugene and continued, "the computer hard drives are being examined. One of my colleagues thinks it's a set up by someone."

"What does the alleged material comprise?" asked Dr Bekhit.

"I don't know what it's supposed to be."

"So, all that remains under investigation?"

"Yes."

"How does it all make you feel?"

Eugene thought and then replied, "Angry, scared, perplexed, a mix of emotions really. I keep telling myself that it's all a mistake, a silly unfounded allegation made by someone, but then I doubt myself".

"What have you told your wife?" asked Dr Bekhit.

"I haven't told her much, just that the computers were taken because of some sort of allegation against a number of officers, 'trolling'."

Dr Bekhit didn't reply. He was writing in his notebook. He then took out a prescription pad and said, "I'm sorry for this, but I have to ask you - have you ever thought of ending your life, either now or previously?"

"No, never."

"Well, Gene, thank you for being so honest with me. It's been a long and difficult session for you, I'm sure. I think that you're showing the symptoms of depression, but I also think that a lot of this is reactive to your current situation. You are also enduring some PTSD which has historic origins and which I believe has been present for some time. I would like to treat the PTSD but can't do that until the depression has been dealt with. I think the depression will lift quite quickly once the current situation has been dealt with and ideally you return to your work."

He paused and continued, "I'm increasing your dosage of Amitriptyline to 25 mg at night. Please don't exceed the dosage, so do not take the 10 mg tablets that Dr Bennett gave you, and have a glass of water next to your bed as your mouth will become very dry. You may also have some constipation and be careful about driving or operating machinery." He gave the completed prescription to Eugene and said, "I'd like to see you again in 4 weeks' time at the same time". He gave Eugene an appointment card and said very much as an afterthought, "Is that OK?"

Eugene nodded his head, shook the doctors hand and before he knew it he was outside the building. Looking at his watch Eugene realised that he had been with Dr Bekhit for just under two hours.

CHAPTER 7

Eugene couldn't really remember much of the journey, as he arrived at his driveway. He couldn't remember leaving Dr Bekhit's office, the walk back to his car or the journey home. He put it down to automation as his mind dwelled on other things but could not even recall what he was dwelling on. It was a scary thought and Eugene just sat in his car for a few minutes. He could see the kitchen light was on and was aware that Sandra and Katie would be at home. As he got out of the car, he thought he just didn't want to go over everything with Sandra, and realised how exhausted he felt.

On entering the kitchen Katie ran toward him put her arms around her father and said, "Dad, I love you."

This was the best thing Eugene could have heard right then. Sandra looked up from her meal preparations and just said softly, "You OK, love? We'll talk later."

Eugene didn't reply but excused himself and went upstairs. By the time he returned the meal had been prepared and they all sat down together.

Katie was quite loquacious and spoke at length about her day at school: hockey, friends and so on. Neither Eugene or

Sandra stopped her, and Eugene was grateful that he didn't have to go over his day's events. After the meal Eugene offered to clear up and did so with Sandra but they were both silent, consumed by their own thoughts.

Sandra then broke the silence and said, "Do you want to talk about it, Gene?"

"I'd rather not…not now. I feel exhausted. I'm not sure how I feel really."

"OK, tomorrow maybe."

Eugene watched TV with Katie for a while, and then he made his excuses, kissed Katie, and retired to his room and bed.

The burnished rails were reflecting the light from the powerful lights which illuminated the expanse of multiple tracks on the far side from where Eugene stood. The beams also accentuated the persistent and penetrating drizzle that was falling. Eugene negotiated the somewhat flimsy wire fence and walked toward what he thought might be a bundle of rags or a sack that had fallen from a passing goods train.

Suddenly he was under the road bridge where there was a dry and dusty ledge several feet back from the track. He was looking at the spent matches and cigarette ends, at the letters and notes that had been carefully placed under a stone. He was conscious of snippets of conversations, the voice of a hardened CID officer, 'There's nothing for us here son, get this handed over to BTP as soon as you can'.

The voice of the vile inspector addressing the WPC, 'Not you love, this is a bit too gruesome for you.'

Eugene felt angry about this man with his stupid coal miners' type lamp fixed somehow to his raincoat. Suddenly, Eugene was back, walking toward the shape lying next to the track. Now he could see it was a woman, but he couldn't see a head. He came close and saw that her brown coat was over where the head should be. Eugene slowly reached for the coat and awoke with a start.

The room was dark, pitch black. He grabbed to switch the bedside light on and sat upright sweating, and his heart was pounding in his chest so hard he believed he could hear it, pounding so hard he believed he was about to have a heart attack and die. He couldn't breathe properly; he was able to breathe in but couldn't breathe out. He wanted to shout out for Sandra but couldn't – was he going to die, was this it?

Eugene then gave out a large sigh and his breathing returned to normal, his heart stopped pounding and he lay back on the bed, realising that he could now breathe deeply and effortlessly. It was just a dream, a dream that he had had before but not for a long time. That arm reaching toward the coat was always the nightmare contingent. Eugene was aware that Dr Bekhit had opened a can of worms that had lain undisturbed for a while. He looked at his watch - 3:20 am; he wondered if he would be able to sleep anymore. He looked at his bottle of tablets but did not take one. He would get more tomorrow.

*

Superintended Dave Matthews had spent a quiet, reflective weekend with his wife. He didn't do very much, washed his car, pottered about in his garden, read the papers on Saturday and Sunday, the only time he seemed to have time to do so. He wasn't sleeping well; it was nothing to do with the Elphick case although the details of that were occupying his thoughts from time to time. It was more about his impending retirement; he was 57, and had completed well over the usual 30 years. He had joined as a young man of 24 and really didn't know anything other than policing. The printing trade in which he was engaged in before joining had changed radically and wasn't the same anymore.

He reflected and fretted about what was to become of him once he left. Subtle remarks had already been made that he should think about retirement now and he wondered if the

Deputy Chief would mention such when he saw him later on. Dave had no idea why the Deputy Chief wanted to see him.

He had worked out his pension on several occasions and realised that he and his wife would be financially secure but nevertheless the thought of retirement filled him with dread. He reflected on his career as a whole; he had done reasonably well, had been sponsored by his first inspector in the early days, had kept his mouth shut and followed the 'party line'. Don't make waves, he was advised, and he didn't. There were times that he wanted to speak out but didn't. He had never witnessed overt corruption but had witnessed a more subtle corruption; of how the 'job' promoted in its own image, rejected 'gobshites' those who had a lot to say about everything, and stabbed others in the back. Yes, he had witnessed that, and to his shame had been party to it from time to time.

There existed, certainly in his early service, a bullying culture that still existed but was much more hidden and less overt, but it was certainly still there. There was much less racism and sexism, both of which were indeed overt up until the Stephen Lawrence enquiry which led to the police being accused of 'institutional racism'. Every police officer at the time knew that was true but didn't necessarily say so. Racism was then covered up, forced underground as the service in general tried to belie it's 'institutional racist' tag, but it still existed. Gone were the appalling tags of 'Spook,' 'Stani,' 'Jungle Bunny,' 'Coon,' but racism still existed, especially amongst older officers and those who could be described as being part of self-proclaimed 'elite teams'.

Sexism had all but been eliminated. The days of a young woman police officer entering a CID office and being told to "Get your tits out," which he personally had witnessed, had long gone. Indeed such a situation in modern times would be unthinkable and if it did occur the culprit would not only be reported by his fellow colleagues, but he would be sacked without a doubt. But this level of sexism existed. He witnessed it, but did nothing and said nothing, so in a way was complicit with it, something he was now ashamed of.

Women were viewed much more differently today; they have risen to the top of the profession and are often extremely proficient in what they do. Women were now a force to be respected within the service, often middle class and assertive. His thoughts turned to Detective Inspector Helen Callaghan, and he felt a sense of annoyance which he quickly dismissed. However, he didn't realise that this officer would feature in his life again sooner than he would have liked. He looked at the clock – late Monday morning already and he had spent a long time just cogitating. He was seeing the Deputy in a couple of hours' time and needed to get up to speed. He called the office manager and together they would work through the weekend events.

Sandra Elphick wasn't working that Monday morning; she should have been, but having dropped her daughter Katie off at school had phoned the surgery saying that she was seeking an emergency dental appointment and didn't think she would be in that day. She felt guilty when her supervisor sympathised with her, and Sandra just hoped she wasn't tempting fate. She made her way to Windsor, parked her car near the place where the tour coaches parked and made her way through a small park to the river. There were not many people walking near the river at that hour and Sandra found a park bench. She wanted time to herself; she had spent the majority of the weekend with Katie, either ferrying her to hockey practice or spending time with her at her parents' home. She had spent little time with Gene and realised that the time she actually spent with him was becoming less and less. She wanted this space to explore her thoughts, explore what she really wanted.

She was aware that her time living with Gene as man and wife was really at an end. She realised that the present was a bad time for him and had seen how he had aged ten years in a very short space of time. He looked haggard, often did not shave, and seldom showered. He spent hours in his room alone, didn't eat much and she was aware that his sleep remained poor despite him having medication to help him. She should have been sympathetic or at least empathic, but she wasn't; she couldn't bring herself to be so and wanted to examine her thoughts as to why.

Sandra looked around her and remembered how she and Gene used to often walk here before they were married. Gene would enthusiastically explain his plans for the future, his vision of how the police service would develop and his place within that vision. That was a time when they were blissfully happy. Sandra remembered her then boyfriend, PC David Osborn, but poor David was a plodder and although pleasant Sandra saw no future, or future security with him. She remembered how upset he had been when she unceremoniously dumped him in favour of Gene. David never married, was still about, working as a PC at Burnham, near Slough. They occasionally spoke on the telephone and had met for coffee, but not recently. Now, considering all things, perhaps, David would have been a safer bet, she thought. However, she quickly mentally scolded herself because she had Katie, and Katie would only exist because of her and Gene.

She remembered her wedding; it was a large affair with mostly police personnel in attendance, lots of drinking and male humour. She remembered her early married life; it was more than reasonably good on reflection, money a little tight but the police rent allowance, money that was paid in lieu of couples living in police married accommodation, something that hadn't exist for new officers now for some time, helped and allowed them to purchase their first home in Langley. Gene's promotion facilitated a move to their current home. After moving there Katie was born.

Gene was a uniform sergeant for about a year and then returned to the CID. Sandra stopped working for the police then and was for a while a stay-at-home mum. It was during this period that things became much worse. Gene was working long hours, or at least said he was. He was drinking more, and she was aware that he often drove home the worse for wear ,and that worried her. Arguments increased; she dwelled on that period thinking about how coarse in his speech Gene had become. How unforgiving, lacking in compassion, judgmental, exploiting right wing views only just short of being blatantly racist. And worst of all, especially when the worse for wear through drink, him talking in a stupid pseudo cockney accent - why, she had never fathomed out. He wasn't a cockney, he came from Shaftsbury; he had probably never been to an area of London within the sound of Bow Bells, and whatever is 'spinning a drum'? Something he often said at that time.

Sandra suddenly wanted a cup of coffee; she knew there was a kiosk a little way along the tree lined avenue where she was and thought it might be open. Sandra walked towards it knowing that she was engaging in a displacement activity as the overt reflection on some of the things would trouble her. Sandra obtained her coffee in a polystyrene cup with a plastic lid and returned to the bench that she had been sitting on. She placed the coffee on the bench and thought back…there was violence, too, once when Gene was drunk having driven home in that state. Sandra confronted him calling him 'stupid and selfish' whereupon he had slapped her hard across the face. At the time she had been shocked, even now thinking about it she felt shocked. At the time she felt such pain, both the physical pain of her face burning and the worse psychological pain of someone she loved, admired, and respected doing that to her. She cried and cried. Gene was later all apologetic, saying how such a thing wouldn't ever happen again. He pleaded with her not to leave him, and she didn't. She forgave him believing his words that such an appalling incident wouldn't be repeated, but it was.

A few weeks later, again after a late arrival home following a drink fuelled evening, a row erupted between Gene and Sandra, she couldn't even remember over what. On this occasion Gene had punched her in the abdomen which winded her, causing her to fall to the ground. She had difficulty catching her breath and thought she might be seriously injured, but although gasping for breath she could only think of her young daughter Katie upstairs and hopefully sleeping through this trauma. She was thinking what would become of her. Gene had left the room leaving her on the floor gasping. After a little while Sandra was able to compose herself and she calmly walked to the telephone and called the police. At that time police control rooms were controlled locally, and she was put through to the station at Windsor. She told the operator who she was, where she lived and that she had been assaulted by her husband.

She added, "My husband is a detective sergeant. He's drunk, and has, I think, gone to bed."

The operator merely said, "Someone will attend soon, Mrs Elphick. Do you need any medical assistance?"

"No," and the call ended.

About thirty minutes later a light knock was heard at the front door. Sandra answered and as she did, so Eugene descended the stairs. Sandra allowed a uniform sergeant to enter the home.

The sergeant removed his cap and Sandra said, "My husband here has punched me in the stomach."

The sergeant seemed shocked and after a pause said, "Are you injured?"

"No, no, I'm OK."

The sergeant then invited Eugene into the sitting room and said to Sandra, "Why don't you make a nice cup of tea and let's sort this out."

Sandra recalled the fury she felt at the patronising remark. She remembered that she certainly wasn't going to make any tea. She propped herself up against the kitchen cupboard and waited. She remembered the muffled conversation coming from the sitting room punctuated with the occasional laugh.

After a fairly short time both men reappeared.

The sergeant said, "Mrs Elphick, I think that this is a little blip. I have spoken to your husband, and he assures me that nothing like this will occur again. I think less said soonest mended, don't you?"

Sandra remembered that she had not replied, she was aghast at the seeming inaction of the police officer. The sergeant nodded in the direction of Eugene and let himself out of the front door.

Sandra stood in the doorway as the sergeant walked away, saying into his radio, "I'm leaving the domestic in Old Windsor now. No offences disclosed, suitable advice given, no further action required and by the way can you please destroy the telephone message."

Sandra watched him as he entered his patrol car and drove away without a backward glance. She remembered closing the door and seeing Eugene staring at her with a look of what she could only think of as being one of hatred.

"Thanks for that," he said and walked up the stairs. As Sandra recalled the event she realised that although she had for most of the time suppressed the details, they there were still there. The feelings of hurt, not just the physical hurt of being assaulted, but the deep psychological hurt of being betrayed by the person she loved and whom she believed loved her.

She remembered the feeling of total hopelessness, of being trapped, of being alone with not even the police willing or wanting to help and thinking about her young child asleep upstairs and how difficult it would be just to turn and walk away from that marriage, from that situation which had become now, for her, a toxic union. She felt betrayed by the very authority that should have protected her, ensured that she was safe and that there would be no repetition of such conduct - conduct which surely would be outside some police code of conduct. The betrayal of the police sergeant who clearly thought he was extolling the virtues of being avuncular but was, in fact, just totally inefficient and more afraid of the unwritten rules of closing ranks, of protecting a brother officer in distress, rather that applying the basic rules of policing, the basic rules of humanity and justice.

As she thought about it all she was becoming more and more angry and realised that the injury of that night in all its forms had in no way gone away; it was there all the time, just festering in her subconscious. The hurt so raw, not in any way reduced by the fact that there was no repetition of what…yes, what it was, and to her surprise she said out loud was domestic violence. The recalled details of that night were still so, so vivid. She could even remember noticing for the first time a piece of worn stair carpet as Eugene ascended the stairs. Yes, she was angry, incredibly angry.

She muted on the fact that she had never told anyone of that night, and it had never been mentioned again. Perhaps it was the fact that Eugene had never said sorry, added to the fact that the issue remained unresolved. No, more than unresolved, it remained a gaping unhealed wound. Betrayal, that was the feeling that arose so much and then there were the 'other women' – Ann-Marie Curtis and the dreadful Shelia Marshall, and probably others and that hurt very much. What she knew hurt, but what she didn't know but suspected hurt even more. And the images, those images of intimacy that may have and probably did occur, images of her husband's physical betrayal with nothing she could do about it. She could not ask, could not discuss her inner thoughts and suspicions with Eugene because he would just bat her concerns away with his brutish police vernacular.

She was experiencing such mixed emotions fluctuating between anger, betrayal, hatred, disappointment and an overwhelming sense of self-pity. She looked out onto the river Thames and thought of how she and Eugene walked here along the tow path all those years ago, of how light their hearts were, full of hope, anticipation, optimism and love. And now, their hearts were like the river itself - cold, dark, and deep, hiding a thousand secrets from each other.

"Enough of this," she said aloud. She reached down for her coffee which by now was stone cold, threw the contents on the ground and watched as a rivulet of cold coffee trickled away. She got up thoughtfully, disposed of her coffee cup in a bin and walked back toward her car. She looked at her watch and was surprised at the amount of time she had spent in contemplation, but she knew what she had done, and she now knew what she had to do.

Dave Matthews couldn't remember a time when he had felt so angry and so belittled as he did at this particular moment as he walked from the main police headquarters building, back to his office in the single-story annex away from the main building. Dave walked quickly. A junior colleague, an inspector from communications, tried to speak but Dave ignored the man and walked on and entered the office with a crash, slamming the door behind him with such force that the female admin assistant sitting closest to the door physically jumped.

He said gruffly, most unlike him, "Find out where Inspector Preston is and let me know." He didn't wait for a reply and went into his office again slamming the door hard. The three admin assistants looked at each other and said nothing; one of them started to try and locate Nick Preston.

Matthews sat at his desk. In a way he felt defeated, for the first time in his career he felt old and out of touch, as if he was on the scrap heap, and he wallowed in self-pity until a light knock sounded on his office door and after a second or two one of the admin assistants brought a mug of tea to Matthews and put it on his desk.

She said, "I thought you could do with this sir," and she left.

Matthews said a very quiet and somewhat belated, "Thank you."

After a few moments Matthews' phone rang, and he was told that Preston was on his way back from Oxford.

"Please tell him to come and see me as soon as he gets here."

Matthews didn't wait for any reply and got back to his tea and inner turmoil. He unlocked his filing cabinet and took out the Eugene Elphick file, and placed it on his desk. He began to thumb through it, not really reading anything; after all he knew exactly what is contained. He closed the file again and felt quite uncomfortable in respect of this case.

It wasn't long before there was a knock on the door immediately followed by Preston entering the room.

"Afternoon, Guv."

"Come and sit down Nick," instructed Matthews.

Preston somewhat unusually sheepishly took a seat opposite Matthews who remained at his desk. Preston could see that Matthews looked uncharacteristically angry; his face was slightly red, and his jaw clenched. Preston's overdeveloped super-ego, or perhaps his aptitude for self-preservation went into overdrive and he steeled himself, convinced that he had done something to evoke Matthews anger.

Nothing was said for a few moments, the time span seeming much longer to Preston.

Matthews looked Preston straight into his eyes, making Preston nervous, and then he said, "Who the hell is this Helen Callaghan?"

Preston knew that he had had nothing to do with Helen Callaghan and whatever this was about it didn't involve him. He immediately felt relieved and his normal bravado returned.

"You know Guv, she's the DI in the Paedophile and Cyber Investigation Unit at Oxford."

"Yes I know," said Mathews with a slightly irritated tone, "but who is she? You've served at Oxford. Tell me about her."

"Well, she's certainly an interesting character. She's got about ten years' service, I suppose, always been at Oxford, and there's a rumour that she only did about four weeks of night duty in her whole service, she rarely did any outside patrol work as a probationer and spent a lot of time in the station." Preston paused looking for a reaction from Matthews and continued, "She moved to Crime Prevention toward the end of her probation and then on to what used to be the Child Protection Unit. She passed her exam, got promoted to sergeant and didn't go back into uniform, but remained in the CPU. Then, and this shocked us all, she got made a detective sergeant without attending any CID courses, the rest his history as they say. She moved into her present job from CPU."

Matthews was quite silent looking down at his desk.

"But she's a DI now?"

"Yeah, she must have passed her exam and then moved from CPU to her present job as a DI. Almost unbelievable, isn't it, Guv?"

Matthews was again silent and didn't speak for several moments, then he said in quite a quiet tone, "How the hell can someone have such gold plated career path?"

Preston gave a little laugh and said, "That's easy, Guv, it's who you know isn't it?"

"What?"

"Well, her old man is a landowner, somewhere out between Witney and Chipping Norton, Charlbury, that way. You know the sort, Guv - riding, shooting, fishing, hunting, that sort of bollocks. He's said to be well connected with businessmen, politicians, the Chipping Norton set. A powerful man by all accounts."

"Why ever did she join the police?" enquired Matthews.

"Who knows, but whatever, she's well connected within the job. She must be to have such an easy existence - it used to be Freemasons, now it's other types of connection, - not what you know, but who you know and who's looking out for you."

Matthews nodded thoughtfully and said, "Yes, I suppose, it's always been that way to an extent. Do you think our senior officers are connected with Callaghan's family?"

"Without a doubt Guv, they would want to be in, or at least on the edge of that scene, that's obvious by the way dear Helen is protected."

"I thought that might be the case. As you are aware I had to see the Deputy today. I thought it was for him to brief me on a case but no, he bollocked me - yes bollocked me - for the way in which I had spoken to Helen Callaghan. He accused me of bullying her. Can you believe that? Me being accused of bullying her?"

Preston could see that his boss was quite emotional, more than that, angry to a point of unsuppressed fury, and Preston had not seen that before. In a way he was surprised, but also internally relishing the moment as Matthews' defences were down.

Matthews continued, "Do you know, he even said that perhaps I should consider retiring, that I'd given thirty-plus years' service, and it may be time to put my feet up. Cheeky bastard! I was policing when he was in primary school. I couldn't believe the way he spoke to me."

Preston thought it best to say nothing and just let Matthews unload.

Matthews was quiet, looking down at his desk. He felt both angry and hurt, and he could not believe that he was relating his thoughts and feelings to Preston.

He continued by looking up.

"Do you know what, Nick?" and not waiting for Preston to reply, "he's told me not to interfere with Helen Callaghan's work and that she will make contact with me in her own time, that she's an efficient dedicated officer who will prioritise our job as best she can. Can you believe that, Nick?"

Preston didn't reply.

Matthews sounding like a rebuked child reiterated, "Bullying! He accused me of bullying her."

Preston said, "Bullying is the in word now. Supervisors can't do their job anymore, - merely tell someone off, and it's viewed as bullying. The job's weak now, and supervisors frightened to do their job."

Matthews wasn't really listening to what Nick Preston was saying and continued,"It's that bloody case, Nick," pointing to the Eugene Elphick file which he then picked up with a flourish, dropping it back into the filing cabinet, slamming the drawer and almost ceremoniously locking it.

"The bloody case is jinxed, I've felt that from the start."

After a moments silence Matthews returned to his seat and Preston thought he should say something reassuring.

"We'll soon have it covered, Guv. Once we have the evidence from Helen Callaghan we can sort out Elphick and bring this matter to a close. Straight forward once we have the evidence."

"I hope so Nick, I hope so, You crack on with what you're doing. Sorry to burden you with all this."

"No trouble, Guv," said Preston. And, "I'll see you later," as he left.

CHAPTER 8

When Sandra arrived home she found a note on the kitchen table; it was from Eugene and said that he had gone to collect Katie from school. It added that he had been trying to get hold of her. She took her phone from her pocket and saw that it remained switched off. She just hoped that Eugene had not contacted the surgery. She switched it on and saw that there had been missed calls from Eugene but thankfully no one else. It wasn't long before Katie burst in through the door chattering ten to the dozen, never quite finishing one thing before moving on to the next. She was followed by the more sedate Eugene carrying Katie's bags.

"Anything to eat, Mum?" pleaded Katie and Sandra replied,

"There's a little cake, and help yourself to a glass of milk."

"I've loads and loads of homework; can I take it to my room and start work straight away?"

"Start looking at Facebook straight away, you mean," interjected Eugene and they both laughed.

At such times as this, when Eugene was being the good father that he could be, Sandra had such mixed feelings. At that precise moment she loved him, at other times she loathed him with a vengeance but most of the time there existed a state of mere indifference. The fleeting loving moment disappeared as soon as her daughter left the room.

Sandra looked at her husband and she realised that she found him so unattractive now. He looked as if he had aged considerably in the course of a week, he was more stooped, distant, and in the main, except when interacting with Katie, self-absorbed.

Sandra did not want him, and she wanted to be rid of him as soon as was possible.

"You go and watch some TV; the news will be coming on. I'll start to prepare dinner."

Eugene shuffled away into the lounge and Sandra started the dinner preparation. The family reassembled for dinner and as usual Katie did most of the chattering - the usual things, hockey, friends, sports. Eugene and Sandra responded to her but hardly interacted together at all. Post-dinner followed into what had become something of a pattern with Katie and Eugene going to bed around the same time, around nine. Sandra enjoyed this time when she could indulge in some TLC for herself, relaxing with a glass of wine or three. Tonight she thought very much of the future and what that would hold for her and Katie.

Next week it would be half term for Katie and Eugene had already hinted that he wanted to take Katie to see her grand-mother in Shaftesbury. Although Sandra wasn't happy about it she realised that the absence of husband and daughter would give her the chance to mention the difficult subject of separation and ultimate divorce to her parents, who would not be at all happy at the thought of that. As she helped herself to another glass of wine, Sandra decided that she would spend a couple of days with her parents so that there would be plenty of time for her to properly prepare them.

On the following Monday Eugene and Katie set off for Shaftesbury. Sandra waved them off and as she did so, she was aware of the mixed emotions that occupied her conscious mind as they often did of late. She felt the almost crippling sense of loss, knowing that Katie would be apart from her for only a few days but seeming so much longer, coupled with the feeling of relief to be apart from Eugene for an all too short time: part ambivalence, but also feelings of dislike, distrust and contempt for a husband all mixed in with the feeling of total and unconditional love for her daughter. As Eugene's car disappeared from view she realised that she had to rectify the situation and her mixed emotions by at last bringing to a close this loveless marriage.

It was a quiet period within the Professional Standards Department and Dave Matthews decided that he would take some leave. Initially he thought to lick the wounds inflicted by the Deputy Chief Constable but, in fact, to have what was to become quite an enjoyable break, spending time with his wife and planning for his retirement. When he had announced that was what he was going to do his wife could not have been more pleased and insisted that they set about making a bucket list of what they would do with the precious time that they would spend together.

They both delighted in the time that they were spending together, that they had rekindled a spark to their union that had been missing for so long, with Dave becoming aware that the 'job' was very much a destroyer of marriages and relationships, but gladdened by the fact that his, although rocky at times, had survived and had awoken into a new dawn that would not, and he would ensure such, ever suffer again.

From this time on his wife and family would be his priority and not the all-consuming requirements of Thames Valley Police. During those few days leave Dave enjoyed a feeling of almost rebirth and he knew that things were about to change very soon and that he and his wife would start fulfilling that bucket list.

Nick Preston was always pleased when his supervisor was on leave; it gave him a sense that he had overall charge of what was going on in his subdepartment. Work was in fact light with just a few statements to obtain from complainants about the most innocuous matters. Nick Preston regarded complainants with as much contempt as he would afford the unfortunate officers who would eventually be interviewed in respect of such pettiness.

Preston had little regard for anyone; he lacked conscience, and was devoid of compassion and kindness. Concern for anyone other than himself alluded him. He was ideal material for a Professional Standards inspector, he knew that, and the powers that be knew that, too. Ideal material or not, he remained as someone who had few if any friends, certainly none in the department where he worked. He wasn't liked and, in fact, was most unlikeable. That said Preston had a perpetual belief that someone somewhere was plotting against him, conspiring to cause him mischief and his level of internal paranoia only made his personality that much more 'unfortunate', a description given him on an appraisal carried out by a seemingly wise but now forgotten supervisor of some years ago.

Nick Preston was concerned that when Dave Matthews retired he may not be replaced, and that the department may move from three superintendents and accompanying inspectors to two, which could result in him being moved back to divisional CID or worse, uniform. He also felt that Dave Matthews may seek to retire sooner than anybody realised. Nick Preston's uncanny sense of self-preservation kicked in and he spent the rest of the week trying to convince the head of department, a Chief Superintendent, that a move to a different investigating team under a different superintendent might be good for Preston's ongoing development and of his views on how the department should evolve. In the process he didn't miss the opportunity to bad mouth Matthews a little, indicating that Matthews was indeed past his best, and it might be the time for him to retire gracefully.

Eugene Elphick enjoyed his time with his mother and daughter in Shaftesbury. The weather was good, and they enjoyed walks in the countryside, long lazy afternoons in the garden, and evenings playing board games or watching TV. A few days of innocence, a time where father and daughter could relax with Katie enjoying the company of her grandmother who she did not see nearly enough.

Sandra called each evening to talk to Katie but her conversations with Eugene were curt and somewhat hostile. Eugene's mother actually mentioned the fact that the calls between Eugene and Sandra were so short and asked if there was anything wrong. Eugene lied saying that all was well, and the point of Sandra's call was to talk to Katie. On the last evening after Katie had gone to bed Eugene's mother wanted something of a heart to heart with her son. She said to him that Katie had said that Eugene wasn't working at present, and Eugene again lied by saying he had accumulated a considerable amount of leave that needed to be taken.

His mother went on to say that she thought he was looking much better as a result of his short holiday and that she had been worried when he had arrived because in her words he had, 'looked like death warmed up'. Eugene admitted that the short break had done him good; he had slept better, ate better, felt better and the quality time with both his mother and Katie has been very much a tonic. His mother again asked just before they retired if everything was alright, and Eugene again lied, assuring her that all was well both at home and with the job.

The following morning Eugene and Katie said their good-byes and Eugene, seeing his mother in his rear view mirror waving goodbye from her garden gate, brought a lump to his throat with him not quite knowing when and in what circumstances he would see her again. The long journey home was pleasant with Katie in her usual mode, talking about how much she had enjoyed the break with her grandmother and how she would like to see her again soon. She said that her grandmother had told her of the holidays that she and Eugene had taken at Carbis Bay in Cornwall and that it sounded 'so cool'.

Eugene remembered, too, and told her a little more about the holidays. There had been three in total. He told her of the long bus journey to Taunton and then catching the train all the way to Cornwall and the little scenic railway that took them from a station called St Erth to Carbis Bay, how the hotel would send a Land Rover to collect their luggage, but they would walk down the steep hill to the Carbis Bay Hotel which was virtually on the beach, of how his mother would hire a beach hut for the week so that they could go to the beach even when it was raining, which it did on at least one day of the week. He told of the sandy beach, the warm sea, the safe bay for bathing, the little trains running high above the beach in one direction to St Ives and in the other back to St Erth. Of the walks along the costal path to St Ives, of having Cornish pasties for lunch and sometimes a Cornish cream tea. Of the all-enveloping sadness as they climbed the steep hill to catch the train home, but sadness cushioned with his mum saying, 'We'll come back again'.

Katie was silent for a few moments and then said, "It sounds so fantastic Dad, we have to go. We have to repeat the holidays that you had as a child, taking Mum and Granny, too. Please say yes, please say we can all go this summer."

"Yes," said Eugene, "yes we'll go."

"Thanks so much Dad! The summer holidays aren't that far ahead, are they?"

Eugene thought to himself that, yes, they would go, as soon as all this difficulty was over, when life eventually got back to normal. But he didn't quite know when that would be.

Sandra Elphick spent some of the time that her daughter and husband were away with her parents. She wanted to fully brief them as to her feelings about Eugene, her loveless marriage, and her need to end it. She did not want to burden her parents with the facts relating to past domestic disputes, the real and supposed infidelity, but she did tell them that Eugene was currently off work and that she believed, although she didn't know for sure, that something serious was occurring within his work. Sandra's father was most unhappy with Sandra's decision and her reasoning behind it. Sandra knew that he would think differently if he knew about the domestics and infidelity, but she was determined to keep that to herself although she didn't quite understand why.

Sandra's mother was aware of some of Gene's infidelity but now seemed more concerned about Katie and what effects a separation would have upon her granddaughter. She refused to even contemplate what difficulties a divorce might cause her. She was, after all, doing so well at school and this was a critical time in her schooling, and how would her school fees be met if Sandra and Eugene separated? The trio worked through the pragmatics during the week and both parents came to the conclusion that if Sandra and Eugene were to separate, hopefully for a trial period, then it might be best if Sandra and Katie came to stay with them. It would be easy enough for Sandra to get to work, and to take Katie to and from school; it would just take more time. Sandra explained that she would be talking to Eugene soon and she would let them know what was happening.

As Dave Matthews entered his office after his short leave it struck him that for the first time in his whole career he didn't want to be there. He was fortunate in that through the whole of his working life he had never awoken in the morning and not wanted to go to work. That was certainly something for a work span of over thirty years, but today he just did not want to be there. He wanted to retire and to do so as quickly as possible and with as little fuss as he could. He would see the dreadful Elphick case through and once that had been finalised he would submit his resignation; 'put in his ticket' in police colloquial terms.

He sat at his desk and as he did so he heard Preston talking in a loud voice in the outer admin office. There was then a light knock on the door followed by Preston entering the office carrying a large brown envelope under his arm.

"Moring Guv. Hope you've had a good few days off. It's been quiet except this arrived yesterday afternoon."

Preston held the envelope up. "It's from the office of the Deputy, marked 'Urgent' addressed to you with the stamp 'Confidential - named distribution only."

Matthews held his hand out and Preston handed the envelope over.

Matthews started to open the envelope and motioned to Preston to sit. Matthews turned the envelope over in his hands; both he and Preston were silently anticipating what lay inside. Matthews inserted a ruler under the flap of the envelope and sliced it open with a flourish. He saw that there was a letter from the Deputy Chief Constable attached to a report. He looked and saw the report was headed "Paedophile and Cyber Investigation Unit" and signed by D/Inspector Helen Callaghan. Matthews read the letter from the Deputy Chief first. It started with a handwritten "Dear Dave" then continued in typed format. He read slowly taking in every word, phrase, every nuance. Preston waited with bated breath eager to discover the contents of the envelope.

"It's from the Deputy," said Matthews. "It has Callaghan's report in respect of the examination of Elphick's computer hard drives."

Preston didn't reply but couldn't wait to hear more.

"Do you know that bitch sent her report direct to the Deputy rather than to me, the Investigating Officer?"

Matthews listened to how calm his voice was. Such an inappropriate action by a junior colleague which undermined him so would have, as recently as a week ago, caused him incandescent rage, but not today. Today he didn't feel that concerned, today he just ignored Callaghan's effrontery, today was different for Matthews.

"That's Helen Callaghan, Guv, a manipulative, backstabbing bitch – that's how she works, that's how she gets on."

Matthews looked at Preston, in fact he stared at him and thought to himself that Preston was a fine one to talk about manipulation and backstabbing.

"Go and makes us a coffee each. I'll skim read this and then you can go through it in detail, but I want you to do that in this office. That file is not to leave this office and when you are not with it, it's to be locked away with the other file – OK?"

"OK Guv," said Preston and he left the office to make the coffee.

Matthews scanned through the report, occasionally referring back to the Deputy's letter. He saw that all the computers sized from Eugene Elphick's home had been examined along with his work computer which had been taken from Eugene's office by the Paedophile and Cyber Investigation Unit themselves. He saw that only one computer had material on it and that all the others had no illegal material downloaded on to their respective hard drives. The only hard drive that contained illegal material was the computer labelled as 'Family Computer'.

Reading through the report Matthews saw that what was contained on the hard drive was a number of pornographic images depicting children being abused and one video depicting one child being raped and abused by several men. There was an envelope which displayed the word 'Images' and several reference numbers within the file. Matthews did not open the envelope and did not particularly want to at that time. Detective Inspector Callaghan had suggested charges, which Matthews thought should have been his job in conjunction with the Crown Prosecution Service, but the Deputy in his letter had stated,

'D/I Callaghan has suggested charges which I agree with. Of course, you will need these to be approved by the CPS.'

Callaghan had undermined Matthews, but it didn't perturb him, well at least for the moment. Matthews took the letter from the Deputy and without ceremony fed it into the shredder at the side of his desk and watched and the cross-cutting blades reduced the letter to mere paper fragments. Preston returned to the office with a tray containing two steaming mugs of coffee and a plate of chocolate digestives.

"D/I Callaghan has told us what to do," said Matthews in something of a scathing and sarcastic manner. He continued, "The report correlates with what we already know from the Americans - one of the computers did contain illegal child pornography, the others were clean. The evidence is clear. I want you to go through the report now in detail. What are your commitments today?"

Preston replied, "Nothing that can't wait. I'll get on with this as you say."

Matthews said, "OK, as I said earlier I want you to do this work in this office. The report is not to leave this office. If you have to leave, the report is to be placed in this drawer."

Matthews indicated a drawer in a steel grey filing cabinet and taking a key from his key ring he handed it to Preston saying, "Make sure it's locked away".

"Yes Guv," replied Preston. Then after a pause he said, "Are there any photographs?"

Matthews thought this an odd thing to say when Preston hadn't even read the report but quickly dismissed it from his mind.

"There's an envelope with the report. I haven't opened it as yet. I'm going out for about half an hour. You carry on reading the report. We'll meet later when we can discuss the interview with Elphick?"

"Yes Guv., I think now we have the evidence we should see him ASAP."

"We'll discuss that later," said Matthews almost as an aside as he left the office.

Sandra was standing at the kitchen window as Eugene's car entered the driveway. She was waving and Katie waved back excitedly. She ran to the house leaving Eugene to get all the luggage and paraphernalia from the car. On entering the kitchen Katie was talking loudly and rapidly to her mother, telling her all about her staying with her granny, of what she did, and so on. Sandra appeared to be listening carefully.

Katie then said, "Do you know what, Mum? We're all going on holiday to Carbis Bay, you me, Dad and Granny, all of us. It's where Dad used to go on holiday as a little boy, it's a fantastic place and we'll stay in a hotel and everything, say we will Mum, say we'll go."

Sandra looked at Eugene and then back to Katie and said, "We'll see," which Katie, Eugene and Sandra all knew meant probably not.

Katie's excitement visibly drained away in an instant and she said quietly, "Oh Mum, please say we can go."

"I said we'll see, and we'll talk about it again."

Katie took hold of her case, a pink metal one with a unicorn displayed on the side, a bit young for her really but she'd had it a few years. She left the kitchen slowly and ascended the stairs.

"She seems to have had a good time," said Sandra.

"Yes, she did…we did," said Eugene. He continued, "You been OK?"

"Yes," replied Sandra. She then said, "You unpack, get yours and Katie's washing in the machine and I'll prepare something to eat."

Eugene found Katie upstairs; she was slowly unpacking her case looking sad.

"She doesn't want to come with us, does she Dad?"

"Well, she didn't say no, did she?" He continued, "We're going, you me and Granny and Mum if she wants to. I'll book the holiday for all of us toward the end of August and we'll see what happens. But we'll be going!"

"Thanks Dad, thank you so much. I do love you."

When Dave Matthews returned to his office Nick Preston was sat at Matthews desk engrossed in the contents of Helen Callaghan's report. Preston merely looked up as Matthews entered. He didn't say anything and didn't move from Matthews desk but carried on reading. Matthews sat down at the side of the desk and noticed that Preston had opened the envelope that had been marked 'Images' and he saw that the images, which were computerised pictures, were in a little pile at the edge of the desk. Matthews reached out and took the top picture, he looked, and the contents were so graphic and disturbing that he quickly replaced it knowing that he would have to look at them in detail at some point, a task that he did not look forward to.

Preston gave a large sigh and looked up. Matthews saw how pale Preston's face looked as if it had been drained of blood. He didn't know if this was a result of shock, anger, or an indication that Preston was not feeling well, or perhaps a combination of all three.

"This is awful...no, more than that, it's sickening," he said. "I don't know what to think. All I know is that we need to get hold of that bastard Elphick and take him out of society." He took a deep breath and uttered, "The perverted bastard".

Matthews nodded his head, looked at his watch and said, "What are you doing now? It's 12:15."

"I've nothing planned; I don't know if I can do anything right now, Guv."

Matthews looked at Preston and for one instant felt just a little sorry for him.

"Right, take a long lunch and be back here for 2:00pm. We'll have a look at this together then and plan our interview with Elphick."

Preston said a quiet, "Thanks, Guv," and exited from Matthews office.

Matthews placed the images in the envelope without looking at them and placed the file in the filing cabinet, locking the same with the key that Preston had left on the desk, and then replacing the key on his key ring.

"It's going to be a difficult and draining afternoon," he said quietly to himself.

Eugene and Katie had been back from Shaftesbury for four days and Sandra had not yet approached the subject with Eugene of her separating from him. She didn't know exactly why she couldn't broach the subject and thought it might be something about having to deal with the fallout from Katie. Her parents had asked her what was happening, her mother secretly hoping that a reconciliation might take place. Sandra had made the excuse that she was waiting for the right moment. Sandra knew that she couldn't delay the inevitable for much longer. Life had gone on in a mundane way and there was no change in her feelings. She muddled through her busy morning at work and as she did so she rehearsed the speech that she would make to Eugene when the moment came, but she knew that it would not be today.

CHAPTER 9

Eugene tried to do various things during each day when his family were out at work or school, but it was hard. Concentration was difficult and motivation even more so. Long periods were spent sitting staring into space and thinking. It was the nonstop thinking that was so exhausting; The constant thinking about the job, about what he had achieved, what he had not and most of all what he had lost. He thought so much about his situation, trying to unravel the puzzle that placed him in the position that he was now in. But no amount of thinking could do very much to help. His sleeping was poor, but he had not taken any of the tablets that had been prescribed to him. He now had quite a lot and should stop getting them from the pharmacist. He didn't want to take them although the ruminations at night were worse than during the day; everything he thought about at night seemed that more complex. Sometimes he dozed in the afternoon but always set the alarm on his phone just in case he went into a deep sleep. He didn't want Katie worried and left waiting for him at school wondering where he was. It was in one of these moments of light slumber when he jumped at the sound of his phone ringing. It was Benji.

"Hi Gene, sorry I've not been in touch of late, I kept meaning to call..."

"It's OK, Benji, don't worry," interjected Eugene and continued, "How have you been?"

"More important, how have you been Gene?" enquired Benji."

"Well, not too bad. One day merges into another very much. I try to keep busy gardening, odd jobs, that sort of thing," he lied.

"Good, keeping busy, I would think that's important. How do you feel in yourself Gene?"

"Well to be honest, a bit down. I miss the office...the lads you know."

"Any of them contacted you?"

"No," Eugene said quietly.

"Well they were told not to, so I suppose it's understandable. Anyway, just to keep you up to date, I've been unable to find anything out. Professional Standards are being very tight lipped about all this. I've not been able to find out if the Dodsons made any compliant. I did speak to a contact who's a 'screw' at Bullingdon where they're banged up, but he wasn't able to find anything out either. We have a new DI. A woman called Jenny Cobb. Have you heard of her?"

Eugene sat on the bottom step of the stairs and let this latest blow sink in.

"No, I've not. Is she temporary or permanent?"

"Well, we've not been told that you aren't coming back to us, so I suppose she's temporary although she's a full DI and not acting. She came from Newbury. But to be honest, although pleasant enough, she's no thief taker, more of an admin person if you know what I mean."

"Yes, the modern way, Benji. Still hopefully when this is all over we'll get back to what we're good at, taking a few villains out."

"Sure thing Gene, that's the spirit mate. Keep thinking positive. How's the family?"

"Yes, they're fine, Benji, thanks. Do you fancy meeting up for a coffee or a pint?"

"Yes, I think that would be a good idea. I'm off next Thursday. I'm seeing someone in Bracknell. We could meet at a pub called The Old Manor. It's got a car park and is right in the town centre. They do a good lunch, so a pie and pint if you fancy it."

"Sounds great," said Eugene.

"OK, meet at 12:30 inside," said Benji.

"OK, see you there."

"You take care," said Benji, "and Gene…keep your chin up, mate."

The line went dead. Eugene was so pleased that Benji had called but really devastated by the fact that there was a detective inspector in his place, and that was made all the worse by the fact that she was a woman. But he was looking forward to lunch and a chat with Benji.

The simple short call with Benji uplifted Eugene and then, hearing the post clatter through the letter box a day later, he saw there was a white envelope addressed to him. The letter bore the colourful Thames Valley Police crest in the top left hand corner of the envelope and looked official. Eugene ignored the remainder of the post and placed the other letters on the hall table. He carried the letter into the lounge, sat down and looked at the envelope feeling a little nervous about opening it.

But open it he did and saw that it was a letter from the Professional Standards Department at Kidlington requesting that he attend Maidenhead Police Station at 1:45 pm on the following Thursday. The first thing that entered Eugene's head was that he would have to cancel his lunch appointment with Benji. He read the letter again. It gave no indication of why he was to attend the police station.

The letter was short and to the point and signed by David Matthews, Superintendent.

Eugene folded the letter and placed it in his pocket. He thought about it and felt that this was a good sign. He concluded that if there was anything sinister they would be at his door, Matthews and the awful detective inspector who would be itching to arrest him. No, this was a good sign. It was probably an official note requesting his attendance to collect the computers and to be reinstated to duty. Thank goodness he thought, this will soon be all over.

He couldn't wait to tell Sandra, but first he must cancel the appointment with Benji. He called Benji's mobile but there was no answer, so he left a voice message.

"Hi, Benji, it's Gene. We'll have to cancel our meeting on Thursday next. I received a letter this morning from Professional Standards asking me to go to Maidenhead on that day. I think it will be to collect my computers, so hopefully this nightmare will soon be over, and I'll be back with you before you know it."

Eugene felt happier than he had for some time. He tidied up the house, cleaned the kitchen, had a bath, and planned something for later. Katie told her dad when he picked her up from school that he appeared to be much happier, and she thought that was good. Eugene told her that he did feel happy - happy enough to get a Chinese take-away for dinner.

"Wowsa," cried Katie, and Eugene started to believe that things might just be getting back to normal.

The Chinese take-away dinner went reasonably well. Eugene noticed that Sandra didn't eat very much and just picked at her meal. Katie enjoyed hers and chatted incessantly as usual. After dinner, and when Katie had gone to bed, Eugene sat beside Sandra and told her about the letter that he had received and his thoughts about it. He said that he felt good about it and had had a good feeling all day. He said that he felt that this was a new beginning and felt that it could be a new start for him and Sandra. He explained that he knew that he had been self- absorbed for a while and somewhat inward looking. He said that he had learned a lot from the process of being on 'gardening leave' and that his priorities had changed; it was his family now that was the main priority and not the job.

Sandra listened to Eugene just wanting to tell him that the marriage was over but couldn't bring herself to say the words. Eugene kept going on about his love for her, Katie and what a new beginning they would have, how important it was to work and function as a family. Sandra felt that Eugene was droning on, and she wanted to scream "Stop!" but she sat passively listening, but not really absorbing what he was saying.

Eugene put his arm around Sandra and said, "Look, now that a future is beckoning for us, I thought this may be the right time for us to share our bed again. To learn to love each other in an intimate way again..."

Sandra said firmly, "No Gene, not now. Such a lot has gone on. I don't know. I don't know where we're going as a couple, as a family...I just don't know."

She was becoming agitated and moved away from Eugene and stood up. Eugene could see she was upset. He stood up and faced her.

"It's OK, Sandra. I understand. It may take a little time. I'm quite willing to wait."

They made their way to their separate rooms and Sandra realised that there was another lost opportunity.

One of her father's favoured and overworked expressions echoed in her head, 'Sandra, procrastination is the thief of time'. "Yes," she murmured aloud 'and the thief of a life'.

Eugene's ebullient mood persisted, despite the setback with Sandra. Thursday came around soon enough.

Benji had replied to his text merely saying, "Great, look forward to seeing you back in harness soon."

Eugene made his way to Maidenhead, parking in the same car park that he had when he had visited Dr Bekhit, a short time ago, but a time that seemed much longer to Eugene. It was still half an hour till the appointed time and he didn't want to arrive at the station too early so he sat in his car mulling over in his head what was likely to be said. He was hoping that the unlikeable Detective Inspector wouldn't be there. He probably wouldn't; there was no reason for him to be. This was just a closure to an unfortunate episode and Eugene wondered if he would be given an apology. However, he knew that the police service was not particularly good at giving apologies, especially to one of its own.

At 1:35 pm Eugene entered the foyer at Maidenhead police station. There was a uniformed civilian at the desk and Eugene told him who he was there to see. He was told to take a seat and did so.

The civilian disappeared from the desk only to return a few seconds later and call across, "Someone will be with you shortly."

Eugene looked up at the somewhat ancient public information notices pinned to a notice board, notices about securing boats, post coding bicycles, etc. Eugene wondered how old the notices were, when and who put them there.

A door on the right hand side of the main desk opened and Nick Preston stood in the doorway. Eugene's heart sank for a second and then thought that because the whole business was drawing to an end he could at least be pleasant to Preston. He wasn't likely to meet him again or at least he hoped not.

"This way," said Preston looking in Eugene's direction.

Eugene got to his feet and smiled, a gesture that was not returned, and made his way to the doorway. Preston stepped inside allowing Eugene to enter. Eugene offered his hand for a handshake but Preston ignored that gesture also and said, "In there," directing Eugene into another office.

On entering the office he saw Superintendent Matthews. Although he had his back to him Eugene could see that it was him. Eugene heard Preston shut the door behind him and Matthews turned to face him.

Matthews face looked stern, and he said in his precise manner, "Eugene Elphick, I am arresting you on suspicion of making illegal, indecent material depicting children and I am further arresting you on suspicion of possessing illegal, indecent material depicting children."

Matthews then proceeded to caution Eugene, but Eugene wasn't listening to that. He could feel his heart pounding in his chest, his legs felt weak as if they wouldn't hold his body up, he could feel his body shaking and he thought he might faint.

Matthews could see that Eugene was in some distress and said, "Sit down."

Eugene did so.

Matthews continued, "Just take a moment, calm yourself," and turning to Preston said, "Get some water please."

Preston left the room, retuning within moments with a plastic cup which he placed on the table in front of Eugene. Eugene took the cup and as he picked it up he saw how much his hand was shaking.

Matthews continued, "Please take a moment and we will then go through to the custody area." Eugene drained the plastic cup of water.

"Ok, follow me please."

The three then walked along a narrow corridor in single file, Matthews at the front followed by Eugene with Preston at the rear. Eugene knew the building and knew where he was within it. The trio entered the custody area and were approached by a male civilian custody officer.

"Get the custody sergeant," barked Matthews and the custody officer hurried away.

Matthews led Eugene and Preston into the charge room and told Eugene to stand in front of the desk. Eugene had been in many charge rooms with identical desks, but they had never seemed so high as this one appeared now. A few moments later a smartly dressed slightly built female sergeant appeared followed by the custody officer.

The sergeant stood behind the ubiquitous computer, entered some details into it and looked at Matthews.

"Please go ahead, sir."

Matthews told the sergeant who he was and which department he was from and then related the details of everything that led up to the present moment: the investigation by the police in America, the first file arriving, the search of Eugene's home, the seizure of the computers and the examination of the computers by the Paedophile and Cyber Investigation Unit. Matthews paused and took some papers from the briefcase he was carrying.

He continued, "This is a copy of the report from the Paedophile and Cyber Investigation Unit which states that on one of the computers seized, a computer owned and used by Mr Elphick and labelled as 'the family computer', there were found 14 images of class A, 25 images of class B and 25 images of class C. A video had also been down loaded which is classified as Class A."

The sergeant took the report looked at it briefly and handed it back to Matthews who placed it back in his briefcase.

He then said, "We wrote to Mr Elphick asking him to attend here today and upon his attendance I arrested him."

The sergeant who had been typing quite a lot of information into the computer said a quiet, "Thank you."

Matthews then added, "We're in a position to go straight to interview". The sergeant didn't reply.

She then turned to Eugene and said, "Mr Elphick, you've heard what the superintendent has said?" Eugene nodded his head and the sergeant continued, "I'm authorising your detention at this police station to secure further evidence by way of interview. Whilst you are here you have certain rights: you have the right to have someone informed of your arrest, you have the right to consult a solicitor and you have the right to examine the Codes of Practice, a book which tells us how you must be treated whilst you are here. Do you understand?"

Eugene understood only too well.

The sergeant continued, "Do you want us to inform anyone that you're here?"

Eugene said, "No."

The sergeant continued by saying, "Would you like to consult a solicitor?" to which Eugene replied in the affirmative.

The sergeant said, "Would you like to consult a specific solicitor?"

Eugene said "Yes," and continued, "Karen Nicholls of Gillespie and Clapton Reading."

"Have you their number?"

"No, not off the top of my head."

The sergeant told him, "We'll make a call and ask Karen Nicholls to contact us. When she does you will be allowed to speak with her in private."

She nodded to the custody officer, and he disappeared out of the door. She then asked Eugene a series of questions about medication being taken, (Eugene didn't mention the Amitriptyline), if he had ever made an attempt on his own life, if he currently felt suicidal and then explained that Eugene would have to place his property on the lower part of the desk especially designed for that purpose.

Eugene emptied his pockets placing his wallet, car keys, a photo of Sandra and Katie and all other paraphernalia, including his police warrant card from his pockets onto the desk.

Matthews stepped forward and said to the sergeant, "We'll take possession of his warrant card."

The sergeant didn't reply; she was busy listing the details of Eugene's property into the computer. The custody officer returned, and the custody sergeant asked him to search Eugene which Eugene found upsetting and, frankly, humiliating. He considered the times, hundreds of times probably, he had searched or had caused people, prisoners, suspects, to be searched and had never, not once, stopped to consider how such an ordeal must feel. He knew now!

"Nothing further," said the custody officer taking a large plastic bag in which he placed all of Eugene's property.

The sergeant said, "We'll take care of your property and it will be returned to you when you leave here. Please sign here to say this is a true record of your property."

Eugene did so without even reading the list of property.

The custody officer continued, "Nothing further can happen now until you have spoken with your nominated solicitor so until that time..." she stopped mid-sentence as a civilian custody officer entered the room.

"There's a solicitor, a Ms Karen Nicholls, on the phone for Mr Elphick."

The sergeant said, "Please take Mr Elphick to the telephone room and allow him to speak to his solicitor in private. He has been searched."

The custody officer said to Eugene, "Follow me please," and Eugene and the custody officer left the room.

Matthews stepped back and leaned against the wall; Preston was already doing so. Preston then took the brief case which was on the floor in front of Matthews. He walked to the front of the desk opened the case and took out a list of suggested charges which had been pre-prepared by Helen Callaghan and supported by the Deputy Chief Constable.

Handing the list to the Custody Sergeant Preston said, "You could start preparing the charges now if you want, love, might save you some time later."

The male custody officer looked aghast, and Matthews thought what a nervous sort of chap he appeared to be.

The sergeant looked up, took the sheet in her hand, and said in a calm and measured voice, "My name is Sergeant Gray. I am nobody's love, and we'll just see what happens, shall we?"

She handed the sheet back to Preston. Behind him Matthews smiled and thought 'good on you'. Preston was taken back somewhat but said nothing, took the sheet, placed it back into the briefcase and returned to his place at the wall beside Matthews. Preston said quietly "Cheeky cow!" Matthews didn't say anything.

After a few minutes, the custody officer and Eugene came back into the room. The custody sergeant looked at Eugene and said, "Did you speak to the solicitor?"

"Yes, thank you, I did."

The sergeant said, "These gentlemen," she gave a slight glance toward Preston, "have said they are in a position to go to interview. Is that OK with you?"

"My solicitor is coming across so I would prefer to wait for her."

"OK," said the sergeant. She continued, "It will take a while for her to get here, and I have nowhere for you to wait so you will be placed in a cell until the solicitor arrives."

Eugene didn't reply.

The sergeant said to the one of the custody officers, "Place Mr Elphick in cell 17 please."

The custody officer made his way to Eugene and said, "Please come with me."

Both men left the charge room and as they did so Eugene noticed Preston staring hard at him with a snarl on his face.

Eugene and the custody officer passed through a barred gate that the custody officer unlocked, along a poorly lit passageway with cells on both sides. Some were occupied but not many. There were some inaudible words issuing from two of the cells, but Eugene couldn't hear what was said. They arrived at cell 17 which was near the end of the passageway. The door was open, and Eugene went to walk in.

"Take your shoes and belt off," said the custody officer, "and place them here outside your cell."

"Is this necessary?" asked Eugene and the male custody officer affirmed that it was.

Eugene did as he was instructed and entered the cell, and the door was shut behind him with a heavy thump. Eugene felt more alone than at any time he could remember in the whole of his life.

He pulled the thick blue plastic covered foam rubber mattress which was propped up against the wall down onto the bench, which would serve as a bed if he were here long enough, and he sat on it. He looked around the cell; it was freshly painted but various names scrawled into the brickwork could still be made out. However, it was clean - cleaner than cells in his experience usually were. Eugene wondered how he had ended up here. He could still feel his heart pounding, his hands still shook and there was a burning in his throat, his eyes welled up with tears. After a few moments Eugene composed himself. He didn't want anyone to see his weakness; logically he had done nothing wrong, what he was being accused of was a massive mistake and he now had to rely on the wisdom and skills of Karen Nicholls. He and she were aware of each other; they had worked together a number of times, albeit on opposite sides. In Eugene's estimation she was the best solicitor locally and he must now put his faith in her.

After what seemed a long time, and Eugene had no knowledge of how long because his watch had been bagged with his property, the cell door opened. There stood a civilian custody officer who Eugene had not seen previously.

Without looking at Eugene he said quite loudly, "Your brief's here, mate - come with me." Eugene wanted to inform this person that he most certainly was not his mate but resisted the temptation to do so. He put his shoes and belt back on and followed the custody officer along the passage and through the barred gate. They stopped at a door and the custody officer knocked and then immediately entered. Eugene followed.

Karen Nicholls was sat behind a desk which was affixed to the floor with one empty chair, which was also fixed to the floor, opposite her.

"Thank you," said Karen, and the custody officer departed.

Karen stood up offered her hand for Eugene to shake and said, "Come and sit down Mr Elphick. I don't think we've seen each other for a while."

Eugene was relieved that she remembered him and said, "Never in these circumstances," as he took his seat.

Karen said, "We just need to complete some boring admin forms first and then we'll see how I can best help you."

She spoke pleasantly and made good eye contact and appeared in no way judgemental. She was a woman of about 35 years of age, quite short, of medium build for her height, with slightly greying dark hair. She was smartly dressed in a sombre coloured trouser suit which befitted her occupation.

Eugene didn't know much about her personally but noticed that she didn't wear a wedding ring.

The administration requirements over, Karen placed the numerous papers she had completed with Eugene back into her briefcase and took another two sheets of paper from it.

She sat back in her chair and said, "How are you feeling?"

Eugene relied, "I feel broken, frightened, humiliated and I suppose, wronged."

Karen looked at Eugene and said, "Do you mind if I call you Eugene?"

Eugene replied, "I prefer Gene".

"Ok, Gene," Karen continued, "I've been given an advance disclosure by the investigation officer; I don't need to explain what an advance disclosure is. It gives me details of the allegations that you, toward the end of last year, downloaded a quantity of illegal child pornography in the form of images and one video across the range of classes A to C. Do you understand the classes?"

Eugene nodded.

Karen continued, "Class A being the most serious, to Class C. It is alleged these were downloaded onto your home computer on three separate dates from a website in the USA and were paid for by a credit card in your name. The rest is as you know. Your home was searched, your computer seized, examined and the images as described found on your hard drive – that is the extent of what I know at this time."

Eugene thought for a moment and said, "When Professional Standards attended my home they told me that they had received information from another police force; I have only learned today that it was an American force."

Karen Nicholls took an A4 sized notebook with a blue cover from her brief case and started writing in it. Eugene noticed that she used a form of speed writing, not shorthand but something similar, which he had observed before.

"What else did they tell you at that time?" asked Karen.

"Um, they said a number of people had downloaded material…" he paused and the continued, "that is to say child pornography, on to their computers and that I was named as one of those persons."

"Did they say how you came to be named?"

"No…no I don't think so. It's hard to remember what was said actually. I was in a bit of a state of shock, I suppose."

"Yes, I fully understand. Did they give you any further information at that time as to what evidence they had?"

Eugene thought and then said, "No, they seemed to want to get on with searching my house and had a search team to do it. They were there quite a while and took possession of all the computers that I had."

"Which were?"

"There was the family computer, a laptop, my daughter Katie's laptop and two old PC's that were in the garage."

"Did the police say there was anything on the other computers?"

Eugene replied, "They only mentioned the family computer when the superintendent outlined his reasons for arrest."

"Did they arrest you at your home today?"

"No, they sent me a letter asking me to attend here today. I thought it was to collect the property they had taken from me. I've done nothing wrong and had nothing to fear. When I arrived here I was arrested and told I'd committed the offence of downloading and possession of child pornography. I've not done that."

Eugene was beginning to feel emotional, and his voice began to falter.

"OK, Gene, just calm down. We'll get to the bottom of all this. Would you like some water?"

"No, I'm OK."

Karen Nicholls continued, "Now, we know that material has been downloaded onto the hard drive of what has been termed the family computer. I must ask you this; how do you think the material got onto the hard drive?"

Eugene said, "I don't know. All I know is that I've never downloaded that material. I've never viewed any pornographic material on that computer. I have a 14 year old daughter for goodness sake."

"Is there a child lock on that computer?" asked Karen.

"Not on that one, there is on Katie's."

"Who uses that computer?"

"Me mostly, occasionally my wife, but not often, and Katie very rarely because she has her own."

"Have the police spoken to your wife and daughter?" asked Karen.

"No."

Karen paused for a moment while she wrote in her notebook in that strange speed writing style.

She then looked at Eugene and said, "So, I will ask again, I'm sorry, but how did that child pornography end up on the hard drive of your computer?"

Eugene replied, "I don't know; I have no idea. I spoke to a colleague and told him I was being investigated following an allegation that I had been 'trolling'. I wasn't going to tell him it was anything to do with what it is." Eugene noticed that he was having great difficulty even saying the words 'child pornography'. "He suggested that someone might have planted things onto the hard drive."

Karen stopped writing looked up and said, "I am no computer expert, but I think that if the material is on the hard drive it must have been downloaded onto that machine. That said, we will be having the report of the Paedophile and Cyber Investigation Unit examined by an expert and go from there."

She continued, "Is there anyone else who has access to your computer apart from your wife and daughter: friends, other relatives, anyone like that?"

"No, there's no one else."

"Is there any way your wife or daughter could have done this?" asked Karen.

"No...no way," replied Eugene.

"The police haven't spoken to them?"

"No, and I don't want them talking to my daughter – she's 14 and young for her age, naive really."

Karen didn't reply at first. She then said "Now we come to the credit card. Do you have a Lloyds credit card?"

"No, I've never had a bank account of any kind with Lloyds."

Karen said, "The police haven't told me very much in the advance disclosure about the credit card and I'll need to ask them about that. There are a few things that they haven't said, in fact."

She was silent for a few moments, obviously thinking, her lawyer brain dissecting, and critically analysing the information that she so far had to hand.

She then looked directly at Eugene and said, "At this moment in time things aren't looking that great. There are further questions that we, as the defence, need answering by the police. There are a number of enquiries that we need to make ourselves. You say that you didn't do this and for the moment I don't think it wise for us to say anything further to the police. We will therefore be answering 'no comment' to all questions put by them. Is there anything else you can think of that you haven't told me so far that may be relevant?"

Eugene hated the 'no comment' interview. He always resented prisoners using it as a cop out. In his view, delaying the inevitable, unable to admit their guilt. He had always assumed guilt when a prisoner opted for the 'no comment' interview.

That said, he believed that sometimes a lazy, incompetent solicitor or one who was out of their depth would elect for it. He knew, however, on this occasion that he wasn't guilty, and Karen Nicholls was in no way incompetent, lazy or out of her depth. In fact she had, despite what she had said, given him a feeling of confidence in her.

"Well, I don't know if it is relevant, but I'm seeing a psychiatrist for PTSD and depression. I've only started seeing him since all this business started but he's said the issues go back a few years."

"Yes, thank you. What's the name of the psychiatrist?"

Eugene gave Dr Bekhit's details and at Karen's request signed a form whereby Karen could make contact with Dr Bekhit and obtain information from him with Eugene's permission. Karen packed her bits and pieces back into her briefcase and snapped it shut.

She said, "Just wait there. I'll be back in a second."

She went to the door, looked out and said, "Excuse me."

After a few seconds a custody officer appeared at the door.

"Please tell the custody sergeant we're ready now and would like to see her."

Karen returned to the room.

"OK, let's make our way toward the charge office."

As they walked the custody officer returned and said, "You can go onto the charge room."

The efficient custody sergeant was sitting behind her computer at the desk, and Karen told her that they were ready for the interview now.

The sergeant somewhat sheepishly replied, "Superintendent Matthews has said he's a little tied up for the moment and can you wait please?"

Karen rose to her full height, all of five feet three inches of her, and said, "Sergeant, please tell Superintendent Matthews that his tired and outdated, nineteen eighties delaying tactics will not work. You told me when I arrived that he was ready to go to interview. If he was ready then, he's ready now. Please contact him and ask him to attend and commence this interview."

Eugene noticed that the sergeant's cheeks turned slightly red, actually enhancing her attractiveness, as she simply and quietly replied "Yes, ma'am."

The sergeant left her desk, leaving a somewhat nervous looking custody officer, the one that Eugene had encountered first on arrival. She clearly wanted to use a telephone out of earshot of Karen.

She returned a few moments later and said, "The superintendent is on his way, ma'am."

CHAPTER 10

Eugene had carried out probably hundreds of tape recorded interviews in his time and walking into Interview Room 2 at Maidenhead Custody Suite he was familiar with the setup of the room: a single table, with a double tape recording machine against the wall, and a video camera in one corner at ceiling level positioned to record all that took place within that small room There were four chairs: Preston took the chair closest to the wall and next to the tape machine, Matthews sat next to him, Karen Neville took the seat opposite Preston and Eugene took the remaining seat. Matthews took some papers from his brief case and then set it on the floor. He also placed a laptop computer wrapped in a plastic bag with a red numbered seal on the table between him and Eugene.

Matthews asked if everyone was ready. Preston took two tapes from a brown envelope and placed them in the tape recording machine banging the little doors closed, each tape in its own aperture. He pressed a red button and there was a long buzzing noise. All this was quite familiar to Eugene. Indeed the process was familiar to all present as all had taken part in many taped recorded interviews through time. Yet, the process was unnerving for Eugene. He could again feel his heart pounding in his chest, his mouth felt so dry, and his hand shook a little. Although familiar with it the process had never before been directed at him as the prisoner, the suspect, the accused. The assumed guilty one.

The buzzing stopped and Matthews read from a yellow plastic laminated sheet.

"We are in Interview Room 2 at Maidenhead custody suite, the time is 4:07pm ..." and on he continued in his detached monotoned voice, saying what the date was, who was being interviewed, that the interview was being tape recorded and videotaped, there were four persons present and asking each to identify themselves - which they did by saying their name and role, with Eugene just giving his name. Eugene was given the caution and told how he could access a copy of the tapes. At the end of the diatribe Eugene was asked if he understood all that had been said. Of course he did! but answered politely that he did understand.

Matthews then took the laptop from the plastic bag by breaking the red plastic seal and placing that inside the bag.

He said, "For the benefit of the tape I am showing Mr Elphick a grey Hewlett Packard laptop computer reference number DM/PS/14/. Is this your laptop, Mr Elphick?"

Eugene could see that it was his family laptop recognising a small smiley face sticker on the right hand corner on the outside which Katie had placed there about a year earlier. He could also see a dark yellow sticker with the words 'Paedophile and Cyber Investigation Unit Oxford' along with a long reference number written on it. There was also another label which stated - Family Computer, and the reference number DM/PS/14

"Yes, that's our family computer."

Karen gave a little cough which reminded Eugene that he should not be saying anything.

Matthews continued, "When did you purchase this laptop Mr Elphick?"

Eugene was silent for a moment and then said, "I've been advised by my legal representative to make no comment to your questions at this time".

Eugene felt awkward and shuffled his feet as the unfamiliar defensive sounding words issued, embarrassingly from his mouth. Both Matthews and Preston were silent for a moment, then Matthews commenced his interview. Eugene quickly became aware that Matthews was in no way an experienced interviewer. His interview had no structure, no technique, he followed no format, had no strategy, and applied none of the accepted interview models. In fact to an experienced interviewer, which Eugene was, and no doubt Preston, too, Matthews' interview was awkward and clumsy.

Matthews went through the stages of events, the use of the credit card, entering the American site and the purchase of material, which Matthews tried to describe with more than a hint of embarrassment, the downloading onto Eugene's laptop and the search of Eugene's house and the seizure of the computers. At each stage Matthews asked his questions in his monotonous, wearisome tone. Eugene could see how increasingly frustrated Preston was becoming, sighing, shuffling in his seat, and tapping his pen on the desktop. He was clearly embarrassed by his supervisor's interview ineptitude. Preston would have probably been a more formidable interviewer, and Eugene was glad that Preston wasn't conducting the interview.

Eugene wanted desperately to answer the questions, many of which were unskilfully closed questions just requiring a 'yes' or 'no' answer. Desperately wanting to say that he knew of none of these things, of his naivety when it came to advanced computer techniques, and scream his innocence, but he continued to answer all Matthews questions with 'no comment' as advised by Karen.

Suddenly Preston got up walked to the rear of Matthews and took the briefcase from the floor to the left-hand side of Matthews. He returned to his seat, rummaged in the briefcase, and took from it a sheaf of papers which he laid on the desk in front of him face side down.

He then said to Matthews, "May I, sir?"

Matthews replied, "Of course," and sat back in his chair with something of a look of relief on his face.

Preston paused and then said in an uncharacteristically quiet and calm tone that surprised both Eugene and Matthews, "Eugene, we're both police officers, both detectives with considerable experience. You know that the innocent will always want to explain their position, in fact will go to great lengths to explain their innocence, non-involvement, blamelessness – you know that. Yet here you are failing to answer what often are non-incriminating questions. Perhaps you'll reconsider, and if you're blameless, give us some reasons why you feel that. You know there's no mileage in saying 'no comment' to everything."

Eugene was silent pondering what Preston had said. He knew that he, before today, and certainly before this hour even, would have thought the same way.

Karen then said, "May I remind you, Inspector, that it is my client's fundamental right not to answer questions put to him, and it is the duty of the prosecution to prove the prisoner's guilt, not the duty of the accused to prove his innocence."

Matthews said nothing and Preston was silent for a moment.

He then continued, "Well, Mr Elphick?" His tone had changed to its more menacing style, "You've heard Superintendent Matthews describe the pornographic material that you downloaded, pornographic material showing children, some very young".

He flicked over the sheets of paper in front of him on which were images copied from the hard drive of Eugene's laptop.

"For the benefit of the tape I'm showing Mr Elphick still images coped from the hard drive of his computer, exhibit numbers HC/PCIU/ 121-164. Here they are, images of categories A, B and C and you're aware of what the categories mean, these images taken from your laptop, downloaded by you."

He pushed one of the sheets toward Eugene and said, "Do look at your handiwork, Mr Elphick."

Eugene could see what the images were; they shocked him. He had never in his experience seen such graphic pictures and he felt sick. He knew that he couldn't have downloaded such material, not in a million years. He turned away.

"Do look, Mr Elphick. As you've done no doubt on many occasions before."

Eugene wanted to protest his innocence and muttered "I...I..."

Karen, who had also had a glimpse of the graphic images, immediately said, "My client does not want to view these images and I find your tactics oppressive, bullying and intimidating."

There was a faltering to her voice, but she continued, "If you have the evidence to charge my client do so or release him."

Matthews and Preston didn't reply. After a few moments of awkward silence Matthews coughed and then brought the interview to an end. Preston stopped the tape machine and ejected the two tapes. Matthews again read from the yellow plastic laminated sheet explaining what would happen to the tapes and so on, again all familiar to those present.

Matthews then said quietly, "Inspector Preston will take you through to the charge office and I'll join you there shortly."

Matthews packed the briefcase and the laptop. He was first to leave the interview room and the others followed with Preston leading the way back to the charge room.

There was only a civilian custody officer present and Preston in his familiar manner issued the order, "You," he commanded, "call the custody sergeant".

The custody officer left the room. Eugene felt a general numbness, he was tense, and there was a sensation of a lump in his throat, he could feel his breathing rate increase. His mouth was dry, so very dry, he could feel his heart beating faster his mind felt blank, and he knew these were the symptoms that he had experienced before.

"Don't lose control," he said silently to himself. "Not here."

The custody sergeant, the civilian custody officer and Matthews entered the room together. Matthews was carrying what Eugene could see was Katie's laptop. He wondered if they had found something there but no, he reassured himself, they couldn't have done. His mouth was so dry.

"Could I have a glass of water please?"

Preston nodded at the civilian custody officer who returned almost immediately with a plastic cup. He handed it to Eugene who drank the entire contents in two large gulps.

The custody sergeant looked at Eugene and said quietly, "Are you OK?"

Eugene nodded and she continued, "I have spoken with Superintendent Matthews; he has presented evidence to me which has already been seen by the CPS and the Deputy Chief Constable. They've deemed that there is sufficient evidence to charge you and I'm in agreement with the CPS. I therefore do intend to charge you. It'll take a little while for me to prepare the charges."

She then looked at Karen Nicholls and said "Are you remaining with Mr Elphick?"

Karen hesitated briefly and then said, "Yes…yes I'll stay."

"In that case," continued the custody sergeant turning to the civilian custody officer, "please show Ms Nicholls and Mr Elphick to the solicitors interview room."

Turning back to Karen she said, "I will let you know when we are ready."

The civilian custody officer led Karen and Eugene back to the room where they had first met that afternoon and they took the same seats as they had previously sat in. The civilian custody officer left, and Eugene felt slightly better.

"I'm not happy with this case, Gene."

Karen settled into her seat, she looked at Eugene and placed her hands palm downward onto the table and continued, "That interview wasn't particularly good, and I've a feeling that they, and especially that inspector, what was it…" she looked at her notes "Yes, Preston, seem totally focussed on you. That's why I've elected to stay until everything is finished. I don't usually stay for the charging and admin but today I will."

"Thank you," said Eugene in a quiet, helpless manner, almost childlike.

"In terms of evidence this isn't looking good; images and a video have been downloaded onto the hard drive of your computer. Someone must have done that; you say that you didn't"... could anyone else in your household have done that?"

"No, only my wife and I use that laptop. My daughter could have access to it, but she rarely uses it, she has her own."

Karen was writing in her notebook and after a few moments looked up.

"They said in interview that material had been downloaded onto your laptop on three occasions: once on 16th October, once on 30th October and once on 13th November. All Sundays. The first at 10.10 am and the others at 10:25am and 10:17am respectively according to the Phoenix Police Department. Now, you have said to me previously, and the police didn't go into this in interview, you could account for those times, saying that you weren't working on those days but were at home with your family. Now, this is the important part..." she paused and then continued.

"So, if we bear in mind," she paused again and said, "that allowing for GMT Phoenix Arizona is some seven hours behind us, the actual time that the material was downloaded here in the UK would have been 3:10am 3:25 am and 3:17 am."

She paused again and asked, "Does that make any sense to you?"

Eugene processed what Karen had said.

"No, that's the middle of the night...no, I don't think."

Eugene's voice got quieter at the end of the sentence; he sat head in hands lost in thought. Karen maintained silence.

Eugene then looked up and said, "Well, I don't know, I mean...um...well it would appear that I've been sleep walking. My wife mentioned it to me a little while back. My sleep has been disturbed that's for sure. I did mention this to the psychiatrist I saw. I don't know."

"Thank you, that may be significant. I'll be making contact with Dr Bekhit." She continued to write into her notebook.

"Are you taking any prescribed medication?"

Eugene replied, "Yes, Amitriptyline, twenty five milligrams at night." He didn't say that he wasn't taking it.

"And that was prescribed by Dr Bekhit?"

"Yes."

Karen then said, "It may be a good idea for you to make an appointment to see him again and update him on what's occurred. That would coincide with me either writing to him or speaking to him."

Eugene didn't have a chance to reply. There was a knock at the door and Karen issued a loud "Yes?"

The door opened and the civilian custody officer with proudly displayed tattoos on both arms said, "The custody sergeant is ready now, please follow me."

They returned to the charge room where the custody sergeant was again sitting behind her computer. Preston and Matthews were standing in front of and facing the custody sergeant, and neither turned as Karen and Eugene entered the room.

The custody sergeant said to Preston and Matthews, "Which of you will carry out the charging?"

Matthews stepped forward and Preston moved away to his left, then turning to face Eugene. The custody sergeant gave Matthews some forms. Suddenly Eugene's sense of hearing became very acute, he could hear someone whistling in the corridor outside the charge room, the heavy thump of a cell door being closed, and an indistinct and muffled shout from somewhere deep in the cell block, a phone ringing somewhere.

Matthews then commenced, "Eugene Elphick you are charged that between the dates..." and on he droned, his face expressionless. He fumbled over his words, and it was clear that he was unused to charging anyone and not with so many charges. Eugene stole a glance at Preston who was staring intently at him with something of a smirk on his face. Matthews came to the end of his charging and cautioned Eugene. Eugene made no reply. The custody sergeant then took the forms back off Matthews and asked Eugene to sign them, stating that he would be given a copy.

She then said, "You will be bailed from this police station to attend Maidenhead Magistrates Court on Thursday 21st of this month, that is next Thursday, a week today. Please sign here for your bail and a copy of the charge sheets."

Eugene did so without saying anything.

The custody sergeant continued, "You will now be photographed, have your fingerprints and DNA taken, you are no doubt familiar with this. Once that has been done I will speak to you again. Ms Nicholls, you can wait in the solicitors room whilst this is going on."

The civilian custody officer then took Eugene off to carry out the tasks that the custody sergeant had outlined. They both returned to the charge room about twenty minutes later. The custody sergeant and Karen were already waiting. Eugene noticed the plastic bag with his property inside on the custody sergeant's desk. The custody sergeant broke the seal on the property bag and carefully laid Eugene's property out on the lower level of the desk. She again asked Eugene to sign for his property and he did so.

Eugene started to place his property into his pockets when Matthews and Preston entered the room. Matthews was still carrying Katie's laptop.

He said, "Now Mr Elphick, you are aware that I took your warrant card from you when you first arrived here."

Karen then said, "Superintendent if you are about to say what I think you are, I think this would be better done in private."

Preston said, "It's nothing to do…" but Matthews quickly interrupted him and said,

"Yes, you're right," and turning to the custody sergeant he said,"May we use the interview room we were in?"

"Yes, but bear in mind I've returned his property to him and will need to see him to formally release him."

They moved toward the interview room and Preston said to Karen Nicholls in his natural menacing tone, standing in front of her almost blocking her way, "You don't need to be present for this."

Eugene, having recovered some of his composure, said in a clear voice, "I'd like her to be present please," and all four entered interview room number two.

All stood and Matthews said, "I have your warrant card, and it's my duty to now inform you that on behalf of the Deputy Chief Constable I'm formally suspending you from duty. You're not to enter any police station or have contact with any police officer or police staff unless in the case of an emergency or seeing your Police Federation representative. I've a form here which points out what you should and should not do whilst suspended."

Preston then rummaged in, and then took from the briefcase he was carrying, two forms which he handed to Eugene with just the hint of a menacing smile on his face.

Matthews continued, "You could now be interviewed in relation to the alleged discipline offences that are disclosed but that would appear academic at this stage."

Eugene did not reply.

Matthews then said, "I have here your daughter's laptop which I'm returning to you."

Preston handed Matthews a pink card which Eugene had to sign. Eugene did so and took possession of the laptop, still in its plastic sealed bag.

Matthews then said, "We've two desk top PC's which you can have back."

Eugene said, "I don't want them. I'll sign a disclaimer."

Preston handed another form to Matthews upon which Matthews entered some details and asked Eugene to sign, which he did.

Matthews then said, "I'd advise you to make contact with your Police Federation Representative. Have you any questions?"

Eugene replied in the negative.

"There's one final thing; because of the nature of the offences that you've been charged with, coupled with the fact that you've a young child, I'm duty bound to report this to your local Social Services Children's Department. I'd assume that they'll be in contact with you and your wife pretty quickly. I'll be informing them by tomorrow morning at the latest."

Eugene felt quite numb, did not know what to say. He hadn't expected this. Matthews again said, "Have you any questions?" to which Eugene said "No."

They returned to the charge room where Eugene was formally released and soon he and Karen were outside in the evening rush hour air. It was 6:35pm. Both walked toward the car park where they had parked their cars. Neither said very much; both were lost in their own thoughts. Karen said that she would be in touch in a day or so and would see him again the following week. They said awkward goodbyes and parted company each going to their respective cars.

CHAPTER 11

Eugene could not remember much of the journey home; it was again one of those journeys that seemed to occur in something of a haze, on automatic pilot so to speak. As he turned into his road he pulled over. He switched on his phone, noticing he had several missed calls, one from Benji and ominously, seven from his wife. He quickly telephoned Sandra and she answered with, "Wherever are you?"

With some apprehension Eugene said, "I'll be home in a few minutes."

He then sat motionless wondering what on earth he was going to say. Eugene didn't know how long he sat there but it couldn't have been that long, or Sandra would have called back. He realised that he would have to tell her the truth; the time for hiding things and telling half-truths or even lies had passed.

He parked in his driveway and entered his home via the kitchen. Both Sandra and Katie were there putting dishes away, and Katie with her usual enthusiasm greeted Eugene.

"Daddy, we've been waiting for you!"

Eugene slowly took Katie's laptop which was still in is sealed plastic bag from behind his back.

"Great!" cried Katie, "I'll be able to transfer all my old things onto my new laptop; you'll help me won't you Dad."

"I think your mum will do a better job."

Eugene then remembered that somewhere on the laptop would be a dark yellow sticker betraying where the laptop had been.

"Wait there," said Eugene as he made to exit the kitchen and retreat to his car.

"Where are you going?" asked Sandra with some surprise in her voice, but Eugene was back at his car removing the plastic bag and tearing off the dark yellow sticker, placing it in his pocket and returning to the house.

He presented the laptop to his daughter and said, "Here you are Katie, good as new. I just wanted to get rid of that old plastic bag."

"Thanks Dad," said Katie. "I'll put it with the other one."

As Katie left the kitchen Sandra stopped what she was doing and said harshly, "Where have you been all this time?"

"Well, I went to the police station as you know, got Katies laptop."

"Where's ours by the way?" asked Sandra looking around as if it would miraculously appear.

Eugene was aware that the time for procrastination, half-truths and lies were over. He knew that he had to be honest with Sandra but made a lame effort to delay the inevitable.

"It's a bit complicated, a bit involved. Let's talk when Katie's has gone to bed."

Eugene thought Sandra would demand to know what, where and when straight away but she didn't - she merely sighed and said, "Katie and I have already eaten; if you want something, prepare it yourself," and she disappeared into the living room.

The journey back to Oxfordshire was made for the most part with neither Matthews nor Preston having much to say. Both were, in fact, tired as they we unused to working such long hours within the Professional Standards Department. Matthews was the first to break the silence.

"Do you want to have a little debrief of today?"

Preston, his eyes rigidly fixed on the road replied, "No, not really. It was pretty straightforward. A no comment interview as was to be expected from a guilty party advised by a solicitor." ,

"What did you think of the custody sergeant, Nick?" asked Matthews with a slight chuckle in his voice. Preston shifted uneasily in his seat, "Arrogant little bitch, another Helen Callaghan in the making if you ask me, Guv."

Matthews laughed, "She had your mark, Nick. I thought she was very efficient."

Preston didn't reply and concentrated on his driving. Little else was said on the journey and the two parted company at Kidlington, agreeing to meet the following day when Preston would start to prepare a file for the court hearing in a weeks' time.

An awkward hour ensued in Old Windsor with the nuclear family sitting in front of the TV, the only person actually watching and taking in what was going on was Katie. Both Eugene and Sandra were very much lost in their own thoughts.

The subdued atmosphere was then punctured by Sandra who said, "Come on Katie, go up now. Busy day tomorrow."

Katie who was unusually accepting of her mother's demands said, "'night" and kissed each of her parents on the cheek and made her way upstairs. An oppressive silence persisted, both Eugene and Sandra thinking of what they might individually say.

Sandra started speaking in a controlled and exact manner. She said with more than a hint of causticness in her voice, "So, I'll start where I left off, shall I? Where's our computer?"

Eugene replied, "The police still have it." He surprised himself in saying the police and realised that he was already seeing himself as distinct, apart from and different to the police. He continued, "Well, Professional Standards, that is."

"So what is exactly going on Gene?"

This was the moment…the very moment that Eugene had dreaded. He didn't know what to say and then commenced, "I went to Maidenhead with the impression that I was going to be picking up our computers: ours, and Katie's. I was under the impression that whatever mistake had occurred had been rectified and the nightmare that I… we, had been living was over."

He stopped; he could feel himself welling up but resisted the urge to succumb.

Taking a deep breath he plunged in with, "When I got there I was arrested".

He stopped again and Sandra broke the ensuing silence by echoing but with great exclamation, "Arrested?"

Eugene took another deep breath and caught hold of the arm of the chair he was sitting in tightly as he feared the now familiar symptoms of panic would return. Sandra got up, walked toward the television and switched it off. She tuned and faced Eugene.

"Arrested for what?"

"I have to be honest with you Sandra but please just listen to what I have to say."

Sandra said with agitation, "Go on."

"I was arrested for downloading and possessing indecent images of children, but I haven't done it."

Sandra, who had been standing up since switching off the TV, flopped heavily onto the sofa.

She said, "What the fuck? What do you mean?"

"They've examined the laptop and images were found on the hard drive. They've said the images were purchased from an American site..."

Sandra interjected, "Which laptop?"

"Ours. There was nothing on Katie's or the old PCs."

Sandra paused and then continued, "If they were on the hard drive, then you downloaded them...how else could they be there?"

Her voice was getting louder; her complexion had gone from slightly flushed to a pale colour as if the blood had drained from her head.

"I don't know what to say...why have you done such a thing? What were you thinking of? Why have you treated Katie and me in this manner? How long...how many years have I been married to a pervert, a paedophile?"

Eugene was silent.

"Because, yes, Gene that's what you are, you bastard."

Eugene responded with almost a pleading in his voice, "I didn't do it."

Sandra stood up again.

"Oh, I see! You didn't do it…it was me or Katie was it?"

Eugene leaned forward in his chair and placed his head in his hands.

"No, no, of course not," he said quietly, as if talking to himself, into his hands.

"Well that's it as far as I'm concerned…that is it. I can't live here; I can't live with you anymore. I've put up with your sordid affairs – Oh yes, Gene, I know about Ann-Marie Curtis and Shelia Marshall – the domestic violence, the late nights, the drinking. Yes, Gene, I've not forgotten, but this…this filth, no, no, I can't put up with this! I'm leaving you, Gene. I've thought about it for a while…"

"Mummy, Daddy?" came the voice from upstairs. Sandra moved quickly to the hallway and saw Katie standing at the top of the stairs. She was dressed in her owl patterned pyjama set clutching a pillow as if it were a comforting cuddly toy and looking very much the child she was not so long ago.

"Is everything alright, Mum?" she asked in a lilting hesitant way.

Sandra responded in a soft maternalistic voice saying, "Yes darling, everything is OK. Daddy and I were just having a heated discussion. Sorry we disturbed you. Go back to sleep now."

"OK Mum, if you're sure."

"Yes, don't you worry, everything is fine." Katie returned to her room and Sandra re-entered the lounge.

Eugene was crouched over with his head still in his hands.

He said without looking up, "I didn't do this thing."

Sandra, who had calmed down considerably, sat down and said in a very calm and precise manner, "Please look at me."

Eugene looked up. His eyes were wide, his expression fixed and rigid.

"Gene, I am incredibly disappointed in you, but it doesn't go beyond that. I was angry but not now, I was hurt but not now. I am not sufficiently interested in you to be any of those things. I have some ambivalence but nothing else. I want you to know that you and I are now finished. I have a daughter upstairs who will be a major, yet innocent, victim in all this and I sincerely hope for your sake that you haven't done anything to her."

Eugene said, "Of course not," and he replaced his head in his hands.

Sandra continued, "I don't want to talk about any of this anymore now, you're effectively on your own. Katie and I will be leaving here in the morning, and I don't want you to contact us. I'll let you know when you can have telephone contact with Katie. We'll be going to my parents, and I do not want you coming there. If you do come there I will call the police. I will be contacting a solicitor. This is very much the end, Gene."

Eugene was silent for a moment and then looking up he said in supplication, "You're going to leave me when I'm needing you most."

"Yes, well in your well-seasoned police parlance, you should have thought of that before. Please go to your room and leave me alone now. I've things that I need to do."

Like a scolded child Eugene retreated to his bedroom. He was aware that his world was falling apart. He knew that he hadn't told Sandra everything, about the solicitor, his PTSD, the fact that the Social Services would be involved and would want to speak to her, no doubt. So many things that needed to be said but were left unsaid. He lay on his bed fully dressed. He could hear Sandra moving around the house upstairs and downstairs. He felt so lonely, so alone, like a pariah, and he was aware that is how he would be treated, a social outcast.

It was something of a disturbed yet surreal night for Eugene; he could hear Sandra moving around the house late into the night. He dozed lightly, was aware of all sounds around him so wasn't sleeping deeply at all. His mind replayed the day's events over and over in his mind focussing on the most irrelevant facts, the custody officer telling him to take his belt and shoes off, of him sitting in the cell, Preston's passive aggression, Matthews' incompetent interview, the voices of the various participants saying over and over, 'Is this your laptop, Mr Elphick,' 'I am arresting you for downloading illegal indecent material depicting children,' 'Would you like to consult a solicitor?' 'Class A being the most serious,' 'Eugene, we're both police officers, both detectives,' on and on it went in a disjointed, unconnected, and disassociated manner.

Eugene awoke, light was coming in through the curtains, but he knew that it was not that early. He was still in the clothes that he had lay on the bed in. His head ached and he was initially disorientated. The events of the previous day came flooding back to him slamming into his brain. How he wished those events were a dream, but they weren't, they were real. He could hear Sandra's voice downstairs and he got up from his bed. He started down the stairs and could see three suitcases in the hallway. The last time they were here like this was when the family were going on holiday – how he desired so much that was happening now.

He entered the kitchen where both Sandra and Katie were. Katie had her untouched breakfast in front of her. She wasn't wearing her school uniform and was crying.

She was saying through her tears, "I don't want to go and live there." When she saw Eugene she appealed to him, "Dad, help me! I don't want to go and live with Gramps and Nanny in Stoke Poges."

Eugene didn't know what to say. He felt quite helpless.

Eventually, he replied in a gentle tone, "It'll only be for a short time, Katie, then all will be OK again."

He knew that he was lying to her; lying had become perennial these days.

"I don't see why I can't go to school today," she sobbed.

"Is she not going to school?" asked Eugene.

"No," replied Sandra, "I won't be able to collect her".

Eugene automatically said, "I could..."

But Sandra turned to him and said through gritted teeth, "You can't".

Katie continued to sob, and Sandra said quite harshly to her, "Are you ready now?"

Katie came to Eugene and put her arms around him.

"I love you Dad," she said through her tears.

Eugene put his arm around her head and kissed the top of her head saying, "I love you too my little princess," something he hadn't called her for a long time.

"Come on!" ordered Sandra, feeling uncomfortable with Eugene being intimate with her daughter. Katie followed Sandra, who had picked up two of the suitcases, out of the house. Eugene, not quite knowing what to do, picked up the other suitcase knowing that he was assisting his family to leave him and their home.

Katie climbed into the back seat of the car and Eugene leaned in and kissed her tear strewn face. Sandra sat in the driver's seat and said curtly, "Shut the door."

Eugene did as he was told, and the car moved out of the driveway. He followed into the roadway and watched Katie waving to him from the rear car window, her face red with crying. She mouthed, "I love you Daddy".

Eugene raised his arm to wave and replied, "I love you too."

Sandra's car turned at the top of the road and was gone. Eugene stayed there for a few seconds, his arm still in the air. He then made his way back into his house. Katie crying like that was always painful to him. Today, her distress and the circumstances causing it felt like a sword was puncturing his very soul.

Matthews came into the office of the Professional Standards Unit that morning in something of an ebullient mood. He greeted the civilian staff in a manner that surprised them, making his own coffee, and offering to make theirs, which was quite unheard of. However, what they did not know was that

Dave had informed his wife earlier in the day that today would be the day when he would be tendering his resignation, putting in his ticket, taking his pension. She had been so overjoyed that she kissed Dave on the cheek which was not something she usually did. A morning of firsts - the first day of the rest of Dave's life, and he wanted to enjoy every moment of it.

"As soon as Nick comes in, would you ask him to come and see me please?"

"Yes, sir," the three ladies replied in unison, and they all laughed.

After a short while there came a knock on the door, followed by Preston entering the office.

"Guv?" he enquired.

"Good morning Nick, come and sit down. Have you had a coffee? Would you like me to make you one?"

Preston thought that Matthews might have come into money - won the lottery or something, or perhaps the events of the previous day had sent him a bit scatty.

"No, no, I'm OK thanks, Guv," replied Preston, as he took his seat opposite Matthews.

"Any thoughts on yesterday, Nick?"

Matthews knew that Preston would be scornful of his interview with Elphick, but he would not say so, not to Matthews anyway, but in all probability to his inspector peers within the unit.

Preston thought for just a moment and then replied, "No, not really, just another bent, perverted copper taken out of the job for the time being until such time as he can be banged up".

Matthews sat back in his seat savouring his coffee.

"I don't know, Nick. He certainly didn't come across to me as that, I must say. He didn't have the look of a bent, perverted copper, for sure."

Preston didn't immediately reply and thought what a naïve comment that was – a naïve comment from an officer with many years' service but little experience.

Preston gave a little grunt and said cynically, "What does a perverted, bent copper look like?"

"Yes, I suppose so, Nick. Any other thoughts about yesterday?"

"No, I need to get the court file made up fully now for the CPS for Thursday. You'll want me to go over to Maidenhead for the hearing?"

"Yes, I think so, Nick. Well, don't let me delay you; you crack on…Oh, there is one other thing I would like to share with you. I did hint at it the other day, but now the Elphick case is all but finished I've decided to retire. I haven't told anyone else yet but will be submitting my intention to resign in writing this morning."

Preston was taken aback that Matthews would share such news with him first. His mind started plotting immediately. He knew that he owed Matthews no real favours and thus did not owe him any loyalty.

Preston knew how his own mind worked; supervisors, colleagues, teams, units – all just ships that pass in the night. He knew that it was a matter of self-preservation now and he needed to fulfil his desire to remain in the department. He needed to ingratiate himself with the head of the department, the Chief Superintendent. He needed to showboat a little, put himself about in a good light and he would start by suggesting to the Chief Superintendent, himself an ex CID man, that officers with a majority of uniform service did not make good Professional Standards Men, and would start by revealing how awful Matthews' interview with Elphick was the previous day.

"Sorry to hear that, sir, I've always thought we were a good team. I'm honoured that you would share this news with me first, and of course I wish you every happiness on your retirement, but we have a few weeks left to work together I'm sure."

"Thanks, Nick."

"You get on with your report, Guv, and don't forget you need to speak to Social Services, Children and families this morning."

"Ah yes, thank you Nick."

Preston moved out of Matthews office thinking, 'The prat would have forgotten; I'm running this team on my own'.

On exiting the office Preston went to a telephone in the corner of the main office and dialled a number. Preston then said in hushed tones so as not to be overheard, "Detective Inspector Preston here, sir. Sorry to trouble you but I wonder if I could come and have a word with you, in strict confidence, at you earliest convenience?" He then said, "Two thirty today, thank you sir."

Eugene didn't know how long he had been sitting there but he became aware that he was still in the clothes that he had been wearing the day before. He hadn't washed, hadn't eaten, and had had nothing to drink. His head ached and he felt nauseous. He felt that his heart was broken. He went to the drinks cabinet and poured half a tumbler full of Indian tonic water thinking it might help his headache. He picked up a bottle of gin and was about to top up his drink but knew that this would be disastrous, especially in his current state of mind. He gathered up all the bottles in the drinks cabinet.

Gin, whiskey, brandy and took them to the kitchen where he poured the contents down the sink.

He then took the few bottles of wine that were in the kitchen and did likewise with them. He drank his tonic water and congratulated himself for doing the most sensible thing he had done for a while. He wondered what else he could do to help himself, help his situation.

He dialled a number and a voice answered, "Windsor and Maidenhead CMHT, how may I help?"

"Um...I wonder if I could speak to Dr Bekhit please."

"Dr Bekhit isn't here today, and we do not expect him in the office until the middle of next week. Is there anyone else who could help you?"

"No, no thank you, I'll call back next week. Could you ask him to call Eugene Elphick, I'm one of his patients, my number is...", and Eugene gave his mobile telephone number.

"I'll pass the message on, Mr Elphick," came the reply.

Eugene pondered what had been said and was aware that if Dr Bekhit were away then he would be unable to answer any correspondence that Karen Nicholls may have sent and certainly not by next Thursday, the day of his hearing at the Magistrates Court.

Eugene felt that this was something of a blow and debated with himself whether or not he should call Karen but decided against it.

He tidied up the kitchen, which was a little painful. He disposed of Katie's uneaten breakfast cereal and placed her special breakfast bowl in the dishwasher. He wondered how she was settling in at her grandparents' house and came to the conclusion that she, like many children, was resilient and would most likely adapt, at least he hoped so. He resisted the urge to call her mobile although he desperately wanted to. He was yearning to hear her voice but decided that it would be better to wait until Sandra called him to make firm arrangements.

Eugene nursed the idea that this was still all a mistake, that right would overcome wrong and that all would be well. At other times he just felt totally despondent, felt the whole world was against him and that no one could help him, not that anyone wanted to. At such times he could see no way out.

Eugene was not in any sense a religious man, but he found himself making deals with God in his head: such things as 'if I come thorough this I will go to church,' 'if this issue passes me by I'll make an effort to be more charitable to people' He made many such deals in silent conversations with an entity who for a major part of his life remained unknown, not thought about, not contemplated, irrelevant and of no consequence.

Yet, lately these silent conversations, appeals and negotiations had become part of his daily ritual. Perhaps, he thought this was part of something he should further explore no matter what happened, although this thought, of course, could be another deal in the making.

Eugene's mobile phone rang making him jump and shaking him out of his deep ponderings on more divine matters. It was Eugene's mother who gently admonished him for not making regular telephone contact.

She asked after Sandra and Katie and Eugene said that they had gone to stay with Sandra's parents for a few days. She asked about the holiday to Carbis Bay which they had spoken about in their last telephone conversation and Eugene said that it was still being sorted out and that he would provide her with dates as soon as he could. She asked him if he was OK, saying that he sounded tired, but he assured her he was, and just a little busy. She said she understood that he must be busy and asked that it not be too long before he called her again. He said that he would and breathed a sigh of relief as the conversation ended.

He disliked either blatantly lying to his mother or telling her only part of the story, but he did so to shield her from hurt and despair. If she knew the truth of what was going on, he feared it could have devastating consequences.

Almost as soon as he had finished his call the mobile rang again. It was Benji and Eugene suddenly remembered there had been a missed call from Benji the previous day.

"Hi, Benji, I'm sorry, I had been meaning to call as I'd a missed call from you yesterday."

"Hi, Gene," Benji's voice sounded rather morose. "How you doing?" he asked.

Eugene paused, then said quietly, "Not so good, mate."

"Yes, I've heard. Um, I'm sorry to say Gene, the news is out. You know how fast the jungle drums beat in the job at such news."

"What's being said?" asked Eugene with a sheepish tone.

"That you've been charged with offences of downloading child porn, have been suspended and are on bail to court." Benji said this in a typical matter of fact way.

Eugene and then said, "That much is true, Benji, but I didn't do what they are accusing me of.".

"The word is that they found images on your hard drive, Gene." Again it was said in a manner that appeared to be devoid of emotion or feeling,

"That's true, too, but I didn't download them."

Benji was silent on the other end of the phone.

Eugene said, "You don't believe me, do you?"

"I want to believe you, Gene," said Benji, in a more conciliatory tone.

"Nobody does! Sandra's left me and has taken Katie with her, I'm living a nightmare Benji an absolute nightmare."

"What would you like me to do, Gene?" asked Benji, knowing that he could do very little.

"Could you come and see me and let me explain to you, Benji."

"I don't know, Gene, it's a bit difficult, you know, you being suspended and all."

Eugene gave a little insincere laugh and said, "That's not like you, Benji, constrained by petty bureaucracy. Help me out, just listen to my story, will you?"

"OK, Gene." Benji hesitated and then said with some determination, "I'll come and see you. This evening is the start of Shabbat and I'm finishing early to go and spend it with my sister and her family. I don't get the chance to do it very often and I've promised her I'll be there. I could come and see you tomorrow, early evening, if you want, say about seven thirty ?"

"OK, thank you. You'll come here, yeah?"

"Yeah, I'll be there about seven thirty."

"Thanks, Benji," said Eugene and the line went dead.

Eugene could tell that Benji wasn't keen on coming to see him and in all probability considered Eugene guilty but out of long term friendship and loyalty would come. Eugene just hoped that he could convince Benji that he wasn't guilty of an act that was so alien to him and others, especially police officers.

Eugene found the telephone conversation with Benji difficult. He could feel some hostility but was sure that Benji hadn't meant to be hostile. The very nature of what Eugene had been charged with would have, in different circumstances, made him act in a similar way. If the shoe had been on the other foot and it had been Benji who had been charged, he wondered if he would have made the effort to call Benji, or would he have just written him off. In all honesty he just did not know. Eugene tried to occupy himself through the day. He found watching TV and reading difficult, his concentration was poor, and he found his mind wandering back to the unpalatable events of the past twenty four hours or so. He yearned to speak to his daughter and held his phone in his hand on numerous occasions debating with himself as to whether he should call or not. On each occasion he decided not to, based on the manner in which he believed Sandra would react. He wondered if he should send a text and again balked at the idea for the same reasons.

Eugene had attempted to find things to distract him, which he knew was a form of escapism. Music, although something that had not previously been that important to him, took on a much more meaningful role. There are always songs, songs that may mean something for someone at significant times. Such songs stayed in the mind giving rise to episodic memory which could transport the listener back to another time and another place. There are songs for happy times, songs for lovers, songs for cleaning the house and songs that are meaningless. But now Eugene wanted to hear the words of songs that reflected his mood, the words of songs and singers who seemed to understand and equate with the depth of his despair. In listening to such songs Eugene felt less alone, less despairing, and more balanced.

The genres of Billie Holiday, Leonard Cohen, Joan Baez and surprisingly, Amy Winehouse, attracted him and gradually became part of him. Eugene could lose himself in their melodious melancholia which seemed not only to compliment, but accept his low mood. When listening, time passed in a manner where Eugene wasn't constrained by thinking about himself and his situation and was indeed a form of therapeutic escape. The vinyl records, CDs and tapes were Sandra's, collected over many years, some even before they were married. Listening to the music he thought it brought her closer to him and although Sandra and Katie had only been gone a few hours, it seemed longer almost permanent, and he missed them so.

A day that was lost in nostalgic despair, Eugene settled down for the evening just hoping that the phone would ring and that it would be Katie or Sandra. A while later the phone did ring, and Eugene gave a sigh of relief – here they were at last. He looked at his phone and it read 'Restricted number'. It must be the police station thought Eugene or maybe Karen Nicholls, but it was a little late for her. He answered, there was a pause at the other end and then one word uttered in a kind of long drawn out forced whisper,

"Pervert."

"Who is this?" demanded Eugene but the line went dead.

Eugene was shocked, he was convinced that the call had come from a telephone in a police station somewhere. It obviously came from someone close enough to him to know his mobile number and that made Eugene feel very uneasy.

The fact that it could have even been a member of his own team made him feel worse. Eugene know that this was only the start of the hostility that would be directed at him. He was fully aware how unforgiving the job was of those who were seen to betray it and what he had been charged with, irrespective of whether he actually had done it, would be seen as the ultimate betrayal. No other calls came, and Eugene went to his bed, and tonight he chose to sleep in the matrimonial bed. He felt a complete absence of hope and as with most nights everything felt wrong and exaggerated and as if nothing would turn out well. Eugene could feel himself sinking lower and lower into a bottomless pit, a sea of despair and the fact that he was sleeping in Sandra's bed with her smells and her things around him just made everything worse. He reluctantly retreated to the room which had become his for a while now.

Sleep these days was a rarity; it occurred but only superficially and intermittently. He remained in a state of almost semi alertness although did not think he was currently sleepwalking. Indeed he had not thought about the issues that allegedly gave rise to his PTSD since seeing Dr Bekhit and his head was full of more current concerns – concerns that haunted him nightly, concerns, thoughts whatever they were, became torturous to him. Tonight was no different. He thought about the events of this morning and could see his daughter's tear strewn face in the rear window of her mother's car and her mouthing, "I love you Daddy."

He thought about Sandra saying, "I'm not sufficiently interested in you"; the disturbing anonymous voice whispering, "Pervert"; Benji saying "I want to believe you". Brief flashes, images, words all jumbled up with the pervading thought that there was no possible way out of this, that jangled through Eugene's brain preventing that therapeutic sleep, a sleep devoid of anxiety and fear that he desired so much. He wanted so much to take one of Dr Bekhit's tablets but resisted the urge to do so.

The morning came; it was still early. He looked at his watch - 4:40am. He knew that he probably wouldn't get back to sleep again and although he in no way felt refreshed he got up and set about his daily routine. During the morning Eugene looked out upon his garden; it had been neglected, the grass was long and the whole garden needed a tidy up, but he was just not motivated to do it. He wanted to and although not a keen or knowledgeable gardener, usually liked it to be kept neat. If felt that the untidy garden was in some way a microcosm of his untidy and confused mind right now. Perhaps he could motivate himself sometime, but he was unable to do that today. Having looked into his fridge, however, Eugene realised that like it or not he would need to go to the shop for basics: eggs, milk, bread. He thought he would walk to the village shop, which was in itself a mini supermarket, that stocked most things and was within half a mile from the house. He hadn't been there for some time and certainly hadn't walked there for a long while.

Eugene set off and as he walked along the cul de sac where he lived he saw some of his neighbours working in their front gardens. It was a beautiful day and a fine morning for gardening. As he passed each of them acknowledge his presence, a "good morning" through to "Ah, Mr Elphick, I haven't seen you for ages, keeping well?" - brief friendly conversations which were quite unexpected, but which gave a boost to Eugene's state of mind and put a spring in his step. Florrie, the lady that ran the mini supermarket, greeted Eugene like an old friend returning from a long absence. She asked after his health, enquired after Sandra and Katie, and spoke about life in the village generally.

As Eugene walked back to his home he felt that something had been accomplished; he felt better, better than he had in a number of days. He vowed to do this more often.

CHAPTER 12

Eugene looked at the clock in the living room. It was one of those mock Victorian square box shaped clocks with a large white dial. It ticked too loudly and needed frequent winding. Eugene disliked that clock but as it was an anniversary present from Sandra's parents it was destined to take pride of place. In fact, the very presence of the clock had caused light-hearted arguments between Eugene and Sandra, and Eugene smiled at the thought of those more carefree times.

Eugene was never sure if Sandra liked the wretched clock any more than he did - probably not. The clock nosily ticked away the seconds and Eugene could see that it was approaching seven thirty when Benji had said he would arrive. Benji was, at least for a hardened detective, unusually punctual and Eugene had no doubt he would arrive shortly. He went to put the kettle on and before it had a chance to boil there was a loud knock to the front door. As he went to answer Eugene was overcome with an inexplicable sense of nervousness.

On opening the door he saw that Benji was not his normal cheerful self but looked as he had sounded on the telephone the day before, morose, even despondent. He entered without saying anything and followed Eugene into the living room.

"Would you like a tea or coffee?" asked Eugene over his shoulder as he started for the kitchen.

"No, you're OK," replied Benji.

Eugene went to turn the kettle off and they then both sat. There was a short period of silence with neither knowing quite what to say to the other.

Eugene started by saying, "Thanks for coming, Benji. It's much appreciated." Benji didn't reply but seemed to be thinking about what exactly to say.

He coughed and said, "I know what's being said Gene, but I would like to hear about this from your perspective."

"What is being said?" asked Eugene apprehensively.

"It's like I said yesterday," commenced Benji, again employing that matter of fact voice and perching on the edge of the sofa, "one, that you've been charged with offences relating to downloading indecent images of children; two, that the images covered all categories and that such were found on the hard drive of your computer; and three, that you've been bailed and will be attending Court next week; that's about it."

"Yeah, well, all that's true but as I told you yesterday, I did not do it". Eugene emphasised the word not.

Benji was silent for a short time. He then looked straight into Eugene's eyes and said quite slowly, "If that's the case, Gene, how did they get there?"

"I don't know, Benji." Eugene was beginning to sound defensive, knowing that he would rather not talk about this but accepting that he must, and seeking to justify in some way the complexity of the situation.

"I've seen a psychiatrist and he's diagnosed me with PTSD. It would also appear that I've been sleepwalking. I don't know…I've been thinking…, perhaps…perhaps I could've done something whilst in that state. Sandra did find me downstairs, like, in a trance at least once."

Benji was again silent and then asked, "PTSD from what?"

"Oh, it was a railway suicide I attended when I was a PC. It was a long time ago but apparently it's still affecting me."

Benji was silent, looking at Eugene who could see that this man, his friend, was evaluating everything he was being told, like the detective he was.

"So, how does that lead to sleep walking, I suppose, years after?"

"You sound as if you're interrogating me Benji."

"I'm not interrogating you, Gene; I'm trying to find something which would give me a base to fully believe you. I want to believe you, Gene. I want to believe you and support you." To Eugene this sounded as if it was said with sincerity.

"Thanks. To answer your question, I don't know. I'm hoping the psychiatrist will know."

"When are you seeing him again?" asked Benji.

"I have an appointment for the week after next. I've tried to see him before, but he's away until the middle of next week. I've asked that he call me but, sadly, I won't be able to talk to him before my court hearing".

"When's that?" enquired Benji.

"Next Thursday."

Benji was obviously thinking, drawing little circles with his finger on the arm of the chair in which he was sitting.

He said slowly, "You are on bail?"

"Yes, unconditional."

"Well nothing will happen on Thursday. This'll go up the steps to the crown court and it won't be at Reading for obvious reasons; they'll arrange for it to be heard at Guildford, may even be Salisbury."

"I thought that might be the case," said Eugene.

"There is just one thing, though, and that'll be that the press will be there on Thursday so be prepared for that. They probably know already, some bastard in the job would have leaked it by now."

Eugene did not reply but the very thought of this being all over the local press was especially daunting.

"Who's your brief again?" asked Benji.

"Oh, it's Karen Nicholls, Gillespie and Clapton."

"She's good," said Benji nodding in a knowing sort of way.

"Who did the interview?" asked Benji.

"A Professional Standards Superintendent by the name of Matthews, he's been assisted throughout by an obnoxious DI called Preston. Matthews' interview was pretty poor. I think he might've been phased by the fact that we'd elected to go 'no comment,' plus the assertive stance of Karen Nicholls".

"It's probably best to say nothing until we get the full spec from the psychiatrist," said Benji.

Eugene noticed that Benji had said 'we' and that engendered a little confidence with him feeling that Benji was on his side, and he no longer felt that he was being interrogated.

"Have you contacted your Police Federation rep?" asked Benji

"No, I've not as yet," replied Eugene.

"I've never seen them as being that helpful," said Benji and continued, "I've always found them a bit right-wing to be honest, more inclined to support the organisation as opposed to the individual. They could be extremely powerful in the political sense but rarely have been. There've been one or two individuals in the past who tried to change things, but they disappeared into obscurity in a very short time. They've never affiliated to the TUC which they should. They seem such a secretive bunch, lacking in transparency. Something like the Freemasons, that's how I've seen them, anyway. They never really did much for me."

Eugene didn't reply he had had no dealings with the Federation up until now, so he didn't really know how to respond.

"Do you pay your subs?" asked Eugene in order to break a prolonged period of silence,

"Oh yeah, I do, as most of us do. Oh, and we do get a poxy pocket diary each year, I had forgotten that." Benji gave a cynical laugh.

There was again a period of silence and then Benji asked, looking directly at Eugene, "What about Sandra leaving you?"

"Yeah, well, I had to tell her what'd happened, what I'd been charged with. She couldn't deal with it and left taking Katie with her." This was said with no emotion and Eugene was anxious not to get emotional in Benji's presence.

Benji again thought about what had been said and replied, "Well, put yourself in her shoes…."

"Yes, I have, and I know," said Eugene a little irritated with what Benji was alluding to. "I feel so betrayed, betrayed by her, betrayed by the job, betrayed by people. Someone called here last evening and just said one word in a sort of whisper. Said 'pervert'. The number wasn't' shown, it just said 'restricted' and I've no doubt that it came either from our station or another. It was, I believe, a police officer."

Benji was again looking preoccupied, he was fiddling with the lapel of his jacket, there was a pause and he said thoughtfully, "Yeah, betrayal" he paused again, "I think that you may experience more of that...probably was an officer."

"Do you know how that feels?" asked Eugene.

Benji echoed the question, he paused again and gave a little smile seemingly more for his own benefit and relating to his own thoughts,

"Do I know how that feels? Yes, yes, Gene, I do. I'm Jewish - my people have been betrayed for thousands of years."

"But that's historical," said Eugene.

"Is it? How many Jewish officers do you know?" asked Benji.

"Only you, I think."

"Yes, only me! There were a few in the Met, and a few who successfully hide the fact that they're Jewish. You see the job itself is anti-Semitic just as the country is, just as the whole of Europe is come to that. And, joining the job didn't win me much approval with a large number of the people I knew, Jewish people."

But that's not being betrayed is it?" said Eugene.

"Yes, it is because betrayal is experiencing disloyalty, treachery, deceit, and downright racism. Not once, not even occasionally but being aware of it constantly. That's the betrayal that I have experienced within the job, let alone outside of it. You see, trust is the currency of democracy. The job is supposed to be, and should be, an example of democracy at work. But because there's mistrust pervading throughout and within, it never can be. The job therefor fails it's very reason for existing. It's the raison d'etre."

"I hope that I've never made you feel any, if that," Eugene said in an almost pleading apologetic way.

"No, you've not, and that is why I'm here now." He gave a heavy sigh and sat back in his seat. "You see, Gene, society, and the job with all its platitudes and its attempts at being politically correct is a fallacy, a falsehood, because racism, anti-Semitism, homophobia or whatever, never goes away, it gets buried and then resurfaces when it's safe to do so, that applies to both society and the job."

Eugene thought about what Benji had said, being previously unaware of the strength of Benji's feelings.

"Benji, What do you think about my current situation?" asked Eugene. Benji looked at him and again sat forward on the edge of his seat.

"Gene, believe me when I say I want to believe that you are innocent of this thing, but it's not looking good. You now have to rely on that psychiatrist, and I don't know what he may come up with. But to me, a hard assed copper, only dealing with facts and evidence, what you've told me is not even plausible and you're not in a good place right now."

"You don't believe me then," said Eugene with disappointment obvious in his voice.

"I find it difficult, but you're my friend and I choose to believe what you've said because I want to believe you. As I said, it depends on the psychiatrist now. But don't expect any favours from any quarter. I will support you as a friend and we'll talk again after next Thursday. I would like to support you at Court, but I think that would be futile and would probably cause me difficulties. Karen Nicholls will serve you well."

With that Benji stood up and made his way to the door. Eugene followed, opened it for him and said, "Thanks for coming, and thanks for being a good and honest friend."

Benji didn't reply and exited the house, realising that the meeting with Eugene had been something of a cathartic release for him.

Eugene looked at the living room clock and found that he and Benji had talked for just over an hour. He didn't know how he felt about the meeting. Benji had certainly been honest but perhaps he would have wanted him to have given him greater hope about the future. Benji obviously had his own agenda, too, and Eugene had never heard him speak in the way that he had before. Eugene could feel those now common feelings of worthlessness and guilt, creeping up on him, even though he knew he wasn't guilty. Sandra hadn't called and if she was going to she should have by now. He thought about making a call but again dismissed the thought not knowing how Sandra would react.

*

Eugene negotiated the flimsy wire fence and walked toward what he thought was a bundle of rags, he soon saw it was a woman lying on the ground, a woman with a brown coat over her head or where her head should be. Eugene slowly reached for the coat and as he did so, he awoke violently with his whole body seeming to leap off the bed. For a moment he didn't know where he was; he was sweating, he was frightened, he could feel his heart pounding in his chest getting tighter, his breathing more difficult. He felt a lump in his throat as if it were obstructed, and he couldn't breathe. He reached and turned on his bedside lamp, swung his legs out of bed and sat up. His whole body was shaking and then as quickly as it had occurred the feeling started to ease. He could feel his heart slowing down, his breathing was becoming easier, and he could breathe again.

He took slow deep breaths savouring the smooth passage of air in and out of his body. He felt much calmer. He looked at his watch and saw it was 3:50. He sat there trying to remember coming to bed but couldn't. Things slowly started to order themselves in his mind, the discussion with Benji, the fact that Sandra hadn't rung, the dream. What was it about that dream, he asked himself? Was the dream the precursor to him sleep walking? Had he been sleep walking? He didn't know, how could he?

He sat there on his bed, and tried to order things. He tried to analyse what was going on, was the PTSD giving rise to the dream? Maybe, because he had mentioned the PTSD to Benji and that may have triggered something. When he dreamed like that did he sleepwalk? Perhaps it was a toss-up, he either walked in his sleep or woke up in a state of panic. Perhaps he could have done things whilst sleep walking? He didn't know. Was he a victim of, what was the medical term for sleepwalking? – Somnambulism, that's it, he had looked it up. Was he a victim of somnambulism induced by PTSD? It sounded plausible, or did it?

Eugene lay back down staring at the ceiling thinking so much. Selfish, self-pitying thoughts at first wondering why all this had happened to him and then a more pragmatic examining of the facts, the evidence, like a police officer, like Benji had said. He recollected Benji's hard but honest analysis and the words "What you've told me isn't even plausible," came back to him. Perhaps what he was thinking was not in the least plausible. But Eugene felt that he must hang on to something; if he didn't, then there would literally be no hope. Eugene was aware that the middle of the night was not the time for logical examination. It was a time when those negative and catastrophic thoughts had their way.

He remembered that his mother had a name for such nocturnal dissenting ruminations. She used to call them the 'Night Najjars' and even wrote a poem about them when he was little. He couldn't remember all of it now, but remembered some of the last few lines: '*As the sun shines through the night Najjars abate, like vampires they creep away....*" He couldn't remember the rest but that seemed so absolutely true. He distracted his negative thinking into more positive things and reflected on his childhood in Shaftesbury and upon the love that had clearly been given him which unaware of at the time, he was immensely grateful for now.

There was a ringing and Eugene awoke with a start, it was his mobile phone. Who could be calling at this hour he thought, but upon picking up the phone he saw that it had gone nine. The Night Najjars had indeed abated and had allowed him some gloriously refreshing sleep. He felt buoyant as he answered his phone.

"Hi Gene." it was Sandra. "I hope I'm not disturbing you."

"No, no, not at all I've been waiting for your call," Eugene attempted to put on a cheery tone.

Sandra paused and then said, "I've told my parents all about what's occurred. They, as you would expect, are not happy and my father has asked me to reiterate that you're not to visit or telephone here. I'll telephone you - are you clear on that?"

Eugene noticed that Sandra had now adopted her most brusque and impersonal conversational style, honed over her time as a doctor's receptionist.

"How's Katie?" asked Eugene.

"She's fine, she's settling in here. I'll be taking her back to school tomorrow and that is another thing I don't want you going to the school to see Katie, collect her or anything else."

Eugene said, "May I speak to her?" as pleasantly as he could; he was anxious not to antagonise Sandra in any way.

Sandra replied, "Yes, but keep it short, I don't want her getting upset again." The line went silent for a short time and then Katie came on.

"Hi Dad, are you OK?"

"Hi Katie, yes I'm fine. How are you getting on there?" Eugene was relieved to hear his daughters voice.

"Oh, OK. I was helping Gramps in the garden yesterday and I've been helping Nanny sort out some old photos."

"You've been busy then."

Katie laughed and said, "Sort of." She continued excitedly, "I'm back at school tomorrow and I can't wait".

"That's good," said Eugene, pleased to hear his daughter sounding so ebullient,

"Oh, Mum wants a word."

Sandra then said, "Ok Gene, that's enough for now".

Eugene could hear Katie's protests in the background,

"But we hadn't finished talking…"

"She's right, we hadn't finished."

Sandra said, "I'll call you again in a little while".

Eugene remembered and said, "Just before you go, I should've said this the other evening, but Social Services will be getting in contact with you".

Sandra paused and then with obvious irritation in her voice, "What the… what have you told them?"

"No, I haven't told them anything," he paused, and then said quickly, "It's because of the nature of the charge, they have to be informed."

"That's simply great, that's fucking great. I can't talk to you anymore right now," and although Eugene could hear Katie continuing her protests the line went dead.

Eugene lay back in bed just wishing that all this would just go away.

*

Sandra didn't call back and that last phone call had done little to help Eugene's mood, very much to the contrary. It was the day before his Magistrates Court hearing, and he had heard from no one further. He realised that his mood had dropped considerably. He felt low in spirit most of the time every day and had little interest or motivation. He was currently trying to motivate himself to sort the clothes he was going to wear to Court, but everything took so much effort.

He spent long periods just sitting staring into space, listening to melancholy music, or laying on his bed trying to sleep. He wasn't eating much; the fridge stank because food inside had gone mouldy.

The place was getting increasingly untidy, but he just could not seem to keep it tidy. He was aware that he wasn't attending to his personal hygiene as well as he should and believed that he must stink. He wasn't eating and if he did eat it was comfort food: crisps, biscuits, chocolate things that he knew were not doing him very much good, and despite the high sugar content of those foods he was aware that he was losing weight. He did not feel particularly well and that was on top of him feeling desperately sorry for himself.

He became aware that someone had driven into the driveway and parked in front of his car. He saw two women alight from the vehicle and make their way toward the house. Eugene moved toward the front door upon which there was a light knock. There were two women, one about 45 years of age and of large build, wearing a brown dress with big yellow flowers on it, and she clutched a brown document case to her chest. Eugene noticed her large dangly earrings which seemed to be customary amongst social workers, which Eugene sensed they were. The second woman was much younger, in her early twenties perhaps, slightly built wearing a white top with a navy blue skirt. She was at least smiling, the older one certainly was not.

The older woman spoke, "Mr Eugene Elphick?" she asked. Eugene replied in the affirmative and she continued, "We're from the Windsor and Maidenhead Children and Families department within Social Services. May we come in?"

Eugene stood to one side and gestured with his hand to invite them in.

"You'll have to excuse the place; I haven't got around..."

"That's quite alright, Mr Elphick, we won't take much of your time," interjected the older social worker whilst looking around the living room in which they stood. Eugene invited both to sit, the younger social worker sat in one of the armchairs, the older one took the settee and made a big issue of moving some articles of clothing to one side. Eugene took the remaining armchair.

"I am Miss Waldock, and this is Miss Jane Morrissey, as I have said we are from Children and Families. May I ask where your wife is?"

Eugene said, "She will be at work by now."

"Where does she work?" The social worker was looking intently at Eugene.

"She works at the local GP surgery."

"We have been informed by Thames Valley Police Professional Standards that you have been charged with a number of offences which relate to downloading indecent images and a video of children, – is that correct?"

Eugene nodded and noticed that Miss Morrissey had ceased smiling and was looking down at the floor.

Eugene couldn't help but think that Miss Waldock looked and sounded like he would have imagined Agatha Trunchbull, the tyrannical headmistress in Roald Dahl's 'Matilda' would have looked and sounded when he read it to Katie a few years ago.

She continued, "We, having been given such a report, are required to investigate matters from our perspective, or more correctly from the perspective of child protection. So, this is very much a visit and inquiry in relation to safeguarding. I understand that you have a daughter."

Eugene again nodded and the tone of Miss Waldock was beginning to irritate him; she was seemingly talking down to him or at least that is how it felt.

"How old is she?" enquired Miss Waldock.

"She's fourteen," replied Eugene.

"Have you any other children?"

Eugene shook his head.

"Where is she now?" enquired Miss Waldock, rapidly asking the questions,

"I would imagine in school."

Miss Waldock gave him a quizzical look and delved into her document case. She pulled from it a form which she handed to Miss Morrissey along with the case saying, "Complete this please as we go along."

Miss Morrissey took the form and case which she used to rest the form on and seemed relieved to be doing something rather than just staring at the floor.

Miss Waldock continued, "What school does your daughter attend?" Eugene told her and she said, "That's a private school," in which there was a hint of surprise in her intonation. "You're a policeman, is that correct?"

"You would have been told that in the report from Professional Standards."

Miss Waldock looked at Eugene her eyes just a little wider than before and said in a deliberate manner, "I was only checking."

Eugene was beginning to really feel irritated by this woman; he didn't know why. He had worked with many social workers in his time, but this woman really irritated him. He didn't know if it was the way she looked, sounded, or acted but there was something about her he really disliked.

Miss Waldock continued to ask fairly superficial questions in rapid succession about Katie such as her date of birth, likes, dislikes and so on.

She then asked, "Do Katie's friends come here, say for tea or to stay over?"

Eugene thought for a moment and said, "I can't remember any staying over. I think some have come for tea, but not recently. This sort of question would be best answered by my wife."

Miss Waldock continued, "Do any children ever stay here, such as nephews or nieces, that sort of thing."

"No."

Miss Waldock paused and then more or less as an afterthought looked at Miss Morrissey and said, "Is there anything you would like to ask?"

Eugene thought that Miss Morrissey must be a trainee and she was certainly somewhat subservient to the domineering Waldock.

Miss Morrissey gave a little cough and said, "Mr Elphick, could you please tell me if Katie knows anything about your current situation?"

Miss Waldock expressed a small sigh as if the question were irrelevant whereas Eugene thought it most certainly was not. He thought he would give Miss Morrissey a positive stroke if only to annoy Miss Waldock.

"That's a very relevant question Miss…" he paused, and she quickly said, "Morrissey." "Yes, Miss Morrissey. "Yes, very relevant. At this moment in time she doesn't know anything."

"Thank you," said Miss Morrissey in a quiet, almost child-like voice. She reminded Eugene of a little mouse.

"We will be needing to speak with your wife and your daughter," commanded Miss Waldock. "When will they be home?"

Eugene said, "They're not living here at the moment. They are, since recent events, living with my in-laws. I'm not expecting them to be living back here in the immediate future."

Miss Waldock seemed to become quite annoyed, her face reddened noticeably and she took on more of an Agatha Trunchbull type persona.

"You could've told us that much earlier; it would have saved us a lot of time."

"You didn't ask," said Eugene relishing the slight feeling of pleasure he had at Miss Waldock's annoyance.

She said, "What's the address where they're staying?" Eugene gave it.

Miss Waldock stood up and Miss Morrissey clumsily stood as well, dropping the document case and form she had been filling out onto the floor.

"So sorry," she said, retrieving what had been dropped whilst Miss Waldock glared at her.

"We will be speaking to your wife, daughter, and your daughter's school," said Miss Waldock as she moved toward the front door. Eugene opened the door and Miss Waldock walked out. Miss Morrissey followed, awkwardly clutching the document case and said a quiet, "Thank you," as she left. Eugene shut the door and leaned his back against it. He remained annoyed with Miss Waldock but pleased that he had annoyed her, too. However, he knew that Miss Waldock was about to initiate a set of circumstances that were going to cause immense difficulties not only for him, but for his entire family.

CHAPTER 13

Eugene had not slept particularly well; he was anticipating what would occur at the court and kept going over the interaction with the two social workers. In his state of shallow sleep everything seemed exaggerated. He had expected a telephone call from Sandra, a fraught angry call as a result of a visit or phone call from Miss Waldock, but no call had come. He had considered calling Sandra to warn her of a visit by Waldock but seeing he had already told her that Social Services had been informed he thought that this would just cause additional problems.

He managed to have a shower and had donned his sombre coloured business suit, the one he had worn so many times to court but in entirely different circumstances. Today he would very much be the defendant and not a prosecuting agent. Today, he would not stand in the witness box giving testimony in his normal professional manner; today he would stand in the dock with all eyes upon him, accused of the most heinous of offences, where others would judge him even before the first words of evidence would be given.

There had always been a feeling of nervousness about attending court but today was different and he could feel his level of anxiety increasing. He calmed himself by breathing deeply and consoling himself that today would only be a preliminary hearing where a committal to the Crown Court would occur. He wouldn't be expected to say anything, and Karen Nicholls would be there.

There was plenty of time and he did not want to arrive too early. Looking around the kitchen. There was a pile of dirty dishes, the floor was dirty as were the worktops, the cooker hob was stained with particles of food deposited on it. He realised that he was not coping, and his home was a mess. As Eugene was convincing himself that he would get matters sorted the landline telephone rang.

Eugene hoped that it wasn't Sandra as he didn't think he could deal with any form of argument this morning. He tentatively answered and a female voice said, "Good morning, Mr Elphick, my name is Lorna Symonds from the Berkshire Enquirer newspaper, can you speak for moment?"

He was shaken and did not immediately know what to say.

Lorna Symonds continued, "I understand that you will be in Court this morning..."

Eugene interrupted, fumbling over his words said, "No, no…um…no, I don't want to speak to the press. Where did you get this number from?"

"I understand, Mr Elphick, but if you change your mind, I will treat your story sensitively. Perhaps you would consider giving us an exclusive."

"Where did you get this number?" asked Eugene again, more forcefully.

"Like the police, we have our sources, Mr Elphick."

Eugene didn't say anything, and replacing the receiver he thought, 'Your sources are the police.'

Eugene parked his car in the shopping centre at Maidenhead, less than a ten minutes' walk from the court but he was early so decided to walk around for a while. He eventually came to the court some five minutes before the bail time of 10 am. He knew that he would not be dealt with at that time because experience dictated that any overnight prisoners would be dealt with first, but that, because he had a solicitor, he might get dealt with within the hour.

Maidenhead Magistrates Court was situated upstairs in a building adjacent to the police station. As Eugene entered the foyer on the ground floor he noticed a few people milling around and a man sat behind a makeshift desk. He spoke to Eugene.

"Your name please?" asked the man.

"Eugene Elphick."

The man ran his finger along a list of names and said, "Have you any ID?"

Eugene produced his driving licence which satisfied the man who then said, "Upstairs, Court One."

Eugene moved to the stairway and as he started to ascend a young woman about 26 years of age, with jet black hair and a heavily made up white face, wearing dark eyeliner and dark lipstick, making her look like someone following the Gothic fashion but in a sophisticated way. She was smartly dressed in a dark blue trouser suit.

She approached him and said, "Mr Elphick, I'm Lorna Symonds, we spoke on the telephone this morning. I wonder if we could have a chat?"

"I've nothing to say to you," said Eugene in an annoyed tone. Lorna Symonds followed him still talking but Eugene wasn't listening.

As he got to the top of the stairs Eugene saw a throng of people. Some were sitting on plain brown benches against the wall, others gathered together in small groups. There were some dressed in smart suits looking nervous, probably in Court for the first time in their lives, no doubt to answer some motoring charge or other.

There was a heavily tattooed young woman speaking loudly to a pale faced and nervous young man who was obviously a social worker or probation officer, saying and repeating, "I want it fucking dealt with today."

There was a nonchalant adolescent leaning against a wall with his anxious mother sitting on the bench beside him picking at her badly bitten nails. There were a group of young men dressed in tee shirts and track suit bottoms talking loudly in an effort to make everyone aware that they had done it all before.

Eugene saw a harassed looking usher wearing a black robe which was torn at the shoulder, moving through the assembled people with his clip board. Lorna Symonds had finished talking and had moved toward some men who were dressed in tired looking suits who Eugene thought must be other members of the press. He felt relieved that none of those assembled were known to him but at the same time nervous within in this environment.

He saw Karen Nicholls at the far end waving to him and he moved toward her.

"Good morning, Mr Elphick," she greeted him as she ushered him into a room where a notice on the door indicated 'Solicitor'.

They moved into an austere room painted beige, with a table and three chairs.

"How are you?" asked Karen.

"A bit nervous really," said Eugene.

"Of course," said Karen and continued, "I've been in contact with the police, that Inspector Preston, as I was in the dark somewhat about the credit card that was used to pay for the material. Not much was said about it at interview and not much was said in the initial disclosure either. What we did know was that material was downloaded onto your computer on three occasions in the middle of the night. What we did not know, and this is what I wanted to know was – if the credit card debt had been paid off and if so when."

She paused but Eugene didn't say anything.

Karen continued, "I've been informed that the credit card debt was paid off on two occasion, on 2nd November when the transactions of 17th and 31st October were dealt with, and on 18th November when the transaction of 13th November was settled. They were paid off in cash at the counter of Lloyds Bank, Broad Street, Reading; you would be familiar with that location?"

Eugene said, "Yes, of course. But I've never been inside that bank."

"Well someone paid off the credit card debt in person, during banking hours, which blows any suggestion of sleep walking out of the water."

Eugene didn't know if Karen Nicholls was being sarcastic or factual and he chose to believe the latter, more or less because he had to.

"What about CCTV?"

"Precisely," said Karen.

She continued, "I've put that to, what's his name, Preston. I put that very thing to him. He had not requested any CCTV coverage for the days in question, but I have now asked him to do so, and he assures me he has. In my view he should have done that when he became aware of the dates and times when the credit card debt was paid at the bank counter."

Eugene didn't say anything but was thinking about what had been said.

"This doesn't weaken their case very much, if at all, but it just shows a level of incompetence in the investigation," said Karen.

Eugene could hear the usher outside calling out names – "Bishop and Stern to Court 2 please".

Karen then said, "Today will be a committal to the Crown Court no doubt, there's a Stipendiary sitting so we should be done and dusted fairly quickly. Is there anything you want to ask?"

"As this is going to the Crown Court what about briefing a barrister?"

"We have approached the chambers that we use on a regular basis, but they were unable to take your case. However, they have recommended chambers that specialise in this type of case, and we will be briefing them. I will let you know details when we have confirmation that they will be able to take the case."

Eugene didn't reply but wondered why the chambers that usually acted for clients of Gillespie and Clapton did not want to act on this occasion. He came to the conclusion that it must be the nature of the case that was off-putting for them.

A voice called out "Elphick to Court 1 please."

Gathering her briefcase and papers Karen said,"Here we go, that was quick."

She made her way through the door and into the court which was the next door along. Eugene followed and an usher directed him into the dock. Eugene stepped in and sat on the hard wooden bench. Karen sat immediately in front on him and to the right there was a male who was clearly the CPS solicitor. Behind him sat Nick Preston. Eugene was not expecting to see him but wasn't surprised that he was there. Sitting facing them and in front of the magistrates' bench was a middle aged man who Eugene knew was the magistrates clerk. There was some clattering behind him, and Eugene turned and saw that a number of people had entered the court room. Lorna

Symonds and three men took their seats at the press bench. Eugene looked around the room which was a typical 1960's court room with light oak coloured panelling and windows high up on the walls.

The clerk stood and said, "All rise,." and everyone stood. A man of about 60 years, tall and distinguished looking entered. He had grey hair and a small grey moustache. He wore spectacles and carried a sheaf of papers in his hand. He stopped at the big chair in centre of the bench, bowed, said, "Thank you," and sat down.

The clerk said, "Please remain standing Mr Elphick ." Everyone else sat down.

The clerk stood and said to Eugene, "Please give the Court your full name and address."

Eugene did so hesitating when saying where he lived, knowing that the press and others in the court now knew where he would be. The clerk sat back down. The stipendiary magistrate looked up and at Eugene.

He said in a calm voice, "Mr Elphick, the clerk will put to you the allegations with which you have been charged. You will have the opportunity to plead guilty or not guilty to each charge. If you can, please indicate your plea clearly. Carry on please."

The clerk stood holding some papers and reading from them, "Eugene Elphick, you are charged that..." And he proceeded to read each of the charges in a monotonous tone asking after each charge, "How do your plead?"

Eugene said on each occasion, "Not guilty".

After about the third charge was read out Eugene became suddenly aware of the eyes of those in the court, not least the press and Preston were boring into him. He felt unsteady and grabbed the rail in front of him with both hands and held on tightly. Eventually the last charge was arrived at, and Eugene said his final, "Not guilty."

The tedious voice was silenced, and the stipendiary magistrate again looked at Eugene.

He said very much in the pleasant manner that he had used before, "Mr Elphick, you have pleaded not guilty to all the charges. I now need to hear from the CPS so whilst I do that, please be seated."

Eugene sat and the CPS lawyer got to his feet. As Eugene looked across he could see Preston staring at him with something akin to a smirk on his face. The CPS lawyer read out a brief summary of the case which covered the most salient points. He then resumed his seat.

The stipendiary looked at Karen and said, "Is there anything you would like to say in response?"

Karen said, "No sir, thank you." The stipendiary then made a few notes, and the room had an eerie silence about it whilst he did so.

He then looked up, gave Eugene a brief smile and said, "Would you please stand up Mr Elphick?"

Eugene stood and the Magistrate said, "You have pleaded not guilty to a number of serious charges and this case will be dealt with at the Crown Court".

Karen Nicholls stood up.

The Magistrate looked at her and gave her a similar smile to that he had given Eugene and enquired, "Yes?"

Karen then said, "Sir, may the CPS lawyer and I approach the bench?"

The stipendiary replied, "Yes, of course."

The clerk stood up and to the side allowing both lawyers to stand in front of the stipendiary. All three spoke in hushed whispered tones and both lawyers then returned to their seats.

The stipendiary said to both, "Thank you," and again turned to Eugene and said, "As I was saying, this case will be dealt with at the Crown Court and taking into consideration what both your solicitor and the CPS have told me I will commit your case for trial at Guildford Crown Court on a date to be fixed. Have you anything you which to say me Mr. Elphick?"

Eugene replied, "No, thank you".

The stipendiary magistrate looked at both lawyers who didn't say anything.

"Mr Elphick you will remain on unconditional bail until such time as you appear before the Crown Court." He paused and then said, "Thank you, that will be all," and stood up.

The clerk stood and said, "All rise," everyone stood, and the stipendiary walked off to his right and out of the court.

Karen turned to Eugene and said, "Let's go and have a quick chat," and she and Eugene started to leave. Eugene was anxious to avoid looking at members of the press or Preston and made a conscious effort not to do so.

It was fortunate that the solicitor's room was vacant, and this served as a sanctuary for the moment, away from the prying eyes of press, public and Preston.

Karen started by saying, "How do you think that went?"

"Very much as I anticipated. Thank you for getting Guildford Crown Court; it would have been a little difficult if it were at Reading".

"Yes, well the CPS agreed with us on that point."

"I'm a bit concerned about the press; I feel I'll be harassed by them for a while," Eugene told her with apprehension in his voice.

"Yes, I know. It will be a case that attracts press interest, I'm afraid. But my advice is just don't say anything and hopefully they will soon move on to something else." She continued, "Now for the immediate future I'll be back in contact with you when we have secured a barrister who will present our defence. I also have other enquiries to make. Please do get back to that psychiatrist because despite efforts I've not heard from him as yet."

"Yes…yes, I will. I'm due to see him next week, anyway."

"Try to get hold of him ASAP," said Karen. She continued, "Hopefully that press melee will have dispersed a little and we can make our way out of here."

They started their journey away from the court.

They exited from the building with little difficulty but waiting outside was Lorna Symonds and with her was a photographer. The photographer started clicking away with his camera. Karen said, "Just walk on," and they did so. Lorna Symonds looked at them but said nothing and may have been deterred because of the presence of Karen. Karen and Eugene parted in the town centre and Eugene made his way to his car and drove home.

On arrival home Eugene found the place exactly as he had left it and that in itself was depressing. He made himself a cup of tea only to find that the milk had gone off and he was forced to make do with black tea. He ruminated on the morning's events, not believing that he was really in the position that he was. It all seemed surreal, if not totally unreal. It was around lunchtime and Eugene knew he should eat something but didn't really feel like it and there wasn't much there, anyway. Then he made a spontaneous decision, not something he did very much of late. He jumped in his car and drove the short distance to the shop, obtaining enough provisions for at least the weekend. Florrie greeted him very much as she had done a few days before; she always seemed such a cheerful soul, thought Eugene.

Having had a decent cup of tea and a bacon sandwich Eugene made a call to the Community Mental Health Team at Maidenhead. The call was answered in a brusque manner and Eugene thought that it must be the same receptionist he saw when he had attended the office.

Eugene commenced, "Yes…um…thank you. Um…I called last week to speak to Dr Bekhit. I was told he was away and to call back this week".

"Your name and date of birth please," asked the receptionist. Having given both, the receptionist, after a pause said, "Please wait." After a few moments she came back and said "Dr Bekhit is in clinic this afternoon. Could you call tomorrow around two, please?"

"Yes, thank you," replied Eugene feeling disappointed, and the line went dead.

The day wore on and the general malaise of anxiety, lassitude and melancholy returned which had the effect of preventing Eugene doing anything useful or constructive. The television was switched on but not adhered to, Eugene spending time wandering from room to room with no purpose. The hours slipped by. He tried to read but couldn't, then looked through his telephone note pad to see if there was someone to call. He ended up calling his mother who complained that she hadn't spoken to her granddaughter for a while. Eugene bit the bullet and told his mother that there were some difficulties at present and that Sandra and Katie were staying with Sandra's parents. Eugene's mother was asking questions – questions, so many questions, and each time he answered he was aware that he was lying to her. In the end he assured his mother that the issue was one of minor marital difficulties and that it would soon all blow over. This seemed to satisfy her, and the call ended amicably, although his mother insisted that she would like to speak to Katie soon.

As soon as he had completed the call his phone rang, and Sandra's voice said, "I've been trying to get hold of you."

"Yes, it was my mother. She was worried that she'd not heard from Katie. Do you think you could get Katie to give her a call?"

"Yes, OK," said Sandra, sounding quite irritated. She continued, "Miss Waldock, the social worker, called me and then visited me this morning with another woman, I can't remember her name."

"Morrissey," said Eugene, "Miss Morrissey".

"Yes, whatever," continued Sandra, retaining her air of irritation. "Miss Waldock was quite supportive and empathic and told me what I'd need to do to safeguard Katie."

"What the hell does that mean?" asked Eugene with agitation in his voice.

"It means, Gene, that if you see Katie there's to be someone present, me or my parents. I'll also need to talk to the school, and you shouldn't meet Katie alone. I'd ask that you do not contact her either except through me."

Eugene could feel himself getting angrier, but to express his anger would at this moment be counterproductive and he knew that.

"Can I speak to her now please?"

There was a pause and Sandra said, "Look, I don't think that would be a good idea. Anyway she's working in the garden with her Gramps."

"Well, when can I speak to my own daughter?" asked Eugene emphasising the 'when' and feeling his free hand form into a firm fist.

Sandra paused and said, "Maybe it'd be best if we put things on a more formal basis. I've decided to see a solicitor, Gene. You must have one for the, well, the case that you're involved in. I think it would best to arrange things formally."

Eugene didn't quite know what to say. He certainly wasn't expecting Sandra to say that.

"Look, can we not have a talk. Just you and me?" asked Eugene, his voice becoming more conciliatory.

"I'll be coming to the house on Monday afternoon. Can you be there, Gene. I need to collect some things for Katie and me..."

"Yes, yes I'll be here, Monday afternoon, will you bring Katie please?"

"We'll see," said Sandra which meant 'probably not'.

However, Eugene remained hopeful and said, "OK, Sandra, I look forward to seeing you on Monday. Oh, and can you get Katie to call her granny."

Sandra agreed.

Eugene started to say, "I love…" but the line went dead.

He could not quite take in what had been said. He was literally stunned by the conversation, the words floating around his head, meaningless. He needed to sit down and collect his thoughts. Eugene had not considered for one minute that she would go ahead with her demand for a divorce. He had always been able to talk her round to his way of thinking and this time, he felt, would be no different. He had absolutely no intention of discussing his marriage with a solicitor, not even Karen. Especially not Karen.

CHAPTER 14

The bright early summer sun streaming through the gaps in the bedroom curtain awoke Eugene. He lay there in that blissful place betwixt sleep and being fully awake and realised that he had, despite the difficulties and challenges of the previous day, had a good restful and refreshing night, the exception rather than the rule these days. He thought that he must have been exhausted by the events of the previous day and could not quite remember coming to bed.

He wondered if when he enjoyed a good night's sleep that was an indication that he had walked in his sleep. He looked around the room for clues that may have indicated sleep walking but there were none. He promised himself that he would research the subject himself. He pondered the day ahead and knew that he must do something with the untidy state of the house before Sandra arrived on Monday.

He remembered that he must call Dr Bekhit at two. He just wanted to lay there but if he did he knew in his present state of mind he might just drift off into heavenly sleep again. With determined effort he arose and for once was motivated to take a shower, something he knew he didn't do regularly enough.

The assault on the kitchen and living room had been going well until Eugene realised that he needed more cleaning products. He knew that if he didn't obtain them quickly the desire to complete the task would fade and that old enemy, procrastination, would take over. He thought that a brisk walk to the shop would invigorate him.

Eugene set off walking along his cul de sac. He saw his one of his neighbours, the one who had greeted him warmly recently, working in his garden.

As Eugene approached he said a cheery, "Good morning!"

The neighbour looked at Eugene; his expression was featureless, and he turned and walked away inside his house. Eugene thought the behaviour somewhat odd but didn't pay too much attention to it. Further along was a man washing his car but as Eugene approached the man looked in his direction and left his soap sodden vehicle and retreated into his garage. Eugene carried on, arriving at the mini supermarket, and on entering saw Florrie sitting at her checkout. She looked in his direction but there was no friendly greeting. She looked stony faced and quickly directed her gaze elsewhere.

Eugene issued a, "Good morning!" but there was no response. He was beginning to wonder why these people were obviously ignoring him.

He collected his wire basket and headed for the household goods aisle, collecting the cleaning products that he required. He made his way back toward the checkout and then saw the newspaper stand. He saw all the national papers and the light blue top of The Berkshire Enquirer. It wasn't a paper he read, but his eyes were drawn to the large black lettered headline which read, 'Downloading Detective Inspector.'

There was a picture of Eugene leaving the Court with his solicitor. He read further and saw his name and address printed. He looked and saw Florrie looking directly at him with the blank and non-expressive stony face that he had noticed earlier. He looked back at the newspapers and placed one in his wire basket. He moved toward the checkout, taking the goods and paper out of the basket and placing them onto the small conveyor belt making sure that the paper's front page was hidden.

Florrie checked the items off making no comment and not looking at Eugene. When she got to the newspaper she turned it over with something of a flourish and when the headline was in full view looked directly at Eugene and said slowly and precisely, "Seven pounds forty."

She looked stern and condemning and Eugene could feel his heart pounding, and his breathing becoming more laboured. He just wanted to get out of that stuffy shop, away from that intimidating judgemental woman and into the fresh air so that he could breathe. He fumbled with his money, accepted his change, and placed his goods and the newspaper into his shopping bag. He hurriedly left, assuming that everyone in the shop and primarily Florrie, had judged him and already found him guilty.

At home Eugene stumbled through his front door. He felt ill, his heart was continuing to pound, his breathing shallow and rapid with difficulty in breathing out, he was sweating and fearful. He flopped onto the settee throwing his shopping bag to the side and as quickly as the attack had occurred it abated again and Eugene was able to breathe more easily, his heart slowing and that all enveloping fear leaving him.

He stayed where he was for a while fearing that the attack would resume but after a while he regained his confidence and went into the kitchen, pouring for himself a large glass of water. He looked at the half cleaned kitchen and the half tidied living room but decided to put cleaning duties on hold for the moment. He took the newspaper from the shopping bag, looked quickly at the headline, his name and address and threw the paper onto a chair ensuring that the paper was face down.

The loud tick of the mock Victorian monstrosity of a living room clock told out the slothful misspent hours and minutes of the morning as its grotesque hands moved ever so slowly. Eugene had at least remembered to wind the thing that morning, in anticipation of Sandra arriving on Monday, knowing full well he would have to wind it again before then. Those hands indicated that it was nearly the time he was call to Dr Bekhit. As soon as the clock indicated it was ten past two Eugene made the call.

The usual receptionist answered the call, he recognised her voice and her brusque style. Eugene identified himself and asked to be put through to Dr Bekhit. He was duly connected, and Dr Bekhit said, "Good afternoon, Mr Elphick, how may I help you?"

"I'm due to see you next week doctor, but there have been some changes and I was hopeful that you might be able to see me earlier."

There was a pause and Dr Bekhit said, "Yes, I am aware of the changes in your circumstances." There was another pause and Dr Bekhit continued, "You see, Mr Elphick, I saw you as something of a favour at short notice, but really you should have been referred in the normal manner. So, I think we should cancel next week's appointment and that you return to Doctor David Bennett, and request a formal referral."

Eugene was shaken by what had been said and asked apprehensively, "I'm not your patient now?"

"Not really. I think I would prefer it if you went through a formal referral from your GP."

"You don't want to see me, do you?" said Eugene, quickly followed up by, "You've clearly read the paper and made your own decision, your own judgement." Now he was sounding more assertive.

"That is not so, Mr Elphick. I'm aware of your circumstances and just want you to be properly referred. That can easily be done, and you will then be properly seen by someone from this team."

"Not you, then?" asked Eugene with a hint of sarcasm in his voice.

"Not necessarily, we're a team here."

Defeated Eugene merely replied, "I see."

"Your solicitor has written to me, and I have replied to her letter; she should get that in a day or so."

There was another pause and then Dr Bekhit said, "I don't think there is any more to say today, Mr Elphick. My advice is to return to Doctor Bennett and seek a formal referral. You will then be seen here."

Eugene uttered a quiet, "Thank you," the wind very much taken from his sails and the call ended.

Eugene could only see that conversation as another nail in the overall coffin of rejection. There seemed to be rejection at every turn, and he was beginning to wonder how he was going to cope with all this.

Eugene felt very alone. He fumbled with his mobile phone and saw that there was a missed call from Benji.

Eugene called him and Benji answered, saying, "I'll call you back."

He did so after a few minutes and started the conversation by saying, "I wanted to get out of the office to talk in private," he continued. "How are you, Gene?"

Eugene took a deep breath and told Benji about the court hearing, about the reporter, Lorna Symonds, and the headlines in the Berkshire Enquirer.

Benji listened and then said, "Yeah, I've seen the paper. It's also on the BBC Berkshire website but no picture there."

"I just hope it doesn't get to Dorset where my mother can see it," said Eugene.

"I doubt it," said Benji, trying hard to bolster Eugene, "It's news of local value only."

Eugene, sadly, was not that reassured. They both knew how fast bad news travelled where badly behaving police officers were concerned.

"Have you contacted the Federation yet?" asked Benji.

"No, no, I haven't," said Eugene slowly and quietly, as if he was thinking about something else.

"Well, you need to. They'll appoint their own barrister, and they're well used to dealing with this sort of thing. You're not the first police officer to be accused in this way. Contact them."

"Yes, yes I will," said Eugene, in a murmured voice which still seemed distant.

"Think of the money aspect, it'll be an expensive job and you'll not get legal aid. The Federation will foot the bill and you will get something out of them in addition to that poxy diary every year," Benji laughed.

Eugene hesitated but then said, "Benji, can you come and see me again, or perhaps we could meet up for a drink or coffee or something?"

"To be honest Gene, it's a bit difficult."

"Why difficult?"

"Well, it just is. It's difficult to explain really."

"You mean you don't want to be seen associating with me in any way, is that what's difficult?"

There was a moments' silence and Benji replied, "It's just the nature of the thing. I just can't get my head around it and that's what's difficult."

"You believe I did it," said Eugene, his voice going up an octave.

Benji paused, "Maybe not consciously because of the sleep walking thing if that's possible. I don't know. I'm finding the whole thing difficult to take in."

"So you're abandoning me like everybody else?"

"No, I'm not, I want to believe you and I want you to come through this."

In an attempt to defuse the situation and to let Eugene know he really did want to help, despite what his friend was thinking he asked, "Have you got back to that psychiatrist?"

"Yes, I've spoken to him and like you he's finding it difficult, too. He's abandoned me just like you're doing. I'm sorry that you, too, feel like I am some sort of social leper."

Eugene felt both angry and hurt and he realised that was coming through in his voice.

"Look, I'm here," said Benji. He took on what he thought was a more conciliatory tone, "You can call me if you want to."

"But you don't want to see me?"

"It's difficult," said Benji and added after a pause, "Try and understand my position, mate."

Eugene thought for a moment and then said quietly, "OK, Benji, I understand. Thanks for the call." He then pressed the red button on his phone ending the conversation.

Eugene stood in silence, the only noise being the loud tick of the mock Victorian clock which seemed in a way to be contemptuous in its persistently loud movement. Not for the first time Eugene wanted to smash that miscreated, mocking eyesore to pieces. He wondered just how much more rejection he could endure. But, deciding to finally grasp the nettle he made telephone contact with the Police Federation Office at Thame. Eugene spoke to a receptionist who said that there were no Federation representatives available. Eugene thought well, typical, it is Friday afternoon. The receptionist took his details, and he merely told her he was currently suspended from duty, nothing else. She said someone would contact him on Monday morning.

Eugene thought that whilst he was on something of a roll he would complete his phone calls for today and immediately dialled the GP's surgery. His call was answered, and a recorded voice told him he was 'number 1' in the queue.

This was a new system for the surgery and whilst he waited Eugene contemplated how almost everything was becoming less personal. His call was answered fairly quickly, and he recognised the voice at the other end as Mary, a colleague of Sandra's. He asked to be put through to Dr Bennett and when asked his name he gave it.

Mary simply said, "Oh," and then, "Please wait."

Dr Bennett then came on the line and said, "Eugene, I was hoping you would call," in his normal convivial style.

Eugene explained the conversation he had had with Dr Bekhit, and Dr Bennett said he was aware as he had spoken to Dr Bekhit recently. Eugene asked to be formally referred to him and Dr Bennett explained that he could only refer him to the Community Mental Health Team and not specifically to Dr Bekhit. Eugene didn't say anything as he was convinced that Bekhit didn't want to see him anyway. It was agreed that Dr Bennett would refer Eugene and he was told that it could take anything between eight and twelve weeks before he was seen. Eugene again did not argue the point as he felt that there was no point in doing so and meekly accepted the doctor's advice.

Dr Bennet asked if Eugene needed a prescription and Eugene informed him that he did not. Dr Bennett then said,

"I want to speak to you on a more sensitive issue now Eugene," in a much more sombre tone.

Eugene remained silent.

"I wonder of you'd consider voluntarily changing surgeries. The fact is, I'm aware of the situation regarding you and Sandra and well, you know, I wouldn't want any embarrassment or unpleasantness here at the surgery."

Eugene responded angrily and loudly, his pent up frustration and hurt coming to the fore.

"Is it to do with Sandra, or is it to do with what you have clearly read in the paper today?"

Dr Bennett replied, "Well," he hesitated and then said, "A bit of both really I suppose. One thing impinges on the other to an extent."

Eugene felt more angry than hurt or disappointed and for a moment regained his old assertiveness and said slowly, assertively, and precisely, "I've done nothing that would cause me to be barred from your surgery. So, no, I'm not changing surgeries."

Dr Bennet responded in an equally assertive manner, "Then in that case, I would ask you not to come to the surgery casually, but to make an appointment with me and I will see you and I will arrange that for a time when Sandra is not at the surgery. Am I clear on that?"

"As you wish," said Eugene and retaining his assertive stance continued, "I would be obliged if you would make the referral as discussed at your earliest opportunity," upon which he terminated the call.

Eugene said to himself , 'What a cheeky bastard' but at the same time was pleased in that for the first time in a long while he had stood his ground and been forceful and that, for what it was worth, felt good. He was also pleased that he had actually achieved something by making those telephone calls, yet at the same time distressed by the attitude of his friend, Benji, who he had helped, supported, and protected for a long period of time, but who now was more interested in protecting himself. However, Eugene decided to put hurtful thoughts about Benji to one side and just hoped that his self-pitying slothfulness would abate, and he could become more motivated.

It was while Leonard Cohen was singing about his imaginary sexual encounter with Suzanne that Eugene was jolted from the phantasmal shores of Montreal back to the reality of a heavy crash at the front door. Eugene tore the headphones from his ears and rushed to the door. A perpendicular pane of glass to the right of the door had been smashed, the one to the left remained intact. There was some splitting of the wood surround to the broken pane.

Eugene opened the door and went outside but could see nothing. The man that lived opposite came out, he must have heard the crash, and Eugene shouted to him,

"Did you see anything?" but the man just turned and went inside his house.

Eugene started to look around his property and saw that his white garage door had been emblazoned with bright red paint and the word 'Nonce' crudely sprayed in large capital letters on the door. Eugene went inside and dialled 101, he thought about dialling 999 but thought it best to dial 101. A recorded voice answered informing him that he was being connected to Thames Valley Police.

A female voice answered, "Thames Valley Police, how may I help?" Eugene could feel his heart racing and saw that his hand was shaking.

He said, "Yes, the window in my front door has been smashed and there has been paint sprayed on my garage door."

The voice was quite calm, and she asked, "When did this happen?"

"Just now, a few minutes ago."

" Are there any offenders there now?"

"No, not that I can see."

The voice that was getting more disinterested with each interaction said, "I will give you a URN number". and proceeded to give Eugene a long reference number which he wrote down. He was used to URN numbers and knew that it was the incident number followed by the date.

Eugene asked, " Are you sending someone?"

The disinterested voice said, "No, there are no units to send out for this at the moment. I suggest you make enquiries with your neighbours and possibly the Neighbourhood Team will contact you in due course."

Eugene could feel himself getting angry.

"Are you telling me that you're not sending anyone to deal with this criminal damage to my property and are asking me to make my own enquiries. What is this, detect your own crime week?"

"Don't take that tone with me," the disinterested voice had become assertive.

Eugene said, "

I'll need a crime reference".

The voice replied, "Call the crime desk".

What's your name?" enquired Eugene but the line went dead, and the disinterested female operator had clearly hung up on him.

Eugene could feel his anger rising even further and he contemplated calling a supervisor and making a complaint knowing that the operator could be contacted via the URN number. He started to dial but then realised that he would get nowhere. He was, in the eyes of the police and everyone else come to that, a pervert, a nonce, a sex offender! Who would listen to him?

Eugene sat for a moment and then worked out what needed to be done. He needed a boarding up company and set about finding one and calling one out. The other issues could be dealt with in the morning. There followed a disturbed night where Eugene was listening for, and hypersensitive to, any noise.

Eugene rose early, not having slept very much. He set about trying to erase the red painted word 'Nonce' from the garage door, but it wouldn't shift with detergent, bleach or elbow grease. In the end he just painted over the word with white paint, successfully obliterating it.

It was Saturday morning, and as is the want of the lower middle class people in the cul de sac, they were washing their cars, mowing their lawns, attending to their roses, and doing those acceptable sedate and non-interfering roles that make them tolerable within that assemblage. Young working class men and women who are accepted into the police service seem to have a direct entry to the lower middle class but never seem to fit in and are not received that well, especially so when one retained a regional working class accent as Eugene did.

Standing there feeling totally rejected Eugene could feel nothing but contempt for his neighbours living their uneventful, dull, humdrum, insipid lives where the only excitement was the demise and downfall of someone other than them.

Eugene despised them and wondered which of them had summoned the courage to smash his window and vandalise his garage door and the more he thought about it the more he realised that it would be none of them – they were incapable of making any form of statement about anything. Nevertheless, his contempt for them didn't override his wish that someone, anyone, would reach out and say hello or something. He stood and watched his neighbours for a short while, busying themselves, and avoiding him. Eugene turned and retreated inside his home and again started to try and make the place presentable for Sandra's visit on Monday.

CHAPTER 15

Eugene had done very little for the rest of the weekend, which summed up his forlorn and solitary time. He did call his mother, but this was to ensure that she had not learned of his current situation and he was pleased that the news of his court case had not reached North Dorset. He was also glad to hear that his mother had spoken to Katie.

Eugene had managed, however, albeit at a very slow pace through the weekend, to make the home presentable for when Sandra, and hopefully Katie, would visit later. After a very meagre breakfast that Monday morning, Eugene put the finishing touches to his domestic work, not forgetting to wind the mock Victorian clock in the living room. Quite early and just after nine Eugene received a call from Mike Parsons, who introduced himself as the Thames Valley Police, Police Federation Inspector's representative.

Parsons asked for the details of the case which Eugene supplied. Parsons listened without much comment but employed reassuring para language. Parsons did not sound in any way judgemental. He asked about Eugene's current solicitor and said he would make contact with her to obtain details of the case. Eugene insisted that he spoke to Karen Nicholls first and that when he had done so he would get back to Mike Parsons. Parson agreed but indicated that such should be done with some haste.

Parsons then went on to explain that once he had details from Eugene's solicitor he would make contact with the Federation solicitors' Slater and Gordon and once he had done that he would be in contact with Eugene again. He indicated that their next meeting would probably be held at the Federation offices in Thame and that he would write to Eugene covering all that had been said and giving directions to the Thame office. In coming off the phone Eugene felt that Mike Parsons had sounded very professional. That said, he wondered why a police inspector was devoting himself so much and for so long to Police Federation work and he wondered, when was the last time Mike Parsons actually felt a collar.

Eugene's phone blipped to indicate a text message, something of a rarity of late. It was from Sandra, who didn't text that often, indicating that she would be at the house around 4.30pm which pleased Eugene as it meant that Sandra would be calling in, having picked Katie up from school. Eugene was excited to see Katie and that simple message placed Eugene in a buoyant mood for the rest of the morning.

A lightly boiled egg spooned out of its shell onto warm buttered toast and generously covered with black pepper sufficed as lunch for Eugene. As he devoured the last delicious morsel there was a loud knock at the front door. Eugene, upon opening the door, saw a man of about 35 years of age. He was dressed in what Eugene knew to be the uniform of a PCSO: a blue shirt with a rather grubby florescent vest which had pens, a small torch, a camera, two name badges, and keys affixed to it.

The officer had about a four day growth of beard on his face which was dark, but also showing grey patches. The man had dark coloured hair, short at the sides but long and untidy on the top, His arms bore numerous tattoos with various bangles around both wrists. Some way behind him stood a young female about 19 years of age, short, but wearing her uniform in a much smarter manner. Eugene noticed how wide her eyes were as if she was expecting something significant to happen. Behind her was a marked police vehicle parked in the driveway.

The male PCSO spoke first, "You called the police, mate?"

Eugene smarted at the word 'mate' but didn't mention it and replied, "Yes, that was on Friday evening."

The PCSO, who Eugene noticed was not making eye contact with him but looking around as if to ensure his female companion was still there, said, "Yeah, well we're busy. What's all this about?"

Eugene who was beginning to feel quite wound up by this individual said, "Yes, I'm sure Old Windsor is something of a hub of crime and debauchery these days."

"What?" enquired the PCSO, with a flash of annoyance passing over his face.

"Nothing," said Eugene and continued, "On Friday, about eleven I suppose, there was a crash at the door and as you can see the door was smashed. My garage door was daubed with paint which I've now painted over."

"Did you see anyone?"

"No, I came out but didn't see anything."

"Have you made any enquiries with your neighbours?"

"No, have you?" asked Eugene.

The PCSO looked directly at Eugene for the first time. He then said, "There's nothing we can do with this mate; you've a URN?"

Eugene said, "Yes, I was hoping that you'd give me a crime reference number."

The PCSO smirked and said, "No can do, mate, you'll have to contact the crime desk via 101."

Eugene could feel himself becoming angrier with this man and asked, "What's the point in you coming here then?"

"You asked for the police to attend, and we've done so, there's nothing that we can do with this, mate."

Eugene was reaching boiling point; he could feel his hands clenching into fists and experienced an overwhelming desire to punch this interlocutor.

He said angrily, "For a start you're not the police..."

The PCSO interrupted and said, "We officially represent the police and are police staff."

Eugene continued, "You're not the police, and for your information I'm not your mate. I'm a Detective Inspector."

Eugene immediately regretted saying that. He could see the young female PCSO nervously moving from foot to foot as if she were bursting for the toilet.

The male PCSO looked directly at Eugene his eyes fixed, his chin rigid, he then said slowly and quietly, "Not for much longer from what I hear," and then added sarcastically, "sir."

"Just go from here now," said Eugene and shut the door.

He could hear the police vehicle backing out of the driveway and found the whole interaction with that PCSO upsetting and something which spoilt his hitherto good mood. Eugene could feel his body trembling with anger, and he knew that he needed to control himself. He did not want to end up with a panic attack, especially as Sandra and, hopefully, Katie, would be there in a while.

Eugene was angry at himself for allowing the PCSO to have the effect upon him that he had. He reflected on the whole encounter and was aware that some of the poor interaction that took place was entirely his fault. He started to reflect on why he clearly had a dislike of PCSOs in general rather than a specific dislike for that PCSO in particular, although it was obvious that he had some sort of chip on his shoulder which added to the fuel of Eugene's dislike.

When Eugene joined in 1995 there were no PCSO's; they started to be recruited into the Metropolitan Police around 2000 but did not arrive in Thames Valley Police until much later. Eugene had moved to CID in 2003 and had little to do with them when they did arrive. When he was promoted to sergeant in 2006 and moved back to uniform, there were two but they seemed to provide a service to a semi-rural area and again Eugene had little to do with them. He recalled that some hard line veteran officers and equally hard line Federation Representatives of a now bygone era were vehemently against them, stating that we, the rank and file, should have nothing to do with them, not train them or work with them, as they would erode traditional British policing, which Eugene thought was probably true.

Policing, thought Eugene, was to encounter all aspects of life and death and everything in between and that takes training and a certain mind set which PCSOs cannot attain without the same training. Some would argue that that PCSOs brought back to the public that reassurance of seeing a uniformed presence on the street, but that argument was lost in the fact that most PCSO's now travelled around in cars and public reassurance cannot be given from a car in the same way. Equally, every yob on the street was aware that PCSO's had as much power as a broken lawn mower and, for them, were fair game for abuse and insolence.

Having thought it through, the process gave Eugene some solace and he no longer felt angry with the PCSO, and more importantly, no longer felt angry with himself. He settled down, making a final cursory inspection of the house, and awaited the arrival of Sandra and Katie.

The mock Victorian monstrosity of a clock ticked and moved laboriously toward and past 4:30. 'She's late,' thought Eugene but satisfied himself that of course she would be, she knew how much he wanted to see Katie, and this was a way in which Sandra could exert her control.

Sometime around 5:00 Eugene heard the chugging sound of a diesel engine in the driveway. He thought the PCSOs had returned which was a most inappropriate time for them to do so. He went to the front door, opened it intending to give them short shift but was confronted with Sandra and her father walking toward him. The diesel engine had belonged to a white Mercedes van with the words Northgate Vehicle Hire painted on the side. Eugene stepped aside and let Sandra and her father into the house. Sandra walked into the sitting room and Eugene followed, her father remained in the hallway.

"Where's Katie?" asked Eugene.

Sandra, who was looking much older than her years replied, "I'll come to that in a moment."

Eugene went to say something, but Sandra raised her arm with her palm outstretched.

"Please, just listen to me. Please don't interrupt. I just want to say what I have to say, do what I have to do and get out of here. I've come here this afternoon to collect the remainder of mine and Katie's belongings. I don't want you to obstruct me in anyway. I've contacted the police at Windsor and have told them what I'm doing and if there are any problems they'll come here. I don't quite know what to say about all this, but since your court case and the following article in the paper both your daughter and I have been living a nightmare. Your poor daughter can't even switch on her laptop without being inundated with the filthiest and condemning abuse. She's been called 'pervert's daughter,' 'paedophile,' and all sorts of other things which almost defy imagination, and all, mainly it would seem, from her so called friends."

Eugene went to speak, but Sandra again raised her arm in a similar manner as before and just said quiet sharply, "Please!" She continued, "Katie has spent the whole weekend in a state of extreme distress, so much so that I had to call Mum and Dad's GP to her. Of course she didn't attend school today, but I was summoned to her school and spoken to by the headmistress. She quite politely said that it would be best for the sake of Katie and the school if Katie didn't attend school up until the summer holidays which start in a couple of weeks. She said the whole situation will be reviewed at the start of the new school year. As you might imagine I'm off work with stress, and I don't think I will be able to return to my job at the surgery. So, your perversion, your perverted actions, your utterly selfish behaviour has affected both your daughter's and my life. I don't know what damage you have done to your daughter."

Sandra paused to take a breath. Eugene felt thoroughly drained by what had been said. He didn't know what to say and flopped into a chair.

Sandra continued, "I've spoken to my solicitor, and I don't want you contacting or speaking to Katie right now. If you do attempt to see her or contact her I'll seek an injunction against you. I advise you to contact a solicitor and arrangements can be made in time for you to see Katie at a contact centre or something. My dad and I are now going to clear our things and I suggest you stay in here out of the way."

Eugene looked toward Sandra's father, who he had always found a reasonable but guarded sort of man. He was standing with his head lowered, clearly embarrassed and not knowing what to say, so choosing to say nothing.

Sandra moved out of the sitting room and shut the door, moving with her father upstairs. Eugene remained where he was. He felt nauseous and was glad that he had had only a light lunch as he feared he would vomit. He just did not know what to say or do, he was in all senses defeated and drained of all emotion. He didn't feel angry, he didn't feel sad – he felt nothing. Eugene continued to sit where he was; it was as if his legs were cased in concrete, and he didn't think he could move even if he wanted to.

He could hear Sandra and her father moving around; up, and downstairs, in and out of the house. After a while Sandra came back into the room.

She looked hot and red in the face and with her breathing a little laboured, she said, "I'm leaving here now, and I don't expect to return for a while. Please consider seeing a solicitor and let's get all this done."

She left the room and closed the front door behind her. Eugene said nothing and remained where he was. He heard the diesel engine of the hire van start and reverse out of the driveway.

Eugene didn't know how long he sat there trying to take in process and analyse what had taken place. He then suddenly stood up, walked to the garage selected a claw hammer, and returned to the sitting room. There, loudly ticking, was the monstrosity of a mock Victorian clock. Eugene raised the hammer and smashed it into the face of the clock. The hammer buried itself within the interior and Eugene yanked the hammer pulling the clock from the wall and onto the floor where he, in a manic rage, smashed it into hundreds of pieces which scattered around the floor until there was no indication that it ever had been a clock. Having completed his destruction Eugene fell to his knees, the hammer still in his hand, and sobbed uncontrollably.

Eugene was able to find some solace in the disconsolate musings of Leonard Cohen and Amy Winehouse, both in their own way geniuses, but crippled by a level of anhedonia whereby they were unable to recognise their own masterful achievements, and such came through in their mournful modulations. Eugene was aware that this musical genre was not the best to be listening to in his present mood but in a strange way it seemed to comfort him.

He was grateful that Sandra had not taken the CD player or the large collection of music which were rightly hers. He was aware that if she knew the comfort that the music was able to give him right now she would have made sure she had taken it. Having calmed himself sufficiently Eugene knew that sleep would be denied to him that night, so he took some of the Amitriptyline medication that had been prescribed . He made his way upstairs remembering to take with him a glass of water as advised when taking that medication.

Eugene was drawn to Katies room, he drew the curtains switched on the light and stood there. Katie's bed with its blue and white duvet cover, and the blue and white pillowcases remained untouched but everything else seemed to have been removed. The posters on the walls which gave a graphic pictorial history of the transition from pre-pubescent girl to young woman remained, from pictures of horses and cats through to pop stars and sports icons. Eugene looked at the colour of the room, which was a 'princess' pink that he had decorated a number of years ago. He had, on several occasions, promised Katie that he would redecorate her room but never seemed to get around to it. Standing there now he wished he had.

He saw that the drawers of her cupboard were half open and bare and that the room had an echo type sound, an empty sound: empty of presence, empty of Katie's presence, empty of her existence within it. Even Sir Carotene, Katies soft toy rabbit, was gone from the chair that stood in the corner.

Eugene sat down on the bed recalling the significant events that had occurred within the room.: of the bedtime stories told, of the reassurance given after a terrifying nightmare, of the tender nursing of a sick child enduring a childhood complaint, of the dreams and aspirations told by a child full of the expectations, of a good life ahead. This room had purpose, this room had life this room had a dynamism all of its own, but that, this very afternoon, had been wrenched from it and what was left was just an empty and soulless place.

Eugene lay on the bed and could smell the faint soapy smell of his daughter. He wanted to weep – to weep for her and for him and for what was lost, but he could not weep. He was all cried out. The amitriptyline took effect and even with the light on Eugene fell into a deep sleep.

CHAPTER 16

Eugene could not work out where he was at first; his mouth was so dry, and he was fully dressed. He slowly realised that he was in Katie's bedroom. He thought at first that he must have been sleepwalking as he was coming to from his sleep and then remembered that he lay down on Katie's bed after taking his medication. He reached for the glass of water and was glad that he remembered to bring it with him. Eugene, although feeling groggy, started to remember the events of the previous day but he didn't feel that upset; in fact, he wanted to get things done. He had things to do and wanted to do them.

He showered and prepared for his day. It wasn't long after contacting Karen Nicholls and Mike Parsons that he called the Carbis Bay Hotel. They had no vacancies but gave him the number of a guest house in Carbis Bay - The Anchors Rest. Eugene called there and in the early afternoon of that day found himself with a weekend bag packed and with his railway ticket in hand on Platform 7 at Reading railway station. He had managed to organise everything in a few hours and was determined to take at least part of the holiday that he had promised Katie. The train due at 14:29 pulled into the station on time and Eugene settled himself in his First Class seat which was a little treat for himself. He had never travelled First Class before. As the train pulled smoothly away from Reading, Eugene looked at the travel inventory. The train travelled non-stop to Taunton and thereafter would seem to stop everywhere. He would get to St Erth just after 7:00pm with a short wait until he would travel along the scenic route to Carbis Bay, and it was that part of the journey that he looked forward to the most.

The first part of the journey seemed fast but was uneventful apart from the tea and biscuits served along the way. Pulling into Taunton Eugene recalled that this was the station he and his mother would join the train on their annual 'pilgrimage' to Carbis Bay. The station looked familiar with its seemingly very long platform, but Eugene did not feel the nostalgia that he thought he might. The rest of the journey seemed long, if not torturous, but eventually the train pulled into St Erth.

Eugene alighted and as his train pulled away he stopped and looked around. Yes, St Erth was exactly as he remembered it . The little booking hall with its mock gothic windows, the iron overbridge, the platforms and the three small steps to platform three which one descended to catch the train to St Ives with Carbis Bay en route. Eugene remembered sitting here in almost uncontainable excitement as a child, but that level of excitement or nostalgia evaded him today. In fact he wasn't thinking about that much and on one or two occasions thought that it might have been better not to have come. He looked at his phone. No one had called him or messaged him, and he felt surprisingly alone in a place where no one knew where he was and probably didn't care anyway.

The incoming train from St Ives arrived and Eugene boarded. The train commenced its return journey. It was a ride of less than 10 minutes after which time he climbed the steep slope at Carbis Bay Station to the car park and beyond to the roadway. He looked down toward the sea, which was a dark navy blue; he would go and look at it more closely tomorrow he thought. He turned right as he entered the roadway then left into Headland Road. He easily spotted the Anchor's Rest Guest House with its large blue anchor picked out in illuminated fairy lights. Eugene pondered the name, Anchor's Rest – it seemed a strange name for a Guest House so high up on the cliff above the beach.

Eugene checked in for his two nights at the small desk in the foyer, having to ring a small bell to attract attention. A pleasant young lady with a pronounced West Country, probably Cornish, accent took his details, told him he was a little too late for dinner but offered him sandwiches in his room if he would like. Eugene then settled into his room. He demolished the ham and mustard sandwiches along with a packet of crisps and a pot of tea that had been brought to him. He sorted out his meagre bag, showered and went to bed well before 10pm. He lay in his bed with his window open, he could just hear the murmuring of the sea as a background. He thought about his past holidays in that place but could not summon the nostalgia that he wanted to relive. He just couldn't.

A pleasant awakening with the sound of sea and seagulls followed with a more than adequate Cornish breakfast, after which Eugene set off. He was trying to recapture those past holidays that he had enjoyed so much, holidays that stood out as a significant part of a childhood when he was loved so much. He reflected on that love and realised that he had in no way appreciated it at the time but now that he had seemingly lost others' love, he did not only appreciate it, but longed for it.

Walking from the front door of the guest house he looked out over the now cobalt blue sea. In the distance he could see Godrevy Lighthouse, something which had fascinated him as a child, and he remembered staring at it, wondering what went on there and wondering if he could go there one day. In later years he was told, he could not remember by who, that it was Godrevy that inspired the author Virginia Wolfe in her novel 'To the Lighthouse' and although the novel was set in the Hebrides it was Godrevy, which she would see on her own family holidays at St Ives, that inspired her.

Enough of daydreaming thought Eugene and he walked on into Headland Road and then started to descend the steep hill to the beach. He remembered the hill well and looking to his left he saw the bank that had been covered with both cultivated and wildflowers had been replaced with a number of apartments facing the sea. Small, but no doubt expensive, the buildings were not that obtrusive but just gave the hill a cluttered feel.

Walking on the seaward side Eugene could now see the sandy beach; the tide was out which revealed a wide expanse of sand. Descending further he came upon a flat roofed house which faced the sea, and which had a revolving shiny metal cowl which picked up any available light and coruscated it with great abundance all around. He remembered always looking to see if the shiny metal cowl was still there when he descended the hill on the first day of his past holidays.

The roadway ended at the bottom of the hill, breaking left, to the Carbis Bay Hotel, and right, to the beach. Ahead was a footpath which would eventually lead one to a hill above St Ives. Eugene turned to his right and walked toward the beach; the uneven concrete footway was as treacherous as it always had been. To his right was where the shop and office had been, the office where he and his mother would collect the key for the beach hut on the first day of the holiday. Gone now, the shop and office replaced by a functional looking café come restaurant where the peppery, fatty smell of Cornish pasties being warmed for the anticipated throng of holiday makers who would descend here in an hour or so, punctuating the fresh breeze blowing off the sea.

Eugene walked to the edge of the beach. He looked out at the expanse of fine sand and beyond, the flat and shiny wet sand where the sea had receded leaving small pools and small stretches of minute black stones - which Eugene in his childhood believed was coal lost from a passing coal ship and reduced to a minute size through being crashed by the waves through time. To his left he saw the meandering little stream of water which ran off the hillside and onto the beach, but which was absorbed by the sands long before it ever reached the sea. The stream was something of a mecca for children through the generations who would build castles, harbours, and dams and no less so today as Eugene saw at least half a dozen children busy with their buckets and spades notwithstanding it was just after nine.

Eugene watched the activity for a short while and then made his way to the footpath intending to carry out the walk to St Ives. There were very smart beach chalets where the old beach huts had been, and here you could spend a week living on the beach at a level of luxury. The beach hut used to cost £14 a week and was good value as a shelter from the rain and a place to change away from the public gaze but otherwise basic. Eugene dreaded to think how much a week would cost in one of the chalets. On he walked, over the wooden footbridge and on along a partly made up road which led to the rear of large houses facing the bay. The front of those houses could be seen from the beach with their large scenic windows often glinting in the morning sun.

Eugene arrived at the point overlooking Porthminster beach; here one could look across to the rust red roofs of St Ives itself. There was seating here. Eugene admired the view, one depicted on countless postcards, and remembered standing there long ago with his mother. He started thinking about his mother, who tried so hard to give him a little holiday each year in this place, a mother who was gentle and kind, a mother whose love was absolutely unconditional, not only then, but now, too.

Eugene's mood had changed, he suddenly didn't even know why he was here, why he had come all this way. What was the purpose? All the facts and feelings of the past weeks returned to him; his stomach was churning, and he thought he might vomit. What was happening to him? What was going to happen to him? He felt alone, so terribly alone. There was only one person who would listen, only one person who would care, only one person who would not judge or condemn him. Why had he not gone to her instead of coming here? Eugene could feel his breathing becoming more rapid, he was starting to perspire, he could feel his whole body shaking. 'Not here, please not here,' he thought. How could he cope with a full blown panic attack here?

Eugene sat on the bench closed his eyes and started to breathe deeply and slowly. The symptoms fortunately started to subside, and he was able to prevent the panic attack reaching a crescendo. He placed his head in his hands. After a moment he looked up and saw a middle-aged couple looking at him. The woman went to say something but didn't and both walked quickly away. Eugene gave out a large sigh.

After a little while Eugene felt composed enough to continue his walk into St Ives and did so.

Eugene spent the morning wandering around the narrow streets and alleyways of St Ives which were for the most part crowded with holiday makers wearing T shirts often emblazoned with bizarre, banal, or inappropriate slogans, ill-fitting shorts, and sandals displaying ugly and neglected feet. Wandering somewhat aimlessly about eating – they always seemed to be eating: sweets or the ubiquitous Cornish pasty, ice cream, not helping in many cases, their existing obesity.

Eugene meandered, too, in that aimless fashion where time became something of an irrelevance. He looked in art shops, knick-knack shops, clothes shops and during the early afternoon stopped at a café on the harbour front. After sitting he remembered that this was at a previous time, in a sort of previous life, an arcade centre. Eugene recalled sitting outside and wanting to go in to spend coins on the various slot machines. As he stirred his americano, the memory of that day came flooding back. His mother had declined his request to go into the arcade and Eugene had become very angry, almost to a hysterical level. He was shouting, crying, demanding to go. His mother remained calm but issued a firm, 'No.'

Eugene, with pangs of guilt, remembered shouting in a loud voice, people looking, some laughing others more serious, "I hate you; I hate you; I want you dead."

He recalled the hurt look on his mother's face as she opened up her arms drew him close and said quietly in his ear, "I love you Eugene, I love you more than you will ever know."

He could almost feel the firm embrace; an embrace that lasted until he had calmed himself.

When he had, his mother said, "Let's go and get an ice cream, and let's be careful of the seagulls!"

Eugene could feel the tears welling up into his eyes as he recalled the event. As they sat and ate their ices he remembered his mother saying, "You and me Eugene, we're a team. No matter what happens we're a team, and no one can hurt us. Sadly, your dad is no longer with us, so it's just us two and so our little team needs to be a strong one."

Eugene had not thought of that story for an awfully long time. And, he hadn't, of course, maintained that wise philosophy. He had not been a team with his mother or his wife and child. His 'team' had been his police colleagues - colleagues who didn't care about him now or even think about him, let alone support him. Eugene drank his now cold coffee and regretted the fact that he had made such a mess of his life.

Leaving the café Eugene resumed meandering, not really taking in much of what he saw. He started to walk back the way he had come. He went into a chemist shop and purchased some indigestion liquid, and a little further on he entered a small shop where he was able to purchase a half bottle of Bell's whisky. He walked further on to where the buses stopped. There was a single decker bus there which indicated the destination 'A17 Penzance via St Erth'. Eugene could see the driver sitting on a bench near to the bus and enquired if the bus would be stopping at Carbis Bay.

The driver said that it would. Looking at his watch he continued by saying it would be eighteen minutes before departure. Eugene joined the driver on the bench, but they didn't talk any further except when boarding Eugene asked the driver to stop at the stop nearest the beach. The driver nodded his head.

The bus stopped on the main St Ives Road and the driver said to Eugene, who was sitting near the front, "This is your stop. Just walk along and take the next turning on the left; that'll take you down to the beach."

Eugene thanked the driver and as the bus drove away, he followed the drivers instructions turning into Porthrepta Road, which was a downhill route toward the beach. Eugene vaguely remembered the road from before.

Walking on he saw a church in the distance he walked toward it and as he got near he saw it was a church built in granite and probably not that old although it had a traditional church style. He read the blue board with white lettering situated at the entrance. The board read "St Anta and All Saints" and indicated that it was a Church of England church and detailed the service times. He didn't think that the church would be open, and in any case he hadn't been inside a church for a long time. As a youth he had been an altar boy and server at his local church. However, in his late teens, he felt that he had fallen out with God. He really hadn't thought about God very much apart from the little deals he secretly made. If I get through this I will go to church, and so on. But in reality, religion, God, and the trappings of such had become for him meaningless.

They hadn't even had Katie baptised, much to the distress of Eugene's mother, Sandra had said that it would be better for Katie to decide for herself when she was older. But here, today standing outside this granite church with its imposing square tower, he started to think about God in a different light. Was he not the God of those in distress, those abandoned, those who were rejected? He felt rejected, but wasn't Jesus also rejected? Perhaps it was time, time to make his peace with God and not only to make peace, but to ask for, and accept God's own enveloping peace, he certainly felt he needed it.

He slowly walked toward the door which was in a stone porchway halfway along the outer wall of the building. The heavy wooden door was shut. Eugene turned the black iron handle which had a twisted shape to it. He felt a heavy bolt lift on the other side which made a metallic clunk. He pushed the door, and with a resounding creak he was in the church transept. There were two aisles. The one nearest to him had traditional pews toward the altar and single chairs toward the back. On the opposite side of the aisle there were arches the length of the church and beyond the arches another aisle which was devoid of chairs or pews. There were a number of tables upon which were piled flowers of all descriptions and boxes of fruit and vegetables. There were about half a dozen late middle-aged and elderly women, some wore hats, and all were dressed in aprons. As Eugene entered the building they all stopped what they were doing, which appeared to be arranging flowers into pots and upon stands. They all looked in his direction; they didn't say anything and had fixed stares with not a flicker of a smile or any emotion at all.

Eugene had the feeling that he was an unwelcome intruder. He sat on a pew near to the door and some distance from the women, looking ahead toward the altar at the front of the church and fixed his stare upon a large brass cross. He started to think about his situation, which with every passing hour was becoming more and more desperate. He wanted to say the Lord's prayer and closed his eyes, starting to assemble the words in his mind, but his thinking was disturbed by one of the women calling out, "Father!"

Eugene opened his eyes; two of the women were continuing to stare in his direction, the others had resumed their work. He then saw a tall man, he must have been six feet four at least, and as thin as a rake walking toward him with long strides. In fact he seemed to only take three or four strides to cross the church and end up in the pew in front of Eugene towering over him. He was a man of about Eugene's age, with what Eugene thought was a silly looking goatee beard. He was wearing a black cassock over which was a tatty brown cardigan which seemed out of keeping with the warm day.

Eugene noticed that the man wore a wedding ring but could tell nothing else about him from how he looked.

The priest said, "Um.. I'm Father John…um...the church isn't open at present…um…we are…perhaps you would like to know more about the church.".

Then he bounded toward the back of the church in three or four giant strides, grabbed a handful of leaflets and came back to Eugene, this time standing at his left side.

"Um.. take these, they'll tell you something about the church."

He gave Eugene the leaflets and Eugene placed them in his single use plastic bag which contained his whisky and indigestion liquid. Eugene noticed that the priest spoke with a public school accent with no hint of a regional source.

Father John continued, "Um…as I said, the church isn't open um…we're setting up for a fauna, flower, and vegetable show which we're holding tomorrow evening. Um...we're just here for that; the church is not really open."

Eugene wondered why this man addressed himself as 'Father', this did not appear to be an Anglo Catholic church, but he couldn't be bothered to ask.

"I just came in for some quiet and peace really. I've been having some experiences sort of thing, just trying to sort them out in my head."

Father John, who Eugene noticed was making minimal eye contact but was looking all around the church or up at church rafters when he spoke, paused, and then said, "Yes, well um... every experience has a purpose, often only knowable to God".

"Yes, very helpful," said Eugene sarcastically.

Father John then looked at his watch and said, "Um...yes well, do pray about these experiences of yours, um...I will remember you in my prayers.".

"Yes, that will be very satisfying," said Eugene as sarcastically as he could, but noticed that Father John was quite oblivious to sarcasm; it must have been that public school education that made him immune to it, thought Eugene.

"Yes, well um..."

"Yes I know," said Eugene, "The church isn't really open, and you're busy preparing for a fauna, flower, and vegetable show tomorrow evening".

"Yes, that's right," said Father John with more than a hint of relief in his voice.

"Why don't you join us then and perhaps we could chat over a coffee."

"I don't think so," said Eugene and added, "I'll be home by then."

"Oh, a visitor I see."

One of the flower arrangers then came halfway across the aisle where they were and obviously in an attempt to 'rescue' Father John said, "Can you come and help us with something Father?"

"Oh yes of course, Mrs Fletcher, this gentleman was just leaving." He then asked Eugene,

"What is your name?"

"Gene."

"Jean?" asked Father John with some emphasis.

"Eugene."

"Oh, Eugene! Yes, well…um…good to meet you um…Eugene…um.. safe journey home and God bless."

Father John was saying this as he almost ushered Eugene out of the door which he closed as soon as Eugene had crossed the threshold. Eugene heard the turn of a key locking the door against any other pilgrims who might venture by.

He walked slowly away and said aloud but to himself, "What an absolute wanker!"

As he continued his slow descent along Porthrepta Road the encounter with Father John reminded Eugene of why he had turned his back on the Church of England so many years ago and which in turn caused him to turn his back on God, and he realised that he regretted the latter now.

The Church of England described itself as a 'broad church' and included everything from a form of Catholicism verging on orthodox on the one extreme, to evangelical 'coffee shop' churches which pedal their middle-class values to those 'who don't do church' at the other. In between is the ubiquitous 'Tory party at prayer' stance, and all are marred by the inevitable cliques which form within them.

Those women at St Anta and All Saints were a typical clique of the Church of England thought Eugene, who wanted to maintain an inappropriate status quo, and in order to do so make any 'interloper' feel unwelcome or excluded. The Church of England tried to be all things to all people and ended up being not very much to anyone. An anaemic church that lacks much of a soul with a congregation that in many, if not most cases, further their own or local interests rather than applying themselves to the worship of their creator.

Eugene had made himself feel angry at the Church of England, which was not a new feeling but one which he had not encountered for a long time.

He said quietly to himself, "No, no help at all."

He arrived at the Anchors Rest and spoke to a middle aged woman with a stern face who had her spectacles perched at the end of her nose and was staring over them as a means of trying to make all who she peered at feel inferior. Eugene asked for his room key and arranged to again have tea and sandwiches in his room rather than take dinner in the dining room. Eugene ascended the stairs and noticed the black and white or sepia coloured photographs of Carbis Bay in earlier times. One which Eugene looked in detail at was of a steam locomotive at Carbis Bay with passengers alighting, a man in a uniform with a flat cap who must have been the Station Master, beside him a porter with an upright trolley and on the seaward side, where there are flats now, a beautifully tended garden with the words Carbis Bay picked out in flowering blooms. Eugene remembered the flowers but they and everything else in the photograph apart from the track and platform had now gone forever.

After a shower Eugene dressed in the white fluffy dressing gown which had been supplied in a thick sealed plastic bag. The feel of the gown was quite relaxing, and Eugene settled down in the light green winged and comfortable chair within the room. Eugene wasn't really thinking about that much and realised that he was experiencing a sense of peace, such a feeling for him now was not common and mostly not possible. He may have dozed off, he didn't quite know, but whether just relaxed or dosing, he heard a light knock on the door. The pleasant young lady who he had seen the day before and who had booked him in entered with a tray.

Eugene stood up, slightly embarrassed to be in a dressing gown but the young lady didn't seem at all phased. She placed the tray on the coffee table. Eugene noticed she was wearing a white shirt with a sort of lunji collar, a black skirt which appeared to be just a little too short, black tights which bore a torn hole on the inside of the left knee and cheap, worn, black shoes which bore a little tassel at the front.

"Will this be enough, sir?" asked the young lady.

"Yes, that's fine, thank you very much."

"Just ring down to reception if you need anything else, sir." And she left the room.

Eugene thought a little about her. Working long hours for a pittance, probably seasonal work, what did she do in the winter? Or perhaps she was at university and working through the summer to help pay her way. Where did she live? With her parents, perhaps, maybe in St Ives, Lelant or St Erth. He didn't know and didn't really care so stopped thinking about her. The tray had upon it two beef sandwiches, some horseradish sauce in a small dish, two ham and mustard sandwiches, a packet of ready salted crisps, a tea pot, a hot water jug and some milk. Eugene who had not eaten since breakfast, ate the beef sandwiches, had a cup of tea but left everything else. He just wasn't that hungry.

He turned on the TV in his room and flicked through the channels, but nothing interested him. He went through the radio channels and settled at Classic FM which he had playing softly. Time became something irrelevant for Eugene as he sat and contemplated his situation. He thought about his family, each in turn: his mother, Sandra, and Katie. He had the overwhelming feeling that he had so badly let them all down, but on the other hand he had not done anything out of the ordinary and what he had been accused of was untrue at least in the conscious sense.

He thought about Preston and Matthews and of how his situation would not impact upon them at all and of how they had probably forgotten about him for the time being. He thought about Dr Bekhit and Dr Dave Bennett and how they had let him down, of Karen Nicholls and the very efficient female custody sergeant. His thoughts returned to his daughter Katie, and he wished that he could contact her; he so wanted to, but knew that he couldn't and that she would probably not wish to hear from him anyway. He imagined what his court case would be like; he knew that the evidence was stacked against him. He thought about the jury and press staring at him not believing him, being judgemental from the start.

He thought about the sentence, it would have to be custodial and how would the prison service guarantee his safety? They couldn't, of course. He was, after all, a copper who was a nonce, probably the most despised of all criminals among criminals. He kept thinking about how it could be proved that he wasn't guilty?

He again thought of Katie and realised that it was she who he loved, she who he cared about most and she who he must fight to prove his innocence for. Eugene opened the Bell's whisky and got a glass from the bathroom. Removing the plastic covering he poured himself a good size shot. Eugene grabbed some paper from a maroon folder which contained old and worn leaflets describing what could be seen or visited in various parts of West Cornwall. There were three sheets of plain paper and Eugene started to write things down.

He thought the best way to deal with this was to imagine this was a case about someone else and he was supervising one of his detectives dealing with it. He started to think about every aspect of the case making trigger notes as he went. He didn't know how long he had been there but outside had grown dark. He pulled the curtains of the room and heard the announcer on the radio start reading the news. It was, in fact, midnight. Eugene worked on, time didn't matter – what mattered was examining objectively all the evidence against him as he knew it. He poured another good shot of whisky and carried on with his thoughts and trigger notes which he had to make in incredibly small writing to make the best use of limited space. Then quite suddenly Eugene stopped. He took a large intake of breath and just said, "No, no, no!"

How could he not have seen this before. He couldn't believe what he had discovered. Eugene sat for a while, not thinking, no emotion just totally blank. He then arose and got dressed. He changed into the clothes that he had travelled in: grey slacks, sports jacket, shirt, and tie. He put his shoes on and gathered what he wanted to take with him. He took out the indigestion liquid and drank from the bottle. He placed the whisky bottle in his jacket pocket and his other essentials into his other pocket. He picked up his room keys, switched off the radio and lights and made his way ever so quietly downstairs. He was carrying the notes that he had made. Descending to reception he saw the area was lit with a soft light but there was no one about. The clock in the hall indicated at it was 2:05 Eugene placed his room keys on the reception desk and quietly opened the heavy front door.

He went outside and gave a slight shudder as the cold night air met him. He looked across at Godrevy Lighthouse - he could just pick it out in the moonlight. He noticed the flash of light but was aware that the actual lighthouse light no longer shines out and the pulsating light currently emanates from an LED positioned somewhere near the lighthouse. A pity he thought. Eugene didn't know why he started thinking about that when he had more pressing thoughts. He walked out of Headland Road and down the hill toward the beach. All the streetlights were out at this time, but the road was adequately lit by the moon.

Eugene looked up and saw the moon shinning just above a fluffy grey cloud and it appeared to Eugene as if a great gold coin was being pushed into a lump of grey and dirty cotton wool.

"The moon is like a great gold penny hanging in the sky, I want to go and take it down, and roll it all the way to town, and buy and buy and buy."

Something his mother used to say when he was very young whenever they saw a full moon. He walked on, past the house with the revolving shiny cowl which was picking up the moonlight just as it had picked up the sun earlier that day.

Eugene walked the treacherous concrete path leading to the beach. He could see the little stream unheeded by children's dams making its way across the sand, looking like a silver metal band in the moonlight and disappearing long before it met the sea. Eugene looked at the sea which was like an expanse of dark blue - Quink ink with little white tufts here and there. The sea appeared to be quite calm. Eugene sat on the concrete step at the side of the café adjacent to the sand. He listened to the regular yet soft crash of the sea upon the shore, a relaxing sound.

He started to drink from the bottle of whisky and in between swigs would place a number of amitriptyline tablets in his hand which he would then swallow. Thoughts again started to permeate his mind. They were almost uncontrollable. He was beginning to feel drunk from the whisky. He started to think about the young lady at the Anchor's Rest, a receptionist, waitress, dog's body he didn't know. But what he did know was that at this moment he fancied her more than any woman at any time. He thought about her chunky legs in the black tights with a hole torn at the knee. He imagined removing them and caressing her legs looking up into her once plain but now rapturous face, of him moving his hands beneath her white blouse and feeling her fleshy breasts. Hearing her moan with pleasure as she lifted her chunky legs and draped them over his shoulders. Eugene could feel himself becoming aroused and even wanted to relieve himself whilst contemplating a sexual encounter with the young woman. But, as quickly as they had come, the erotic thoughts subsided.

He took another swig of whisky and more tablets. He felt more drunk, got to his feet but was very unsteady. He went to a rubbish bin nearby and threw in an empty pill box, another box containing some tablets and the paper sheets with the trigger notes that he had torn into pieces. Eugene filled his pockets with stones and bits of the concrete path, he then walked onto the beach and turned right. He walked along the dry sand with each step getting more difficult and requiring more effort. He heard a rushing noise then, out of the dark they came, dark distorted but recognisable faces from the recent past all talking or screaming, all accusing.

Like Dali's clocks they were changing shape like rubber or melting plastic. He saw Matthews face.

"I've been appointed by the Deputy Chief Constable to carry out an investigation..."

Sandra's, "That bloody job, that cancer that has taken over my life as well as yours..."

"My husband here has punched me in the stomach..."

Katie, her little distorted face screaming, "I hate the fucking police...I hate you."

The efficient female custody sergeant, "Place Mr Elphick in cell 17..."

Louder and louder they became.

Eugene drank the last of the whisky, threw the bottle onto the sand and placed his hands over his ears. Music, there was music, too.

He could hear Amy Winehouse with her jazz singer voice, *"I go out by myself and look across the water..."*

Eugene felt a little steadier and looked to see that he was now on wet sand. It seemed easier to walk but he was beginning to feel so very tired.

Leonard Cohen chipped in, *"I guess I miss you. I guess I forgive you."*

So many voices all competing with each other. That vile uniformed inspector's face came into view and his distorted voice issued, "Not you love, this is a bit too gruesome for you."

Eugene felt the wet sand tugging at his right shoe which came off, his right sock coming into contact with the wet sand made him shiver for a moment.

He mumbled in a slurred manner, "Not far now...I just want to lay down and sleep now....But I know, I know, and it hurts."

The voices became softer more friendly and less accusing.

He saw Benji's distorted but smiling face, "What's the score Gene...?" Eugene tried to answer but couldn't.

The frightening sound of Preston's distorted voice came into his hearing and as it did so, Eugene entered the water, he felt his trousers absorb the water like a sponge but on he walked.

Preston continued softly, "Eugene we're both police officers, both detectives..."

Leonard was back with his deep almost subterranean baritone voice, full of mature and mournful pessimism. Dark, like aged mahogany, *"There's a blaze of light in every word it doesn't matter what you heard the holy or the broken hallelujah."*

He no longer felt the coldness of the water, it was warm like a bath. He just wanted to lay down and did so. There was the young lady from the Anchor's Rest.

"Just ring down to reception if you need anything else, sir."

Her face looked beautiful, she opened her mouth seductively and said softly, "Fuck me, fuck me now, sir."

Katie came into view, she looked so young her face distorted, red, and tearstained, "I wish you would trust me…I love you Daddy."

Eugene went to say, I love you, too, but his mouth and nose filled with salt water. He went down under the sea but didn't feel afraid. He couldn't breathe, but it didn't seem to matter. He could hear Leonard Cohen, but he seemed a long way away, as if he were in a tunnel.

"And Jesus was a sailor when he walked upon the water…and when he knew for certain only drowning me could see him…"

Eugene could see the recognisable faces of Katie and his mother although they too seemed a long way away.

Katie spoke first. She was no longer crying, good.

"Hi Dad, great game. I scored. Have a good day. Love you."

Again Eugene tried to reply to his daughter but couldn't.

His mother then said in a soft and loving voice, "We will come back again."

There were colours many of them, and then brightness, sheer whiteness really. Eugene could only think "Wow!" and then blackness, the blackest he could ever know but somewhere, somewhere out there, someone was calling his name.

CHAPTER 17

Stephen Miners tended to walk his dog early on the beach. He was aware that dogs should not be exercised there during the summer months but didn't care that much. The dog did not shit in the sand much, but if it did he would pick it up. This morning he had found an empty half whisky bottle and cursed the thoughtless creature who had left it there. He placed it in his pocket to discard in a bin later. So stupid, it would smash and perhaps injure a child's foot, it didn't bear thinking about.

He continued with his walk. He could hear his wire haired fox terrier barking at something it had seen in the sea. Stephen could see something, a log perhaps it looked like one, but where did it come from? He walked closer and stopped suddenly, his heart started pounding, and he could see that it was a body lying face down in the water.

The sea was calm, and the body which was fully dressed was just slightly bobbing up and down and not too far out. Stephen spoke calmly to his dog and started to wade into the sea. He got to a point where the sea was about waist height where he was able to grab the collar of the person's jacket and start to bring the body back toward the beach. As the body grounded on the sand it suddenly became very heavy and it was all Stephen could do to just bring it out of the water. He turned the body over and could see that it was a man of about his own age, in his forties. What resonated with Stephen most was that the man was smiling the most contented serene and kind smile he had ever seen.

Stephen searched for his mobile phone which luckily was in the top pocket of his shirt. He didn't always carry it but was glad that he had done so today. He dialled 999 and an operator answered immediately. Stephen asked for the police and ambulance and explained what he had found. The operator asked for his details and asked him to stay where he was. He gave his precise location.

"If they come into the car park, past the café onto the beach and turn right they'll see me well enough."

He completed the call, and waited, after turning the body into the recovery position although he knew very well that whoever it was, was dead and had been so for a while. He just thought it would be more respectful.

It wasn't long before Stephen heard the sound of a siren and saw a flashing blue light descending the steep hill to the beach. Shortly after the siren noise had ceased he saw two persons in green paramedic uniforms running across the sand toward him. As they drew closer he could see that they were female, and one was carrying a large green holdall.

On getting to him one said, slightly out of breath, "Good morning, when did you come across this person?"

The other paramedic had gone to the body and had turned it on to its back and was examining it.

"I don't know, about twenty minutes ago now I think, just before I made the emergency call. He was floating face down about 20 or 30 yards out in the sea. I pulled him in. I knew he was dead. I put him in the recovery position."

"Thank you. Have you asked for the police as well?"

"Yes."

The two paramedics continued to examine the body. After a short time Stephen saw a police officer making his way across the sand towards them. He didn't seem to have the same sense of urgency that the paramedics had, but why would he? The police officer introduced himself as Police Constable Herbert from St Ives police station. He spoke briefly to the paramedics and then started to ask Stephen lots of questions. PC Herbert was an experienced officer and knew what to do.

At the Anchors Rest the owner, Derek Trewerne, was opening the heavy front door of the guest house when he heard the siren of an emergency vehicle which seemed to be travelling down Beach Road toward the beach. He returned to the reception desk and saw the keys to Room 4 had been placed there. He hung them on their hook and thought that the occupant had decided upon an early start. It was no big deal because they had the credit card details and would charge the card as normal. Derek went into the kitchen to help prepare for breakfast.

Carol Penhaligon, the young lady who had served Eugene his supper the night before, arrived at work in something of an excited state.

She burst into the kitchen and said to all present, "You'd never guess what, my friend at the Carbis Bay hotel, you know Emily, called me to say that there are loads of police and ambulances on the beach. She said they've found a body and it must be a murder."

Derek mumbled, "I heard a siren going down the hill earlier."

Not much else was said and each got on with their respective work tasks. But each continued to wonder just what had happened down there on the beach.

After the morning rush of breakfast and check outs the staff at the Anchor's Rest would stop for a well-deserved coffee break before they tackled the cleaning of the rooms. Derek Trewerne would retreat to his small office at the rear of reception for his coffee and a read of the paper. Before doing so today he asked Carol to deal with room 4 first as the guest had left early. Before long Carol had reappeared at the office door, she looked a little pale.

"What's wrong?" enquired Derek.

"All his stuff is still there, wallet, phone, clothes everything."

"Show me."

They both went to room 4. It was just as Carol had said.

"You don't think it's him do you, Derek?" she asked in nervous manner and Derek could see her hands were shaking a little.

"I don't know but it could be. We'd better leave everything as it is for the moment. I'll call the police."

Carol went to retrieve the previous night's dinner tray upon which were a couple of sandwiches and an unopened packet of crisps.

But Derek said, "No, leave it as it is, Carol".

There was a cursory look at the scene by a Detective Sergeant and a Detective Constable from Penzance, during which time PC Herbert took a statement from Stephen Miners. The body was photographed by a Scenes of Crime officer. PC Herbert supervised the collection of the body from the beach. The undertakers would take it to the Royal Cornwall Hospital mortuary in Truro as for the moment a post-mortem and an inquest would be required. PC Herbert then made his way to the Anchor's Rest as instructed by his control room. On arrival he saw Derek Trewerne who gave PC Herbert details of Eugene's stay, his home address and credit card details. He also showed PC Herbert Eugene's room and how it was left. PC Herbert set about bagging up and labelling all Eugene's property. He then took statements from Derek and Carol, a process which caused Carol some anxiety. By the time all this had taken place PC Herbert was near the end of his shift. He spoke to his control room and was told to take everything to the Coroner's Officer in Penzance who had been briefed.

There followed communication by way of email between Devon & Cornwall Constabulary and Thames Valley Police which resulted in PC Martin, a young policeman just out of his probationary period, making his way from his patrol in Windsor to an address in Old Windsor. Having received all the information, he was aware that he might have to deliver a death message, which was something he had done before but something he didn't relish. On the way PC Martin practiced what he might say. Arriving at the address in Old Windsor PC Martin found that there was no reply to his persistent knocking. There was a car in the driveway which he did a PNC check on – the details of which came back with Eugene Elphick of that address being the owner.

PC Martin then went across the road to the house directly opposite, the owner of which opened the front door before PC Martin got to it. He was confronted by a man of around 70 years of age, clean shaven and casually dressed. The man looked up and down the road and invited PC Martin inside. The man then started the conversation.

"I saw you at Mr Elphick's address. I haven't seen him this week at all." He was rubbing his hands in ghoulish anticipation.

PC Martin asked the necessary questions and then the man eagerly volunteered the information, "You know he's in the police, don't you?"

PC Martin was astonished as this fact was revealed.

The man continued, "Oh yes, he's been in a bit of trouble. It was in the local papers. Downloading porn if I remember rightly. I thought you were there for something to do with that."

The man seemed to relish the divulging of these facts and was intrigued that the officer in front of him clearly knew nothing about it.

PC Martin thanked the man and returned to his police vehicle, revealing what he had learned to his control room. Armed with other information gained from the man PC Martin then made his way to the GP's surgery in Old Windsor. He found that Mrs Elphick wasn't there but was given an address in Stoke Poges in Slough where she might be. He again contacted his control room, gave full details and was told to return to his patrol in Windsor. PC Martin had a sense of relief that he didn't have to deliver the death message after all but couldn't help thinking about the whole situation. He found that he was in no way judgemental of the man who had drowned in Cornwall, but wondered about what had led up to what had occurred.

Having been given information which he checked fully the control room inspector briefed Police Sergeant Pither. Sergeant Pither was an experienced police officer of over 20 years' service and had probably delivered a score of death messages in his time, and the fact that this related to a police officer did not perturb him too much. It was not long before Sergeant Pither was standing in a reception room in a large, detached house in Stoke Poges.

The elderly man who had answered the door had gone to summon his daughter, Sandra. After a few moments, a woman of about 40 years, of sallow complexion and without any make up entered the room.

"Hello, I'm Sandra Elphick. My father said that you wanted to speak to me. Please sit down, sergeant."

Both sat and Sergeant Pither, who knew it best to deliver sad news quickly, said, "Mrs Elphick, I have some sad news. I am sorry to inform you that your husband, Eugene, would appear to have drowned in Cornwall. He was found on the beach at Carbis Bay this morning."

Sandra gave a short sharp intake of breath and said, "What do you mean, appears to have drowned?"

Sergeant Pither realised that his wording had been clumsy and said, "We're ninety nine percent sure, but enquiries are ongoing."

He went on to explain what had been found in Room 4 at the Anchor's Rest and the enquiries that had already taken place there. Sandra listened to what Sergeant Pither was saying; she felt numb and although she could hear his words she couldn't really take everything in. Sandra's mother came into the room briefly, but Sandra said quite brusquely, "Not now Mum, please," and her mother left the room.

Sandra then said in a very soft tone, "Do you think that he may have taken his own life?"

The sergeant replied, echoing the softness of Sandra's tone, "It's looking that way."

Sandra could feel a burning in her throat. She didn't want to lose control, not in front of the officer, but couldn't help it and started to cry softly.

Sergeant Pither gave her a moment and then said, "Should I call your mother?"

Sandra composed herself, "No, no it's alright. I just don't know what I should do now."

"If you can give me your contact number I'll pass this to the Coroner's Office in Penzance who are dealing."

Sandra gave her mobile number and the house landline number.

Sergeant Pither continued, "I'll inform the Police Federation office and they'll be in contact with you. Both they and the Coroner's Officer, both down there and here, will guide you and I have no doubt the Federation will give you practical support."

Sergeant Pither then gave Sandra a piece of paper with the Coroner's Officer's and Federation telephone numbers written on it. Sandra took the paper but was silent.

"Is there anything else I can do for you now, Mrs Elphick?"

"No, no. I now have to inform my daughter, and Gene's mother and that isn't going to be easy; his mother lives in Dorset, you see, and she's getting on a bit."

"I could have her informed by Dorset Police if you wish," Sergeant Pither suggested helpfully.

"No, I'll do it, but thank you."

Sandra showed Sergeant Pither out and he left, keeping his promise to inform the parties that he had mentioned. As he got back into his police car Sergeant Pither couldn't help but think, "Poor woman, having to contend with that bastard's vile offending behaviour and now, what looks like his suicide. Poor cow."

Sandra's mother appeared as Sergeant Pither left.

"Is it something to do with Eugene?" she enquired.

Sandra replied in an irritated tone, "Yes, I'll speak to you and Dad shortly. I want to make a telephone call and I will do that from my car."

"Why…?"

But Sandra was already on her way to her car. Irene Elphick's number was stored in Sandra's phone and although she initially hesitated, and wished that she had taken Sergeant Pither's offer of the Dorset Police doing this, she proceeded to call the number.

Mrs Elphick answered with a cheery, "Hello."

Sandra spoke, and said what she needed to say.

*

It had been a long and exhausting day and Sandra now lay beside her daughter, who was at last peacefully sleeping with one of Sandra's arms wrapped around her shoulder. Sandra, despite the stress, the emotion, and the chaos was not at all tired, and could not even contemplate sleep. She went over the events of the day from the point of contact with Sergeant Pither. She thought about him and wondered if he knew Eugene or not. He seemed to be a man of experience and Eugene had served at Slough twice, both as a constable and inspector. But he didn't say, so probably not.

She thought about Eugene. She wondered why he was there at that place; maybe it was as his mother had said, planning some holiday or something. She wondered about him and although she felt moved and sorry she could not bring herself to grieve in the conventional sense. She did cry in front of Sergeant Pither, but she was of the opinion that this was more to do with the shock of the moment than a reaction to loss. Sandra felt that this lack of distress, this lack of lament was strange in the circumstances. Perhaps, it was to do with the fact that she had to remain strong for Katie's sake, she had to remain in control, and there was so much that would need to be done. She didn't quite know. Maybe it was because she didn't love Eugene that she couldn't grieve for him; she just didn't know.

Katie gave a little sigh as she shifted her position in Sandra's arm which enveloped her shoulder. She recalled that dreadful moment when she informed Katie and her parents of the awful news, of Katie's loud piercing screams which sounded like an animal in great distress, of her throwing herself on the floor, adopting a foetal position and muttering between screams and gasps for breath, "My daddy, my daddy."

Sandra never wanted to witness such pained distress in anyone ever again.

She thought of her mother wailing and not knowing what to do. The stoic calmness of her elderly father who bodily picked Katie off the floor, sat down continuing to hold her tightly despite Katie's screams, her shouting and punching her 'Gramps' hard in the chest, him continuing to gently speak into her ear, telling her she was safe, that her family were here and that they all loved her. Over and over he repeated it until he felt that he was unable to achieve the desired result and still holding her, asked Sandra's mum to call Dr Clive Pitman, a semi-retired doctor and friend who lived locally. He was informed of Katie's condition and what gave rise to it and was asked to attend in a private capacity, which he did.

Sandra thought about her father continuing to hold Katie, still gently rocking her, and speaking to her, with noticeable tears rolling down his face and dripping onto the back of Katie's pink cardigan.

Dr Pitman, a man of about the same age as her father had attended and Sandra reflected on his kind face, calmness and understanding, of the reassuring way in which he spoke to Katie who had stopped crying and sat up but still on her grandfather's lap when Dr Pitman spoke to her. Dr Pitman had given Katie an injection of Promethazine, which he said was an antihistamine which was safe for a child of her age, and which would allow her to sleep probably well into the next morning.

He also gave Sandra a tablet to give Katie on the outside chance that she might wake up during the night. She recalled how Katie became more placid, how her eyelids seemed too heavy for her and of how she drifted into sleep. Sandra thought about her father carrying Katie up to bed and knew that the task would not have been easy for him, but he did it and placed her onto Sandra's bed. Sandra partly undressed her, darkened the room, and allowed her to sleep.

She recalled then telling her parents that Eugene may well have taken his own life and the short intake of breath given by her mother, who was of a generation where suicide was still, to a great extent, stigmatised. Her father had been a rock, and from today she began to see her father in a new light and without him, especially today, she would not have known what to do.

He just said to Sandra and her mother, "We'll get through all this together."

Sandra thought about Irene Elphick, Eugene's mum, and wondered what she was doing at that precise moment, much like her she thought, but perhaps her thoughts would be more focussed on Eugene.

Sandra wondered why she was not feeling those feelings that a spouse should feel when they have lost their partner: feelings of anger, of rage, despair, overwhelming guilt, helplessness, hopelessness shame, regret. Where were they? All Sandra could feel was a numbness in herself and pity for her daughter, precious little else. And, what about those 'What If's?' that her imagination should be dreaming up, but seemed reluctant or incapable of doing so. The only 'What If?' she could come up with was, 'What if Eugene and I had never met in the first place?' But she quickly dismissed this from her mind because without him there would be no Katie. She continued to muse on 'What If? "What If she had gone to university?' 'What if she had stuck with David Osborne?' "What if?' 'What if?' 'What If? 'What...'

CHAPTER 18

Dave Matthews entered the main office at the Professional Standards Department, Kidlington, in a pleasant mood. He knew that there were only 15 working days left and then he would be able to retire and do all the things that he and his wife had planned. He had no regrets. He wished his civilian office staff a cheery good morning and entered his office. His in-tray had just a few thin files therein for him to peruse, nothing very much it would seem. He sat back in his chair and felt good to be alive.

The telephone rang and Dave answered with a genial, "Superintendent Dave Matthews how may I help?"

"Hi Dave, it's Mike Tadman."

Mike Tadman was the Chief Superintendent Operations; he was technically in charge of the Professional Standards Department, but the Deputy Chief Constable kept his finger on the pulse of the ongoing work of the department, and Tadman dealt with more personnel type issues.

" Are you able to pop across and see me?"

"Yes, yes sir I can. When would you like me to come over?" asked Dave.

"Soon as possible Dave, are you able to come now?"

"Yes sir, I'll be right over."

Dave wasn't fazed by the request at all and assumed that it was something to do with his impending retirement. Within five minutes Dave was welcomed into Tadman's office. Tadman started the conversation.

"Not long now Dave is it, are you having a bit of a send-off?"

"No sir, not long, fifteen working days and yes, just a few drinks and nibbles at The Royal Sun on the Woodstock Road."

"Great, I may pop in."

"You're welcome, sir," said Dave knowing full well that Tadman would not come. Especially so as he didn't ask when or at what time.

"Now," started Tadman, "I had that Inspector Preston in here the other day. He came here to propose the idea that when you retired we should consider making the team leads chief inspectors rather than superintendents and more or less indicated that he'd be right for the job. He then went on to bad mouth you about the Elphick case. I wasn't impressed."

Dave Matthews was not that surprised at what he was hearing. He had never considered Preston as particularly loyal and knew that he would do anything to put himself in a good light.

"I'm sorry to hear that, sir," said Dave Matthews.

"No Dave, I wasn't insinuating I was less than impressed with you. I was less than impressed with him – disloyal traitorous bastard." He paused and then said, "You're on the square aren't you Dave?"

"Um.. yes, yes I am, um.. Didcot lodge."

"Yes, I thought so. I'm at Wallingford. But us brothers must look after each other, Dave. We're not as powerful in this organisation as we were, but we should be seeking to help one another out when we can."

Dave Matthews remained silent. He wasn't an active Freemason and had only joined at the insistence of his father-in-law many years ago, but he went to meetings occasionally.

Tadman was on a roll and continued, "I hadn't told you before because I wanted to make a few enquiries and I can now tell you that when you retire we'll be reorganising Professional Standards but not in the way Preston envisaged. When you leave we'll reduce the investigation teams from three to two and one team will benefit from one, and the other two civilian staff to assist with statement and admin tasks. You'll not be replaced, and we've decided that Preston will be transferred to Cowley uniform as a shift inspector."

Tadman was silent and Dave Matthews, in order to puncture the silence, merely said, "He won't like that."

Tadman said, "Good. Dave, I'm going to give you the pleasure of informing him."

Tadman passed a sheaf of papers to Dave Matthews. He continued, "Dave, I've some unpleasant news to share with you. It's Detective Inspector Elphick, who was suspended pending a Crown Court appearance and you're familiar with that. I'm afraid to say that he was found drowned in Cornwall yesterday morning. The full details aren't known but it would appear that he may have taken his own life."

Dave Matthews was again silent. He thought about Elphick and the last time that he saw him at Maidenhead police station. He immediately thought that perhaps he could have at least been a little more compassionate in his approach.

"I'm very sad to hear that, sir."

"Yes, as I said we don't yet know the details. You'll need to close down the file inform the Crown Court and we will need a full report from the inquest. I don't want Preston swanning off down there. Get him to liaise with the coroners officer in..." he paused to look at an email message, "in Penzance. We'll need a full and detailed report following the inquest, which will need to be sent to the Deputy. I'll forward this email to you which is all the information that we've got at present."

"Yes, sir thank you."

"That's it for now, Dave. I'll see you again before your depart. Thanks very much."

"Thank you, sir," and Dave Matthews made his way back to his office.

When Sandra awoke she could see that her daughter Katie was still sleeping peacefully, now on her side and facing away from her, but clearly remaining in a deep sleep. Sandra quickly washed and put on her dressing gown, and made her way downstairs. It was early and she could hear that someone was up before her. On entering the large kitchen she saw her mother sat at the oak table, a family feature of many years where many discussions some happy, some sad, and some heated had all taken place. She thought that her mother looked a diminutive figure dressed in her floral housecoat against the expanse of the oak table.

"Tea?" she enquired, and Sandra nodded her head.

As they waited for the kettle to boil her mother looked lovingly at her daughter and said quietly, "How are you, my love?"

Sandra nodded and whatever she was going to say was interrupted by the loud shrill of the whistling kettle. The tea was made, and a steaming mug was given to Sandra.

"How's Katie?" asked her mother.

"She's still sleeping very soundly; she had a good night. She didn't wake up at all."

"And you?" asked her mother.

"Yes, I slept a little, fits and starts you know, but I did sleep a little."

They both clasped their hands around their respective mugs seeking the comfort of the warmth.

"I can't grieve Mum, I just can't, I'm unable to."

"It's been a great shock to us all Sandra and especially you. You will grieve; maybe it'll take a little time."

"I think I'd feel better if I could."

Her mother nodded in a seemingly knowing manner.

"Would you like to see our local priest? Your dad knows him quite well; he could ask him to call."

"No, thank you, Mum," said Sandra defiantly,

"I may not have lost faith in God, but I've certainly lost faith in the Church. I don't want some languid creature here muttering their insincere and insipid platitudes, I really don't."

"OK, I understand."

The conversation was interrupted by slippered feet being slid somewhat laboriously across the floor. Katie appeared looking drowsy with untidy hair.

Sandra placed her arms around Katie and asked, "OK?"

Katie nodded and replied, "OK, just very tired."

Her grandma enquired, "Breakfast?"

Katie said to no one in particular, "I'm very thirsty." and her grandma supplied a large glass of orange juice almost immediately. Gramps joined them, and breakfast was eaten with no mention being made of the previous day's events during the meal, much of which was taken in silence.

After she'd had a shower and got dressed Sandra's mother informed her that there had been a call from a police officer in Penzance requesting that she call back. Her mother gave her the number written on a piece of paper. Sandra already had the number and when she had sorted herself out, she called. She spoke to a man who introduced himself as PC Cooper and said he was a coroners officer. He expressed condolences to Sandra in a well-practiced way and then told her that Eugene's body was at the mortuary at the Royal Cornwall Hospital, Truro, and that a post-mortem examination would be carried out on the following morning.

He explained the purpose of the post-mortem and went on to say that an inquest would take place at a later date, again in Truro. PC Cooper explained things in detail in a calm, and Sandra thought, reassuring voice. He then said that there needed to be an identification of Eugene's body and that needed to be done by someone who knew him well, who had seen him recently, and who could attend Truro to carry out the identification by appointment. He said that he realised that Sandra lived a considerable distance away and asked if there was anyone closer who could carry out the identification. Sandra said that there wasn't and that she would attend.

PC Cooper asked if she could do that as soon as possible and she said she would let him know when she could attend. She noticed PC Cooper's tone change slightly. Rather than being focussed on her and her needs he became very much focussed on the process of identification, asking her when she could attend several times. Sandra said that she would need to check when she could attend and again would get back to him. PC Cooper started to sound a little impatient and said that he would prefer that the identification be carried out during the following week so that the inquest could take place soon afterwards. Sandra reiterated that she would call him back. After the phone call Sandra sat in an armchair feeling quite exhausted by the call and at the same time knowing that many exhausting hours were yet to come.

It wasn't long before Sandra's mobile telephone indicated an incoming call. She answered and the caller gave his name as Inspector Mike Parsons; he said that he was from the Police Federation and that he would like to visit Sandra that afternoon at two if possible. Sandra said that it would be, and that she was staying at her parents' house and gave Mike Parsons the address along with the post code for his sat nav. Sandra then wanted to spend time with her daughter and parents for at least a few hours and switched her phone off.

Dave Matthews could not get the thoughts of Eugene Elphick and what had happened in Cornwall out of his head. He went over and over the events and the interactions that he and Preston had had with Elphick. He thought about Elphick's family, his wife and daughter who he had seen albeit briefly on the first meeting with Elphick at Elphick's home. He thought about the way that he and Preston had handled Elphick. He was quite aware that perhaps things could have been handled differently, perhaps more gently, certainly so in Preston's case. That said, he recalled that he had done nothing to curtail Preston's ruthless unfeeling approach.

Matthews knew that there would be some sort of enquiry - here we had a suspended, fairly senior officer, committing suicide and there would be questions as to why. There was talk in the job, always talk, of a not having a 'blame culture' but Matthews, and everyone else for that matter, were fully aware that such a culture existed and would always exist. Where errors, mistakes, neglect and so on occurred someone would have to be blamed. And, after all it was errors, mistakes and neglect that were his bread and butter as a Professional Standards Superintendent. But what concerned Matthews was the question, 'was he to blame in any way?' So, rather than thinking about the demise of a brother officer in any humanistic way Matthews started to examine events from the perspective of whether or not any blame could be attributed to him. Had he, David Matthews, in any way contributed to the death of Eugene Elphick? He didn't think so, and hoped not, especially at this juncture in his career.

Dave looked at his watch; there were fifteen minutes before Preston was due to come and see him. He made himself a cup of tea and planned what he was going to say to the man.

Mike Parsons had some difficulty in finding the address in Stoke Podges, he didn't know the greater Slough area well but nevertheless arrived at the address a mere five minutes late. Following his knock, the door was opened by Sandra who showed Mike Parsons into the reception room that was quickly becoming a reception room for visiting policemen. Mike Parsons gave his condolences and presented Sandra with a cheque for £2,500 which was from the Police Federation and, as Parsons said, to cover any immediate expenses that Sandra might have.

"I realise this is a difficult time for you, Sandra, and I don't want to intrude but is there anything else I can help you with?"

Sandra hesitated but then said, "Well, I was speaking earlier to a PC Cooper in Penzance in Cornwall. He said he was the Coroner's Officer. He explained things like the need for a post mortem and said there was a need for someone to identify Gene. There's no one really except me and he wanted me to do that as soon as possible. I told him I would let him know as to when I could attend but he didn't seem too pleased and wanted an immediate answer which I couldn't give."

Mike Parsons didn't immediately reply and during the ensuing silence Sandra's mother entered to room with a tray of tea and shortbread biscuits. As she entered Parsons gallantly stood up. Sandra introduced them and Parson shook Sandra's mother's hand and thanked her for the tea. Sandra also thanked her, and she left shutting the door behind her.

Sandra started to pour the tea and Parsons said, "Yes, they'll need to have the identification carried out. Is there anyone who could go with you?"

"Well there's my father, and I'm sure that he would come with me. We could share the driving, but I don't want to leave my daughter just yet. I think we could go next week."

Parsons looked into a chunky blue book which was obviously a well-used diary with bits of loose papers protruding here and there.

"Um...would you be able to go on Tuesday?"

"Yes, yes I think so," said Sandra.

Mike Parsons then asked for PC Cooper's details which he noted in his overworked diary. He then called the number. PC Cooper answered quickly, and Mike Parsons introduced himself. Sandra noticed that he emphasised his rank.

Parsons stated that Sandra could attend an identification on Tuesday and that her father would be accompanying her. There was obviously some issue about the day as she heard Parsons say that he was sure the Coroner would appreciate the distance that Sandra would have to travel, the delicacy of the situation and the fact that Tuesday was the only suitable day.

Agreement was reached; Cooper would meet Sandra at the main reception at Treliske Hospital, Truro on Tuesday at 2:30pm. PC Cooper explained that he would also need to take a statement from Sandra and that the whole process would take about an hour. Parsons politely said that Sandra looked forward to meeting Cooper on the following Tuesday. Parsons advised Sandra to leave plenty of time for the trip, taking into consideration holiday traffic making its way to the South West. With a sense of relief that firm arrangements had been made both drank their tea and then Parsons left.

Preston was rarely late for any appointment and as the clock crept toward 2:00pm Matthews anticipated him being there.

In fact, true to form and almost dead on two there was a light knock on the door and Preston entered.

"You wanted to see me Guv?"

"Yes Nick, come and sit down."

"Nothing serious I hope," said Preston as he took his seat opposite Matthews.

"I'm afraid so," said Matthews and continued in a solemn way, "Sadly, Eugene Elphick drowned in Cornwall; his body was found on a beach down there yesterday morning. It's thought that he may have taken his own life."

"Well, that'll save the expense of a court case won't it?" said Preston with no hint of compassion in his voice.

Matthews was taken back by Preston's crassness. He was silent for a moment, and surprised that he was moved rather than angered by the stupid remark.

"Have you no empathy? Can't you even consider what must've been going through Elphick's mind?"

"I'm not really interested, Guv; I just regard him as a pervert. He was obviously guilty and couldn't face a custodial. A pervert and a coward, that's how I see him. Good riddance I say."

Matthews was silent for a moment. Again he was surprised that he wasn't angry with Preston, just embarrassed.

"I fear thy nature is too full of the milk of human kindness."

"What?"

"Nothing."

Matthews continued, "I saw the Chief Superintendent, Operations, earlier. You'll need to close down the Elphick file, notify the CPS and the Crown Court and file the papers locally in case they're needed for any subsequent enquiry."

"What enquiry?" asked Preston. "Nick, for an experienced police officer you remain naïve at times. We exist within a blame culture and somebody, somewhere will be blamed for this."

"Well, we haven't done anything wrong," said Preston with defiance.

"Have we not, Nick? Are we totally blameless?"

"We investigated and brought a filthy pervert to justice, that's what we did Guv."

"That hasn't been proved and never will be now, Nick, and I've never been comfortable with that case."

"There is proof enough for me."

There was a moments' silence as Matthews absorbed Preston's obtuse remark. He then said, "The Deputy needs a full report from the inquest as soon as the inquest has been held. I don't want you going down there, you can contact the Coroner's Officer in Penzance."

He gave Preston a copy of the email he had been given by the Chief Superintendent and said, "All the details are there."

There was another silence as Preston quickly read the email.

Matthews then said, "Nick, I've some further news for you."

Preston did not reply but looked up from the email he was reading.

The look on Matthews face made Preston feel a little apprehensive but he didn't say anything.

"When I saw the Chief Superintendent this morning he told me that the Professional Standards department would be reorganised."

Preston immersed in his own self-importance inwardly smiled to himself thinking that his idea had been accepted.

"When I retire in a short time the three investigations teams will be reduced to two, and work that would normally be attributed to us will be dealt with by Superintendent Simon Green's team."

Preston went to speak but Matthews raised his hand to stop him and continued, "I won't be replaced." He paused briefly, then continued, "Nick, you are to be transferred."

Preston thought that he would be transferred to Green's team, and he was not too unhappy with that. After giving a slight cough Matthews continued, "You're being transferred to Cowley uniform. You will take up the position of shift Inspector there."

"What? You're joking?"

"No, afraid not Nick. Here are your transfer papers."

And Matthews handed over the bundle of papers that the Chief Superintendent had given him.

"This can't be right…this is unfair. I am going to go and see him," protested Preston.

"I wouldn't advise it, Nick," Matthews said in a kindly paternalistic manner. He then continued, "You'll take up duties at Cowley," he looked at his desk calendar and said, "ah yes, seven weeks on Monday. Which is well after I would have left. Your priority is to close down this team, to deal with all matters that can be dealt with and then transfer those that can't to Superintendent Green. Once I leave you'll be supervised by Mr Green."

Matthews could see that Preston was both hurt and angry and annoyingly, he began to feel some pleasure at Preston's disgruntlement.

"That's about it for now, Nick," echoing the impersonal manner in which Tadman had dismissed him.

Preston roughly gathered up his transfer papers and rose from his seat.

"Your priority for the moment, Nick, is the Elphick case."

Preston looked at Matthews and merely said, "Sir," and left the room.

CHAPTER 19

On the Sunday evening, the family, including Sandra's brother Ian, with the exception of Irene Elphick, and this was in fact the entirety of Katie's family, gathered together in the dining room at Stoke Podges. The meal, one of roast beef and all the trimmings was well received but during the meal not that much was said about Eugene and the events of the last few days were not articulated.

It was Katie who broke the somewhat embarrassed subdued atmosphere when she said, "I am glad that my whole family have come together, and I'm aware that this is to both support me and each other".

Everyone had stopped eating and were intently listening to what Katie was saying.

She continued, "No one has mentioned my dad and in the circumstances that's understandable. But please don't think you are sparing me any upset by not mentioning him. I believe that my dad lives on in our hearts and in our minds and he, in a sort of way, comes alive when we think of him or speak of him, and I want him to live on in that way."

No one said anything for a moment, tears were running down her Nanny's face and she placed her arm around Katie's shoulder and pulled her close to her.

Gramps quietly pronounced a, "Well said, Katie," and everyone endorsed that statement.

Sandra had a feeling of great pride in her daughter and having realised that she had matured into a young woman almost overnight, was aware that she was managing Eugene's passing probably better than anyone. Following Katie's heart-rending statement there was some light hearted discussion around Eugene which mainly centred on humorous episodes of the past. No one had cleared their plates and none of those around the table really had much of an appetite. After dinner and following a respectful interlude of pleasant and respectful conversation Ian made his exit, more of an escape really. Gramps and Katie made their way to their respective rooms. Katie would continue to share with Sandra for the time being.

After clearing away Sandra and her mother retreated to the reception room both armed with a large brandy. They sat together not saying very much, both appreciating each other's company.

Sandra's mother broke the silence, "I think Katie is managing this situation incredibly well."

Sandra didn't reply immediately, just sipped her brandy, and then said quietly, "My daughter has moved from a fourteen year old girl who was young for her age into a woman almost overnight. I'm very proud of her and she, very like Dad, has become my rock. She gets upset of course, she cries at night, and I 've even heard her crying in her sleep, but as you say she's managing the situation in a manner far beyond her years."

"And what about you Sandra?"

Sandra again did not reply straight away, she took another sip of her brandy, leaned back and rested her neck on the back of the settee.

"Me?" she paused "I don't know, I don't know, Mum. I just don't feel the guilt that I would expect to feel, grief like a gaping wound, it's just not there. I don't feel the rage or irrational shame that I suppose I should feel. I just feel…I don't know… numb, I suppose."

"I think that may be just transitory, Sandra. Maybe because you have so much going on, so much to do and think about right now that you just can't grieve. It'll come, perhaps later."

Sandra sipped her brandy and thought for a moment.

"I don't think so. I stopped loving Gene, I think, a long time ago. But he was the main provider for us, the father of our daughter; I should feel something."

Silence ensued seemingly for a long while and then Sandra said, "But I can't, and I won't because, well I just won't."

Her mother replied in a motherly consoling manner, "Just give it time Sandra."

"I'll tell you what I do feel Mum, and that's the stigma – the stigma of suicide. Apart from you Dad, and Katie I…we…are isolated, no one outside the family wants to know."

"Maybe a bit harsh Sandra, people may not know where you are."

"They know my phone number. Have any of my colleagues called me? No. Have any of Gene's colleagues called me? No. I'm supposed to work within a caring profession, but no one cares for me. It's not really me though is it, it's because of suicide."

Adopting her consoling tone once more Sandra's mother said softly, "Don't upset yourself Sandra. You'll need to go to go to Old Windsor tomorrow; there may be letters or something there."

"Yes I know. I'm going to ask Dad to go with me. I don't think it'll be advisable for Katie to go. Perhaps you could do something with her."

Her mother thought for a moment and replied, "Um, I'll suggest we go to the Oracle in Reading for some shopping and lunch. Yes, that sounds good."

The trip to Old Windsor was not as bad as Sandra had imagined. Eugene's presence was certainly felt within the home: there were his slippers neatly placed by the fireplace, a pullover draped over one arm of the settee, his favourite armchair, his spare reading glasses on the coffee table. Sandra didn't feel any emotion, just the ever present numbness, a feature of her present existence.

There was some post, mostly charity letters, some bills and one hand written and hand delivered envelope bearing her name but not in a hand that she recognised. She folded the envelope and placed it in her pocket. Sandra's father attended to the practical requirements such as emptying the fridge, shutting down the boiler and very quickly the visit ended. Sandra was unsure if she and Katie would be able to return to live there and if she did she would need to clear Eugene's clothes and personal effects first.

On leaving the house Sandra noticed the man who lived in the house opposite standing in his garden watching. Sandra raised her arm in a form of greeting, but the man didn't respond and just tuned his back and continued with his hoeing. During the drive back to Stoke Poges Sandra opened the hand written envelope and saw it was from Benji Jacobs. The note expressed condolences and a request for Sandra to contact him.

There was a mobile telephone number. Sandra folded the note back up and placed it back into her pocket.

That evening, whilst everyone else was downstairs watching TV, Sandra made her call to Benji Jacobs. Benji answered promptly and as soon as Sandra introduced herself Benji said how sorry he was about the news regarding Eugene. He said that he had been trying to make contact with her but had been unable to do so. Sandra explained that she had been staying with her parents. Benji asked if there was anything he could do to help, and Sandra informed him that as far as she could tell everything was being attended to.

She told him about her forthcoming trip to Cornwall. Benji said he could have helped with that and would have done but Sandra assured him that arrangements had been made. She felt that Benji was sounding quite emotional on the telephone.

He then said, "Look Sandra, I feel so awful. I just want to tell you that I wasn't as much help to Gene as I could have been. I could have been more supportive, more of a friend. Instead I was what I am, a cynical police officer. I should've put that part of me aside and concentrated upon being Gene's friend which I was, but not acting as one. I feel so guilty Sandra."

Sandra was quiet for a moment. Benji's voice had been faltering in a manner that indicated his distress.

"I think that we all feel some guilt Benji. I'm not sure if you know, but I'd left Gene, left him when he probably needed me most, so I feel guilty, too. But as my mother told me, when someone takes their own life we naturally feel guilt, we think of all the what if's. What if I hadn't left Gene, what if you were more of a friend and so on. It's because the whole concept of someone taking their own life and more bluntly, committing suicide, is so…so alien, to us that we have to find some excuse to justify it to ourselves. But remember, and this may seem harsh, but at the end of the day the decision to do that, to commit that violent act, was Gene's decision. Not yours, not mine and not anyone's…his; he decided on that course of action."

Benji was silent, taking in what Sandra was saying as she continued, "I know that sounds harsh, Benji, and it is, but that's the only way I can cope with this, and cope I must for the sake of my daughter if nothing else."

Benji wanted to sound supportive but to his disappointment he could only respond with a saccharine, "I understand where you're at Sandra."

Sandra did not immediately reply but then said, "Do you know Benji, you're the first serving officer, other than the Police Federation, who've been brilliant, who has contacted me?"

"No, senior officer?" asked Benji.

Sandra said quite harshly, "No one. I suppose it's the double whammy of being suspended and committing suicide that makes the precious police organisation come grinding to a halt."

"That's appalling," said Benji and quickly, "Look, if there is anything I can do, Sandra, just pick up the phone."

"I will," responded Sandra.

"Just one other thing," said Benji, "you will let me know about the...you know, uh... funeral arrangements."

"Yes," said Sandra and added reassuringly, "I'll probably be in touch before that."

"Thank you, Sandra."

And the call was terminated.

*

Sandra and her father set off early from home and made their way to the M4. It was decided that Sandra would drive down to Truro and her father would drive back. They travelled in Sandra's father's car which was a BMW 7 series, a car that would eat up the miles and provide driver and passenger with good levels of comfort. The journey was quite uneventful, some traffic where the M4 and M5 merged, but apart from that not the heavy volume of traffic they'd expected. They said little to each other en route; Sandra very much concentrating on her driving. Her father made some reassuring words and sounds which helped Sandra.

They stopped for coffee at Taunton Dene service deck and as they were early, for a light lunch at a place called the County Arms, a sort of gastro pub on the outskirts of Truro. After their lunch Sandra made a telephone call to PC Cooper's mobile phone and he quickly answered. Sandra said where she was, and Cooper said that he would make his way to the main reception at the hospital and would meet her there. The Royal Cornwall hospital was a huge complex, but they found a parking place quite easily and made their way inside. There were a few people at the reception desk but no one who she thought was likely to be PC Cooper.

At her turn to be attended to at the desk Sandra introduced herself and said she had an appointment with PC Cooper, the Coroner's Officer. At that a man stepped forward and said

"Ah, Mrs Elphick…"

The man couldn't have looked less like a police officer in Sandra's view. He was short, bald headed and very plump. He wore a crumpled dark grey suit which had clearly seen better days and an awful patterned brown tie which did not at all match the suit. Cooper stretched out his hand and they shook. Sandra introduced her father and Cooper shook hands with him, too.

"We'll just get you some visitor badges,.." and two were handed over which PC Copper gave to Sandra and her father.

Once formalities were over PC Cooper said, "Do follow me."

They walked along wide well-lit and busy corridors where porters pushed glum looking patients on trollies and in wheelchairs, where nurses scurried quickly which emphasised their busy schedule and what were obviously visitors, clutching bags filled with treats for their loved ones, walking with purpose toward their destination. The trio arrived at a door marked 'Coroner's Officers' and they entered. PC Cooper directed them to two black upright chairs with arms which were surprisingly comfortable whilst he sat behind the desk before them and behind a laptop computer.

Brushing the laptop to the side PC Cooper gave some well worded platitudes, thanking them for attending, and offering his condolences which were obviously well used phrases honed over a long period of his time as a coroner's officer. That said, Sandra thought that although Cooper's appearance betrayed the fact, he was actually remarkedly efficient. He was succinct and was able to impart a huge amount of information in a very short time, detailing what would happen, what needed to occur at the identification, how they could register the death by phone from his office and what they needed to do in relation to Eugene's body being collected. He also gave detailed information about the inquest and asked Sandra if she would like a copy of the Coroner's report and she said she would.

PC Cooper explained that after the identification he would like to take a statement from Sandra and that would be the conclusion of what needed to be done that day. He said he expected everything to have been completed within the hour. Sandra did feel, as did her father, that as a result of PC Cooper's efficiency they were much more at ease.

After a while PC Cooper asked gently, "Are you ready to make the identification now?"

Sandra nodded and Cooper made a telephone call to someone saying, "OK? Yes, we're ready to come through now." He replaced the receiver and said, "This way please."

They went through an internal door into what looked like a little chapel. Cooper, unbeknown to Sandra, signalled for her father to remain by the door and he complied. Cooper and Sandra walked towards a trolly where a man lay. He was covered in a white sheet and only his neck and face could be seen. They both stood looking down. Sandra could see it was

Eugene, but he looked much older, he looked as if he were sleeping, and she felt that he did look at peace.

PC Cooper said the words that he told Sandra he would say, "Do you recognise this deceased person?"

"Yes, this is my husband, Eugene Elphick."

PC Cooper then asked Sandra if she would 'like a moment'. She nodded, and he stepped back to where Sandra's father waited. Sandra looked down. She felt sad but not distraught. She felt her eyes well up with tears, but she did not actually cry. She stretched out her hand and touched Eugene's face, but it felt hard and cold. It wasn't him, not as she knew him. He had gone and she could only view this body as a discarded shell. She said nothing, turned and walked toward the others.

They re-entered the office and without further ado Cooper started to take a statement from Sandra asking questions and typing the answers into the lap top. The finished statement was printed out, read, and signed and having bade farewell to PC Cooper they were back in the car and making for home.

Sandra's father was going to drive back to Berkshire and the conversation flowed more easily. After a respectful period, her father asked Sandra how she was feeling.

"I think that chap, PC Cooper, certainly helped by explaining everything. How did I feel when I saw Eugene? I don't know really. I could see it was him, he looked, what can I say, peaceful. Yes, that's it, peaceful and I was glad about that. I wasn't that upset though, not as much as I would have thought I would have been, should have been, maybe. Sad, yes, upset, not really. I think it may be due to the fact that Eugene and I stopped loving each other. I don't know when, it was gradual, but a fair while ago."

It had started raining and the windscreen wipers were making a slight swishing noise as they transversed the screen, wiping all before them. It was if the soft noise of the wipers was punctuating what Sandra was saying. Swish, a comma, Swish a full stop, Swish a question mark. Sandra continued.

"I touched his face – it was cold and didn't feel like Gene, didn't feel human really. I realised that Eugene as I had known him had gone and what was left was just a shell, nothing really, just not him. I wonder, I think about it sometimes, what happens when we die, where do we go? I'm not that religious, but I sometimes wonder, do we have a soul and what happens to it? We can't remember anything before we were born so what's to say we remember anything after we die?"

The windscreen wipers continued their rhythmic swish, emulating her wiping the inner sanctums of her mind, perhaps. Sandra's father didn't say anything; he was looking ahead but clearly listening to what she was saying as he was making little para linguistic sounds, an um, an ah, a 'go on' all of which helped Sandra. He wanted her to talk and to talk uninterrupted hoping that this cathartic release would prove helpful to his daughter.

"Do you know the worst things about all this?" asked Sandra, but not waiting for a reply, "Well, the worst thing, of course, is the effect that this is having and will have upon Katie – what's going through her mind now? And what will go through it in the future. Will she blame herself for what happened to her dad, blame me, blame the bloody police? I don't know if I should seek out specialised help for her or wait to see what happens."

Again not waiting for any response she continued, "And the other worst thing, and the most upsetting for me, is the way I have been betrayed, abandoned. None of Gene's colleagues have contacted me save one, no senior police officers have contacted me and no one from the surgery have contacted me. Why not, I ask myself? Why have they shunned and abandoned me? I feel so betrayed."

She stopped and for a short while all that could be heard was the somewhat comforting noise of the windscreen wipers making their swishing noise on their ever repeated journey.

Sandra's father spoke. He hadn't intended to, but the silence had been a bit too much to bear.

"I suppose it is the stigma of suicide and the offence for which he was being investigated for. I suppose both are somewhat alien to most people and in consequence people find it hard to cope with and hard to certainly talk about those sorts of things."

Sandra thought for a moment and then replied, "Yes, maybe. Mum said something very similar. But I didn't do those things, I've done nothing wrong, I'm a victim, surely. Don't I deserve a little support, a kind word, a sympathetic ear?"

Sandra's father didn't reply, and Sandra continued, "If Gene had been killed on duty, or had died whilst a serving, I mean 'not a suspended' officer, then I would be inundated with sympathy and help. The only people to help me so far have been the Police Federation who have not stigmatised Gene, well not overtly, so anyway. I'm so glad that I have you and Mum. I don't know where I would be without you. You are my great support, Dad."

With that tears started to trickle down Sandra's face, she leaned back in her seat listening to that heart-warming sweep of the windscreen wipers which comforted and induced shallow sleep. Sandra's father looked across and decided to let her doze.

Sandra slept lightly and could hear the swish of the wipers and the light drone of the engine. When the noise of the wipers stopped she awoke fully and saw that it had stopped raining. Sandra's father asked her in a reassuringly paternalistic way if he was 'alright' and she replied that she was. A fairly general conversation ensued on and off over the miles. No more deep discussion was held. They stopped off at Taunton Dean for a welcome cup of tea, to obtain fuel and to make themselves more comfortable. They had both deduced that Taunton was about the halfway point on the journey between Truro and Stoke Podges.

The second half of the journey passed uneventfully, and they eventually pulled into the drive at Stoke Podges. Katie, who had obviously been watching from a window rushed out to greet them and excitedly told them that she, with only a little help from Nanny, had made supper. A long day was over and all except Sandra's father decided on a fairly early night following Katie's very pleasant pasta supper.

Sandra's father sat, reflected on the long journey to and from Cornwall, the events at the hospital, what Sandra had said, and upon how he could best help and further support his daughter.

CHAPTER 20

Sandra's father had taken her aside and explained that they would have to start planning for Eugene's funeral. He suggested that he took over making the arrangements and Sandra readily agreed. They selected a well know funeral directors in Slough and made an appointment to see a representative at their main office.

In the meantime Sandra and her mum made a few trips to the house in Old Windsor and cleared most of Eugene's clothes which they somewhat unceremoniously deposited in a Salvation Army clothes hopper which was situated in the car park of a local pub. On the final trip to the hopper they decided to have lunch at the pub. The place was not very crowded, and they were able to find a window seat which overlooked the river across the road.

"That was all a bit difficult, wasn't it love?"

Sandra thought for a moment and realised that she hadn't found it difficult at all. In fact, inwardly she saw it as part and parcel of eliminating Eugene from her life, but she lied and said, "Yes, yes it was a bit, Mum."

"How are you doing, darling?" asked her mother very much with a tone of concern. "You don't say very much."

"I'm OK, Mum. You know, I have my moments, but I need to stay strong for Katie."

"Yes, and she seems to be coping very well, too."

The food was brought to the table, and both started to eat.

"It may be different for both of us at the time of the funeral and after," said Sandra, more or less to placate her mother.

"Yes, I think it might be. But you'll be at home with us, and we can support both you and Katie."

"No, Mum," Katie and I will be moving back to Old Windsor as soon after the funeral as possible, in fact, within a day or two."

"Oh!" said her mother in a disappointed way.

"I think it's preferable for us to resume as normal a life as possible as soon as possible. The life we have right now, and I'm grateful to you and Dad, don't get me wrong, but it's a sort of limbo, a false life where we're constantly anticipating something. So rather than anticipate I intend to make it happen."

"How will you manage the mortgage, Katie's school fees and so on. Your father and I could help a little..."

Sandra interrupted, "I don't know if I'll get a widow's pension from the police or not at this stage. No one has told me although the Police Federation rep indicated that I would. But

I don't know for sure, and I haven't been informed officially. I've still not heard anything from Thames Valley Police. If I do get a pension, then all should be OK; if I don't then we will be moving to somewhere else."

Sandra's mother started to speak, "And what about..."

Sandra interrupted, "What about Katie's school? Well, the way Katie and I have been treated by them, I've no intention of her going back there. I'll be looking for another school which will be a priority for me once the funeral is over. I'm going to try to get her into Windsor Girl's School."

"Yes, I've heard that it's very good there..."

Sandra interrupted again, "Please Mum, let's not talk about it. Just let's enjoy our lunch and the view."

The trip to the funeral directors was much easier than either Sandra or her father expected it to be. The person who saw them, a middle aged lady, who perhaps had too much make-up and who wore ridiculously high heels was, nevertheless, very professional.

The collection of Eugene's body from Cornwall, which Sandra's father thought would be an issue was not, and the lady with the make-up assured them that they, the funeral directors, were well used to such scenarios. She explained everything in minute detail but said that a date for the funeral could not be finalised until a death certificate was available. Sandra explained that she expected such to be available within days.

Sandra was asked about the format of the service. She explained that she didn't know but would contact her mother-in-law to find out. They agreed that Eugene would be cremated, and that Sandra would let them know about the service arrangements and service booklets as soon as she could. Sandra and her father left the funeral directors satisfied that things were being properly attended to.

Sandra made the call to Irene Elphick that evening. She always felt so guilty when talking to Irene. They exchanged pleasantries but had been in contact regularly throughout as Katie had asked to remain in regular contact with her paternal grandmother. She discussed the funeral arrangements, and two hymns were selected: The Lord is my Shepherd and Abide with Me, pretty standard stuff. A short reading was also selected. There would be no eulogy – that would be left to the priest and would be arranged by the funeral directors.

It was agreed that Irene would travel to Slough or Reading by train whichever was easier for her and that Sandra would collect her from the station. She would be staying with them at Stoke Podges. Dates and times would be arranged when they had a date for the funeral. Sandra again felt that matters were moving forward. Katie then took over the call and spoke to her granny for a good while; they always seemed to have a lot to say to each other and got along so well.

*

Mike Tadman was not a happy man as he sat at his desk. He had that afternoon received a copy of the Coroner's report in relation to the inquest of Eugene Elphick and it did not make pleasant reading for Thames Valley Police and subsequently for him. Accompanying the report was a hand written note from the Deputy Chief Constable which was direct and to the point, that he and the Chief Constable himself were less than pleased with what had been said by the Coroner.

Tadman looked at the report again and in particular to a paragraph that was highlighted in yellow, fluorescent highlighter:

> *For reasons that I do not need to go into here Mr Elphick had been suspended from his duties by Thames Valley Police. He was under investigation for a suspected criminal offence and the use of suspension would not be that unusual in such circumstances. However, that said, I feel bound to comment that once Mr Elphick had been suspended Thames Valley Police failed to adhere to their duty of care to Mr. Elphick as*

their employee. No welfare provisions were made for him, no one contacted him, and he was left somewhat abandoned by an employer he had worked for, in a responsible capacity, for some time. I have no doubt that the non-action of Thames Valley Police weighed heavily on Mr Elphick's mind. I will be notifying the Chief Constable of Thames Valley Police of my concerns and asking him what provisions for the welfare of suspended officers will be put in place in the future.

Having read and re-read that section several times Tadman picked up his telephone, dialled and asked whoever answered, "Please have Superintendent Green come and see me as soon as." He did not wait for a reply and replaced the receiver.

Within half an hour there was a knock on Tadman's door and Superintendent Simon Green was invited into Tadman's office. Simon Green was a fairly young man; he was a direct entry officer who entered the service as a Superintendent.

The Direct Entry Scheme was intended to attract exceptional individuals with proven leadership and management skills. Simon Green certainly believed that he was exactly that, having held a responsible financial management position in a well-known insurance company before joining. He had no particular loyalty to the police service but felt that time spent in the service would look good on his already impressive CV for the future.

He had completed the eighteen month training programme and now was within his specialist 'attachment'. Simon believed that his skills were in strategy and senior management operations and his current task, as well as running a Professional Standards Investigation team, was to seek to make the unit more specialised, more effective, and more financially viable. The proposed changes to the unit were very much his idea. He believed he was an exceptional leader and an innovative thinker who would help shape the future of policing as long as he wanted to, and until something better and more lucrative came along.

Tadman was aware of Simon Green's history. He was fully aware that he was a high flyer and frighteningly intelligent. Green was the future of policing, there was no doubt in Tadman's mind about that. However, Tadman harboured a resentment for Green and all that he stood for. His privileged background, his cut glass accent, his expensive haircut, suit and shoes.

Tadman had taken twenty six years to get to the rank of Superintendent, twenty six years of scheming, plotting, ingratiating himself, towing the party line, back stabbing and the awful displaying of false bonhomie, and yet the rank was given on a plate to Green. This is the way forward he had been told and do you really have to be a thief taker to manage thief takers? He supposed not.

Tadman welcomed Green and got straight to the point.

"I would think that you are fully aware of the Elphick case?"

Green replied, "I've had nothing to do with it as such. The file has been closed down now and all relevant authorities, Crown Court and so on informed".

"Yes, well as you are aware Elphick committed suicide and there followed an inquest. I have the Coroner's report here."

Tadman slid the report across the desk to Green. "For now concentrate on the highlighted para". Green quickly absorbed the paragraph.

Tadman continued, "You can see, Simon, that doesn't bode well for TVP. The Deputy and the Chief are not best pleased. We need to avoid any 'flack' that may be forthcoming from the press and the media, and the Chief and Deputy have placed that in our lap."

Simon was pleased that the Chief and Deputy must have considered him as the person who would support Tadman in this task.

"I see, sir, yes."

Tadman continued, "I've instructed the press office and the main switchboard, and you will instruct your admin staff, that any press or media interest in Elphick and his suicide will be handled by me or you."

Green was intrigued with the level of passion that Tadman was exuding for the task in hand.

"Have you any thoughts on this yourself, Simon?"

"Um, ah, no sir. I'm all ears."

"Right, well the line we'll take is this: that we are most grateful for HM Coroner's report and fully endorse what she has said; that there is a policy in place to deal with the welfare of suspended officers, but it seems not to have been rigorously adhered to on this occasion which TVP regrets. We are holding a full investigation and we will be re-examining our policy. In relation to the officers who were dealing with Mr Elphick, one has decided to retire, and the other has been posted to other duties. That should satisfy the press-come-media that always like to have a sacrificial lamb. What do you think?

Green was hesitant. "Um, well, yes, I think it's very good; shove the blame onto them, then."

Green hoped that his comment would not be perceived as too derisive, well not as much as he intended it to be anyway.

"Yes, I suppose so. What are they up to now?"

Green replied, "Well, Matthews hasn't got long to go now – about 7 or so working days, I think, before he retires, so he isn't doing that much, just a few tidying up jobs, feeding the birds, and drinking tea. Preston is clearing the backlog of work emanating from his and Matthews' team and constantly moaning about how badly he's been treated. Will you be attending Matthews farewell bash, sir?"

"No, will you?"

Green gave a slight supressed laugh and said, "No, I don't think so".

Tadman, looking out of the window and into space said, "Poor old Dave Matthews has been burnt out for years; it's time for him to go and I'm glad to see the back of that treacherous bastard Preston".

This was said in a way that allowed Tadman to justify his latest episode in his long catalogue of duplicity. He turned back to Green and said, "So, you're all OK with that, then?"

"Oh yes, OK with that, thank you. Just one thing, perhaps we should add to any statement made that our thoughts and prayers are very much with Elphick's family."

"Yes, yeah, that's a good point, Simon. Yes we'll add that in," and with that the two parted company.

Sandra was making another trip to Old Windsor and upon opening the front door was greeted with the ubiquitous pile of junk mail and pizza flyers. She gathered it all up and saw there were three letters of interest. A buff coloured envelope endorsed on the back as coming from the Registrar's Office in Penzance. Another buff coloured envelope endorsed on the back as coming from HM Coroner, New County Hall, Truro, and a white envelope with the crest of Thames Valley Police in the left hand corner. Sandra thought she would open all three letter in private and placed them into her handbag.

Sandra and her mother got on with the necessary tasks, making the house ready for Sandra's and Katie's return there soon. The visit to Old Windsor culminated in a final trip to the clothes hopper in the pub car park.

Back at Stoke Podges Sandra's father told her that the Funeral Directors had collected Eugene's body from Truro and that he was now at their Chapel of Rest. They had asked if Sandra or the family wished to view the body. Sandra said she didn't, and the subject was closed. She did say to her father that she believed the death certificates had arrived and she withdrew the appropriate letter from her handbag, choosing to keep the others hidden. On opening the letter she saw that it contained four death certificates. She didn't look at them but handed them to her father.

He did look at them and said, "We'll need more. I'll get on to the Registrar's office and order another four which we'll have to pay for, that should then be enough. I'm going to the Funeral Directors; they will need one to start the process. Would you like to come with me?"

Sandra replied, "No, thanks."

"Do you know if Gene had made a will?"

"Yes," replied Sandra. "We both made out one of those WH Smith do it yourself wills – quite straightforward, leaving everything to each other."

"Do you know where it is?"

"Yes, they're together in my correspondence file which I brought with me."

"We'll have to sort things out now, banks, and so on. Did he name an executor?"

Sandra thought and said, "No, no we didn't."

Her father said, "Would you like Mr Giles, our solicitor, to do it or I could do it if it is that straight forward?"

"Could you, Dad? That would be a great help."

Sandra set off to find the will and her father set off for the Funeral Directors. He returned later and had a date for the funeral, which was to be Thursday of the following week.

Retreating to her room to find the will Sandra sat on her bed and retrieved the two other letters from her bag. She opened the one in the white envelope first. It was from the Chief Constable of Thames Valley Police. The letter started with *Dear Mrs Elphick* and was written by hand in green ink. The letter was then in typed script expressing condolences for the loss of her husband couched in clichéd terms. As Sandra got to the end of the second paragraph she said aloud, "A bit late mate." The letter continued explaining that as her husband was a serving officer when he died she would receive a Police Widow's pension and that he had instructed the Pensions Team to make urgent contact with her. The author also said that if he could do anything further for her then she should not hesitate to contact his office. The letter ended with the author signing his name in green ink. Sandra read the letter over again and then crumpled the letter in her hand and threw it into the waste paper basket.

She then opened the other letter and saw that it was a report from the Coroner in relation to Eugene's inquest. Sandra scanned through the letter first and then re-read it. She stopped at the paragraph that had caused Tadman such disquietude, but her main focus was on the penultimate paragraph which read:

> *Mr Elphick had not, apparently, left any note informing us of his intentions. However, considering all the evidence we can be assured that Mr Elphick drank a large quantity of alcohol (147mg alcohol in 100 mls blood) had taken a large quantity of the drug Amitriptyline Hydrochloride (1225mg),*

had lined his stomach with an indigestion liquid and had entered the sea fully clothed with stones having been found in the pockets of his jacket.

Mr. Elphick died as a result of drowning. Mr Elphick was under the care of his GP and had seen a consultant psychiatrist who had diagnosed Post Traumatic Stress Disorder and depression. I am bound to say that I am surprised that a Tricyclic drug such as Amitriptyline was initially prescribed, I assume for the depression. It is known that Tricyclics have varying degrees of cardiotoxicity in overdose and Amitriptyline Hydrochloride is particularly dangerous in overdosage. It is therefore concerning that two medical practitioners were prescribing the same drug at the same time albeit in different dosages.

I would remind all medical practitioners that there needs to be careful monitoring of all medications being taken and especially so where Tricyclics are being used. It is apparent that Mr Elphick had been stock piling his medication which is concerning.

Having taken into consideration all the available evidence I am satisfied that Mr Elphick did take his own life but did so whilst the balance of his mind was disturbed.

Sandra skimmed over the remaining paragraph and read the signature at the end.

Davina Tregellas MB, MD, FRCP, HM Coroners Officer, Cornwall District.

Sandra read penultimate paragraph several times and thought on what must have been going through Eugene's mind on that night. She was a little surprised, though, that what was said had not upset or distressed her. She folded the report and placed it in her correspondence wallet whilst at the same time finding and withdrawing Eugene's will.

CHAPTER 21

The following days were busy and passed quickly. The house was ready to move back into at Old Windsor, the funeral directors had been fantastic, and all was prepared. The service book looked great with a very pleasant picture of Eugene on the front cover which had been picked out by Katie. Only twenty books had been ordered as Sandra only expected a few people to turn up. The pensions people at Thames Valley had been in touch and Sandra knew exactly how much pension she would be getting which equated to half of Eugene's basic pay.

There had been two life insurance policies, one with Prudential and one with Police Mutual. Both had a 'suicide clause' but as the policies had been held over two years the clause was not applicable and both companies would pay out, in time. Sandra knew that she would be able to remain in her own home, the mortgage would be paid off and although she would not be rich she would be more than comfortable.

The day then came where she collected Irene Elphick from Reading railway station and brought her back to Stoke Poges. Katie had been the perfect host and she demonstrated that she loved all her grandparents, all gathered together on a rare but sorry occasion, very much.

The day of the funeral arrived. All were dreading it, but they were content that they would all be present together and would get through it. When arranging the funeral Sandra and her father decided that they would meet the hearse at Slough crematorium. The time of the funeral had been set for 10:30 on that Thursday morning.

Crematoriums these days, as her father had said to Sandra, "Are a bit like conveyor belts; we only have a forty minute slot and then another family will be waiting."

The family as it was gathered at Stoke Poges; Sandra, Katie, Sandra's parents, her bother Ian, and Irene Elphick. Two limousines had been ordered and attended the house on cue at 10am. The only insistence as to seating came from Katie who insisted on sitting with her paternal grandmother. Sandra looked at her daughter who appeared very much as a sophisticated and attractive teenager, and one who displayed a compassionate personality. Sandra felt very proud of her daughter.

The drivers of the limousines were well used to their work and drove at a sedate pace arriving at the Crematorium just as the hearse pulled into the entrance to the drive leading to the building. Katie and her grandmother were in the first vehicle and Irene Elphick gave a great intake of breath as she saw the hearse in front of her.

Katie who had been holding her grandmother's hand, squeezed, and just said softly,"It's alright."

At the building entrance the family moved into the building and into an area termed the chapel. It was a multi-denominational building so it was quite plain with varnished wooden walls, a dark red carpeted floor, and light red seats on both sides of what could be called an aisle. The family made their way to the front and were ushed into place by the funeral director. They sat in silence for what seemed an eternity. Some organ music started playing. Sandra's mother cried quietly, but no one else did. Katie held on tightly to her paternal grandmother's hand and was staring directly ahead.

Sandra looked around to the rear of her. She could see Benji Jacobs was there and another man beside him whom Sandra thought must be a police colleague. Mary, one of Sandra's colleagues from the surgery, was there and she nodded at Sandra. There were a few other people who were friends of Sandra's parents. She could see toward the back Mike Parsons, the Police Federation person, and right at the very back David Bennett. The chapel is capable of holding 150 persons but today, now, it contained a mere tenth of that. Sandra could see that the coffin bearers with Eugene's coffin on their shoulders had assembled in the porch and the organ stopped playing. Sandra turned to face the front and heard the words, "I am the resurrection and the life..." in a strong clear voice.

The coffin was brought forward and laid at the front of the aperture through which it would later disappear.

As the coffin passed her Irene Elphick started to cry and Katie put her arm around her grandmother's shoulder and said in her ear, "It's OK, Granny, I'm here."

On the top of the coffin was a cross made out of different flowers and placed in front was a small posey with a card bearing the single word, "Daddy". The funeral then followed the format in the service book. When it came to the hymns Sandra wished that they hadn't chosen any. There were just not enough people to do them justice and a non-melodious dirge ensued. During what could only loosely be described as singing, both grandmothers and Katie cried. Sandra did not. Her father mouthed at her, "You alright?" and she gave a positive nod back.

Mercifully for Sandra the whole proceedings came to an end. Katie had purposely requested that the curtains would not be pulled around her father's coffin until all had left the chapel. Those gathered started to move toward a side entrance and out of the chapel. Katie walked toward her father's coffin and placed a kiss on it, she then, with her grandmother and other mourners, left the chapel without a backward glance. Sandra remained at the door thanking people as they exited the chapel. David Bennett approached her and placed a kiss on her cheek and said, "We'll speak soon," and Sandra thought, "Too right we will."

Benji was the only person left in the chapel and Sandra observed that he slowly and seemingly nervously walked toward Eugene's coffin. As he got close to it Benji donned a blue satin Kippa which he had taken from his pocket. He placed his right hand on Eugene's coffin and recited the Kaddish. Sandra saw that tears were streaming down Benji's face.

It was something of an irony that the day of Eugene's funeral was the day of Dave Matthews' retirement. Not many people turned up at Eugene's funeral and not many people turned up at Matthews' leaving party either.

Within days of the funeral, after Irene Elphick had returned to Shaftesbury, a van was again hired by Sandra's father and all Sandra and Katies possessions were once again transported back to Old Windsor. Sandra drove her own car and her mother, father, and Katie quickly unloaded the van, placing boxes and bags in the living room. Once everything had been unpacked, including a box of groceries thoughtfully obtained by her father, Sandra made them all a drink. The boiler was switched back on and the fridge stocked.

"We'll help you unpack," said Sandra's mother but Sandra said, "No," and continued with "Look, you've all been great, and I don't think we would have even survived without you, but I just want to be here with Katie now, just the two of us settling in again. I'll call you."

Sandra's mother was about to say something when her father interjected, "We understand Sandra," and then to his wife a gentle but commanding, "Come on."

They left and Sandra and Katie were alone.

Sandra looked at Katie and said, "What you thinking love?"

"Do you know Mum, when we drove into the driveway, I was just thinking we would see Dad, here, sitting in his chair, I really thought we would." She started to cry.

Sandra put her arms around her,

"Yes, I know how you feel, I was thinking the same thing," she lied.

Over the next couple of days there was lots to do, and Sandra and Katie were able to spend some quality time together. Things started to get back to some sort of normality, although neither could fathom out what had happened to the mock Victorian clock that used to hang on the living room wall.

Sandra had made the spare bedroom into a functional office and Katie was delighted with it, anticipating studying in there when she moved to Windsor Girls' school after the holidays. She was determined to study hard and do well, just as her father would have wanted.

One evening when Katie was engrossed in the television, Sandra went up to the office to write some letters. She thought about things and was satisfied that she had got Katie into a good school, satisfied that she had got a new job at a GP's surgery in Windsor, and that she would be writing her resignation letter to David Bennet that very evening, and satisfied that she would be, in financial terms, comfortable. Things were looking up.

Sandra went into her bedroom and retrieved her handbag. She sat down at the desk and emptied out the contents of the bag. Lifting the flap at the bottom of the bag, she took out a green Lloyds credit card in the name of Eugene Elphick. She turned the card over in her hand and allowed herself a smile. She then dropped the card into the Fellows paper shredder and heard the crunch as the thick, sharp, cross cutting metal teeth reduced the card to numerous tiny pieces.

Life after Eugene was beginning to look good.

The End

Printed in Great Britain
by Amazon